Watch Me Disappear

Watch Me Disappear

Jill Dawson

ISIS
LARGE PRINT
Oxford

First published in Great Britain 2006
by
Hodder and Stoughton, a division of Hodder Headline

Published in Large Print 2006 by ISIS Publishing Ltd.,
7 Centremead, Osney Mead, Oxford OX2 0ES
by arrangement with
Hodder and Stoughton, a division of Hodder Headline

British Library Cataloguing in Publication Data
Dawson, Jill
    Watch me disappear. – Large print ed.
    1. Missing children – England – Cambridgeshire
    – Fiction
    2. Psychological fiction
    3. Large type books
    I. Title
    823.9'14 [F]

ISBN–10 0–7531–7696–3 (hb)
ISBN–13 978–0–7531–7696–2 (hb)
ISBN 978–0–7531–7697–9 (pb)

Printed and bound in Great Britain by
T. J. International Ltd., Padstow, Cornwall

For Meredith again, with more love

Little girls are cute and small only to adults. To one another they are not cute. They are life-sized.

Margaret Atwood, *Cat's Eye*

Now I wish to introduce the following idea. Between the age limits of nine and fourteen there occur maidens who, to certain bewitched travelers, twice or many times older than they, reveal their true nature, which is not human, but nymphic (that is demoniac); and these chosen creatures I propose to designate as "nymphets".

Vladimir Nabokov, *Lolita*

One

This is the moment Mandy Baker reappears. It's early summer 2002 and I'm with Dean and Poppy on a working holiday on the east coast of Malaysia. Poppy is ten years old, leggy, dark; she has Dean's colouring: great black saucers for eyes. We're staying on the tiny Gem island near Pulau Kapas, where I'm studying the courting rituals of *Hippocampus kuda*. Right now, there's a swishy kind of breeze and the beach is littered with coconuts. Stupidly, we canoe over to Kapas in scalding midday sun. Plastering our skin with Factor 30 lotion every ten minutes makes hardly any difference at all. We've baked to a red glow, though we can't see it yet. The sunlight tricks us, blanching our skin white. We have lunch at Zaki's restaurant of squid, curried chicken and vegetables in soy sauce, followed by chunks of water melon and a huge bottle of water. Some boys at the table next to ours are eating a durian, and they wave the spiky porcupine fruit in our direction, laughing. Poppy bravely agrees to try it. The foul stink and prickly skin is opened with a knife, revealing milky slimy flesh inside. I take one tiny piece and yes, it is more appetising than I expected, but it has

3

a curious after-taste, like an onion. Poppy smiles at first, but soon she's grimacing, glugging back water from the bottle. The boys laugh, knowing she won't be able to remove the taste for days.

There are crusts of sand coating my burnt thighs. Ants crawl everywhere, up the chair legs, across the plastic tablecloth, straggling over every abandoned grain of rice, every flake of bread. Because I'm working, I'm utterly perfectly happy. There's the sound of a boat engine, and a guitar somewhere, strummed here and there by various children, giving off the odd sudden twang like the night call of a frog. In the evening, while Poppy sleeps in the cabin next-door, we sit at the bar and drink the sour green-tasting coconut juice with sugar syrup, and smoke marijuana with another marine biologist, Roni.

Did you know they have the death penalty here for this? Roni laughs, twirling the joint in front of him like Groucho Marx. I shake my head next time he offers it.

Dean often tells me I seem like someone stoned. It's my natural state, he says: no need of illegal substances for Tina. He doesn't say it in a critical way, or complaining. He says it playfully, affectionately. *Wake up, Tina.* Dean would like to call me back from somewhere, a lot of the time. I love this about him. I rely on it.

From our bedroom in the morning we see the giant green whale shape of the island of Kapas, with its strip of yellow beach. In the sea in front of us there are tiny turtles in a netted square hatchery. Grey herons hunch over these like old men, staring into the nets. Two white underbellies of the tiny leatherbacks float upright, the

4

size of children's palms. Dead. Terns wheel overhead. Every few minutes, there is the thud of a coconut falling. When I move I hear the pressing crunch of a rattan chair.

Dean walks towards me, carrying masks and snorkels hired from the hut on the beach, and suggests a swim in the shallows where the coral strip is clearly visible.

Poppy and I stride out into the warm water, fiddling with our snorkels. Poppy's snorkel is tourist fare whereas mine is from home: there's no way I can tolerate a leaky mask or one that fogs. Still, today for some reason the mouthpiece feels big and clumsy — I keep wanting to gag — I'm conscious of it tickling the roof of my mouth. There is a lot of shaking out of water and fiddling with the rubber straps and spitting and cleaning our masks. One of my fins flicks off my foot and bobs up on top of a wave, and Poppy reaches for it and throws it but it's a bad throw and lands far from me, so we giggle a lot about our own incompetence — really, this shared incompetence is always our favourite joke, even here, in what is undeniably my domain. Eventually, waiting for Poppy, I follow her out towards Dean, half-swimming, half-walking, towards the deeper part of the sea. Ghostly white needlefish leap from the water to the left of us, and Poppy giggles nervously.

Here we put our faces in and the coral looms up like a moonscape, full of fat pudding anemones waving brown hair. Poppy points to a large fish, half-black and half-white, and I gesture back excitedly to show I've seen it, though it's one I've seen many times. A shoal of silver needlefish, dream-like and transparent, circle me.

Spiky black sea urchins, coral shaped like crucifixes. Tiny pieces of abandoned cellophane float around us: jellyfish. Poppy and I point them out to one another under the water. Poppy's short braids float around her hair like Medusa's snakes; we try to waft the jellyfish away with our fins, avoiding stings. Clown fish, cleaning the anemones, nose up to us aggressively, swimming close to our masks. I shake my head at Poppy as she goes to bat one away. Never touch anything on the coral! Her frown shadows the mask. I know, I know, you don't need to tell me, her look says. I'm not one of your students.

I can hear the snapping sound in the water of my own breathing popping in my ears. In one spot our skin is stung by piercing pricks, the broken-off jellyfish tentacles. We make more hand signals to one another, gestures of pinching and pricking with finger and thumb to show where the fire corals are and we nod, our movements mired in syrup, astronauts, dreamily slow, and we swim on.

It's deeper here and there are dead coral skeletons, all the same shade of toffee brown, sprouting a pale-brown fur of algae. Impossible for me not to feel sad, noting the coral bleaching, wondering what caused the corals to stress — is it climate change, again? — and expel their zooxanthellae in such huge numbers. Some dark caves gape. Flat hard toadstools, green and brown sea trees. Some huge bulbous brain coral, dotted with chips of green, specks of emerald. Tiny urchins in bright blue and yellow with what looks like a little eye blinking at the centre. I hear something rolling and

6

watery that could be a peal of thunder. I can't see a single seahorse, but that's no more than I'd expect. They don't favour the beautiful coral, but the squidgy mud and grass of the sea-grass meadows, a trip planned for tomorrow. I can't see Dean anywhere.

And then suddenly, here is a black-tipped reef shark, so graceful, weaving towards us. I hold my breath. The sea is abruptly cold, a sharp drop beneath me. I can see Poppy's legs, a strange underwater lemony colour. Sunlight mottling the water makes my own fingers bloodless, white and puffy at the tips. I've seen sharks before. This is not the first time, diving, I've seen a shark underwater but here it is, grey, poised, shadowy: making a bee-line towards my daughter, ten years old, with her skin bared and her feet in their black fins hiding her ten unspoiled toes. Poppy has her back to the shark, she's moving in slow motion in front of me, her legs gently folding the water, like long, languid spoons, idly stirring a cocktail. She hasn't seen it yet and she is so naked, only that tiny blue triangle of her bikini visible; her skin bare, bare and wet and sea-yellow, and unreal: she is paused in time as if preserved in aspic, I'm looking at her through an amber lens, as if she's an eerie specimen in my own tanks in the lab, as if I have all the time in the world to look at her: is this really my daughter? Did I make her, how did she get here?

And then that's it, that's the moment. That's when I see Mandy — her name firmly attached to her — Mandy Baker. She's here in the water with us: yellow and turquoise and stippled, her blonde hair wafting

7

upwards in this ghastly way, great clods of green in it; and something shadowy and appalling, that I really should understand, is zigzagging its way towards her. Something peels away and my stomach drops from me like a stone. Mandy's face, blurred by the green of the water, bobs up beside me, bloated, like a puffer fish. My heart goes beserk inside me, rattling the bars of my ribcage, trying to escape. I can't breathe. I can't move.

My thoughts are moving very, very slowly indeed, like treacle spreading in a puddle. My little girl is ten years old. A shark is weaving towards us. What are you doing here, Mandy Baker? Mandy Baker, where have you been?

But then at last something normal kicks in and the icy chill slips from my skin and my lungs fill with air and I think: it must be the joint I smoked last night, get a grip, Tina, for God's sake! I smash to the surface of the water, screaming: *Poppy!*

And there's the black tube of her snorkel and Poppy comes crashing to the surface too, shaking her braids in a dramatic black spray around her and says: *what, what?* in that American accent of hers, all innocence, and just behind her I see the black fin of the shark silkily gliding away from us. Dean is in the shallows, closer to the beach, standing half-out of the sea, trying to empty his snorkel of water, but he follows the direction of my outstretched arm towards the departing fin and whistles, a wild, impressed whistle, the ear-splitting kind that Dad used to do, to show he's understood.

My stomach rejoins my body with a careering jolt. I pull up the mask from my nose and throw up, a speckled mess spattering the sea.

Poppy stands a short distance from me in the water, adjusting the clasp on her bikini top, the mask pushed back on her head, watching the shark fin melt to a black dot on the waves.

But I don't get it, why were you upset? Poppy says, later. You said that kind weren't dangerous . . .

I know, I know. Black-tip reef shark. They have excellent hearing, so shouting is the right thing to do. Shouting will usually make them disappear.

It was afraid of *you*, Roni says. Needlefish — yes, there is danger. Last year needlefish stab a man in the ribs — like this . . . (he demonstrates with his fork) . . . and kill him.

Yes, sure. I've seen shark before of course, I say. When I've been diving.

I feel foolish now. I don't tell Poppy about Mandy.

Roni is laughing at my worried expression.

You have very nice, very lovely daughter, he says. A big shark — like to eat her up. His eyes slide to Poppy, still practically naked in her damp bikini. They rest for a second on Poppy's sun-burnt skin and then they slide back to me, just in time.

It's not until I'm back at work that I think of her again. Her face suddenly floats towards me, not watery-green and swollen, but heart-shaped, familiar. Mandy. Amanda Baker. Right now it's early in the morning before anyone else arrives in the lab. My favourite time. I have my waterlogged blue notebook in front of me and I'm standing in the dimness, listening to a dripping somewhere, staring at my own handwriting. The lists:

Tank No: Tank Volume: System Volume: Species. Today the overhead light-strip is sputtering — a dodgy thing for me and the seahorses, both, that splintering light. I must let the technician know about that lamp. Changing light levels — they won't like that at all, that'll bugger up everything, the timing, the courtship, light affects all of it. At last the lab comes back to me in full beam: huge and glossy with its rows of benches, computer screens, the familiar hooked taps. And finally here they are, the rows of green tanks, with their tiny inhabitants: the seahorses.

Up close, Henry is bobbing away. All one inch of him, tail hooked around his sea-grass, bobbing like an ice-cube in a glass. *Hippocampus zosterae*. It's hard to describe seahorses as *swimming* exactly, though of course the dorsal fin on Henry's back will be fluttering madly, like the movement of a hand-held fan. Usually he blushes a creamy yellow when I put my face close to his tank. I'll note this, with the time and date. (His name in my notes is always H, not Henry. I do *try* to retain a professional distance from them, from all of them. In my notes, in any case.) I'll scoop some shrimps from the plastic jug beside his tank, and they'll be leaping and tickling my hand. We have tried the frozen kind — defrosted of course — but seahorses need to be trained to recognise them as food if the shrimps don't move. Henry and Anais are young and need to see flickering to help them with their hunting skills. *Hunting* we call it, although to students, to visitors, it often looks like nothing.

My hands always smell of the shrimps. We're supposed to wear surgical gloves but if there's no one in the lab to observe me I never bother. Dean sometimes complains. I mean, if I'm stroking his face or something, trying to be romantic, he'll suddenly go: ugggh, fish-smell! I know I've a rival for your affections, Dean says. How can I compete with something that's less than an inch high and a master of disguise?

It's true I spend a lot of time with my seahorses. They need so much care. But mostly, if Poppy or Dean want to find me, I'm just in the lab, staring at them. Looking is what I do. My research is often just glimpses and flickers, the feeling that soemthing I know to be true, or at the very least possible, is just out of range, out of the corner of my eye.

Henry is the most delicate colour, the colour of a hen's egg, with mottling like splashes of paint, but he can change. A friend of mine, an underwater photographer, she's been photographing a species of seahorse that's really tiny, like mine. They're pink and blobby, exactly like their coral habitat: gorgonian corals. That's the thing people don't know: the disguise bit. They know it about chameleons, but not seahorses. The question I'm most often asked, and not just by children, is are seahorses real? People half-believe they're like unicorns or mermaids: magical, mythical. Poseidon was dragged through his watery universe by four seahorses. But yes, I tell them, they're real.

What are they, fish? That's always the next question, after the "are they real?" one. They are fish, I say. They belong to the family Syngnathidae, which includes pipefish. But I don't think that's what I'm really being asked. I think the question is: if they're real, prove it. What are they? For proof, they need a name. A name is the trick, it's what would convince them.

So here goes:

Her name is Mandy Baker and she went missing in the summer of 1972, the last summer of primary school.

Summer. Primary school. Those words do it. Make stuff crowd in. The smell of warm blotting paper curling on windowsills, growing a lawn of mustard and cress. Jars with tadpoles, turning green in the sunshine. Every day after school we'd buy pink and green ball-shaped sherbet lollies, so hard your teeth barely made a dent in them.

I haven't thought about her in years. Well, I'm not sure that's strictly true but if I've thought of her at all it's been like a lot of things in my life, an undercurrent, an absence. Even now it's only these little details, the lolly, the mustard and cress that drift up to me. I suppose this is my area of expertise. My domain: small things. Small fry. Things other people think are insignificant. After all, I'm not just working with seahorses but the tiniest of seahorses. The dwarf seahorse.

The babies are exquisitely small: about the size of hair lice. Henry's heavily pregnant again at the moment, so he's ravenous. He has a distended belly and what I'm watching for each day is the explosion of babies. This is a regular event — they can have two broods a month — but it's still wondrous, and tricky. Plenty can still go wrong in the timing. That's why the daily mating greeting is so important: they need to

12

synchronise perfectly. We're expecting about twenty to twenty-five babies. He'll usually leak a few in advance to let us know it's about to happen, like blowing a waft of dandelion spores out into the water. They're like *this* tiny, as Poppy would say. Poppy often comes to the lab after school to help with the feeding or just to hang around, enchanted by the various pairs. Everyone is. I've yet to meet a person who isn't enchanted when they first meet a seahorse. Did you have them as pets, when you were a little girl in England? Poppy wants to know.

I tell her I always had goldfish. I wanted a snake. Dad said a snake would escape and strangle my brothers in their sleep. He put his face close up to mine when he said this and squinted one eye like a pirate, and made this snaking movement with his arm around his neck and then stuck his tongue out and rolled his eyes until Mum told him off. He was always joking about and making stuff up. My brothers would get scared and Billy would always ask: is this in real life? I taught myself to stand there, put my hands on my hips and shout: I don't believe you! Then Dad would just laugh even more, say: that's my girl!

So, goldfish it was. The Ely Show. Dad threw the darts, he never missed the bull's-eye and a plastic bag with two fish in it was the prize. Mum bought a bowl at the pet shop and put some water in it but they never lasted long. Still, that idea about goldfish having a three-minute memory is patently rubbish. That was my first bit of original research. I noticed that Moby used to come to the surface when I picked up the tube of fishfood and started rubbing my fingers above the bowl. Why would he do that if he didn't remember from the day before that this meant food? Dad said I overfed him, that this was the reason he didn't last too long: I had loved him to death. You can do that, he told me, warningly. I cried so much it drove Mum insane. I had an aquarium when I was older but that drove her mad too; she didn't like the smell or the gloom or the bubbling sound. She'd hate it now, in my lab. Gloomy, green and a constant bubbling sound. My perfect environment!

Yesterday, I finally told Dean about seeing Mandy.

He's my doctor as well as my husband so I suppose I shouldn't be surprised that he doesn't see it as Mandy reappearing, but my *symptoms* reappearing. The symptoms I used to have — fainting and this weird burning smell, this aura, as Dean calls it, and these other things, the trances and the headaches — well, I haven't had them for years and years. Throwing up, that was part of it sometimes, only rarely. I've been fine since I've been here in the States, fine since I met Dean in fact, and that's nearly fifteen years. He's advised ethosuximide again, four times a day. It has some side-effects: drowsiness, sometimes this little rash on my stomach, a red nest of spots right next to my navel. That I can cope with, but the weirdest thing is what it does to my memory.

Sometimes I can't remember a word and other times a perfectly normal word turns foreign and won't attach to the thing it's supposed to represent. It's driving me mad and it's not as if I'm ancient either: I'm forty years old. To me, that's somewhere in the middle of a long

14

climb and just before freewheeling down the other side. I don't have early Alzheimer's. I've always had a poor memory in some ways; my memory for pictures, scenes from my childhood, that kind of thing, were just . . . patchy. Sometimes vivid; mostly nothing at all. Now that's shifting. The odd word has hightailed it and instead, pictures are hurtling back.

I don't even know if it really is the ethosuximide, or if it had already begun around the time we went on holiday, and a greater dose would be the remedy. I only know it's frustrating, I mean, I can drive and I've held down this job — and now. Now this. Possibly I'm being paranoid and it was just the snorkel mouthpiece, or the sea-water, or the dope. Perhaps it was Poppy, the age she is, ten: the exact same age Mandy was. We were. The year she went missing.

It's a shame seahorses are so passive, Yelena says. Yelena is a big-boned girl from upstate New York, a post-grad who has transferred to me to work on phylogenetic relationships among ninety-three specimens of twenty-two seahorses. She wears her lab-coat two sizes too small for her, with the buttons undone almost down to her waist, and I've heard the boys make jokes about her name. Ya lean any further and we'll see everything. Yelena's a feminist, she says. She despises passivity, and what a shame that it's so . . . female. She's thinking these days that she picked the wrong subject and wishes she'd stuck with the Five College Coastal Program at Smith. It's a real problem.

What looks like passivity can hide an awful lot, I say. It might not be fashionable, but don't be so hasty in your judgments. They're incredible survivors. They're smarter than you think. And then usually, when I'm giving this lecture and we're leaning over the tank, staring at the tiny shapes bobbing in the water, tails curled around a frond of grass, there's a sound like someone flicking the water with their finger. Ping. That's the kill. The shrimp's gone, snaffled. Snorted up their paper-fine snouts, like powder up a straw.

Never underestimate a seahorse, I say. My students laugh politely. I get defensive: we need more humility, I say, when we talk about seahorses. We need to acknowledge how little we know: about their range, their numbers, how long they might live for. Their medicinal properties. (In Asia they claim they can cure everything from sexual dysfunction to kidney stones to asthma.) Their astonishing pigment change — we don't even know how they achieve this, the chemical processes that might be involved. This is my own specialist area of research, and the project I'm currently supervising.

The polite laughter dries up. They've heard plenty of this before. Most have attended one of my lectures as undergraduates — I've been here a while. ("The sea covers seven-tenths of the earth, but we've mapped only a small percentage of it. Of the millions of species of animals and plants, we've only identified a few thousand. The sea controls our climate, but we don't really understand how . . .")

Now I'm muttering: I know it's difficult. We *want* to know — that's why we're researchers . . .

16

Yelena exchanges a glance with another student, but I carry on.

. . . That's good, of course. But for now (I think I've turned my back on my students at this point, I'm bending over the tank and they have collapsed into silence behind me) we need to bear it. Ignorance. Doubt. Learn to tolerate the not-knowing feeling, not rush to the simplest conclusion just because we can't allow another perhaps implausible one to form. It might seem wildly improbable once it comes, the idea. But it doesn't mean it's wrong.

I'm talking to myself, really. I need this lecture. I'm finding my own research rather frustrating just at this moment. Usually I love the incremental aspect of my work. I'm patient, I like doing the same thing every day. I have a heap of data, I have theories. I've been testing the water currents and studying the data on the octopus, which also changes colour, but I'm not much further along. I'm distracted, and something keeps getting in the way. My concentration is shot to pieces.

So it's the end of July now and two weeks after our holiday in Malaysia when I get a phone call from my brother with no warning at all and no sense that we haven't spoken in years and years and that there is such freight, such a huge ocean-dragging net full of stuff between us (green-furred, like the wreckage of the *Mary Rose*) and he just says casually that he's getting married and can I come over to England in August for the wedding.

Where? Where are you getting married? I ask, playing for time.

In Ely of course, at the registry office — where else?

It's 4p.m. on a hot afternoon and I'm standing by the open screen-door, with a coffee in one hand, the phone in the other, staring out at the trees. A squirrel twirls up a tree in front of me in a barley-sugar twist, like the movement on a barber's pole. The coffee-maker in the kitchen behind me sizzles away: the apartment has the warm grainy smell of a café.

Why didn't you give me more notice? I ask him.

I knew you wouldn't come if you had time to think. I don't think you Yanks will fly anywhere any more. Go on, Tina. Ask Dean. It would mean a lot to me if you could come.

You Yanks. He thinks of me as a Yank now. I know I have a hybrid accent. Whichever country I'm in now I sound like a foreigner.

The thing is, I start, you know my seahorses, the research I've been doing for years and years . . . well, one of them is pregnant and it's a crucial time, I mean, it would be quite hard to leave my seahorses right now . . .

There is a long pause, then Andrew repeats, slowly: one of your seahorses is pregnant. You can't leave it behind for a few days? Well —

He's a probation officer, my brother. His job is to be a go-between, to speak the language of his young charges, adolescent boys, mostly in trouble for nicking a car, trying to start a boat, under-age drinking. I get the impression I'm hearing his professional tone: he probably spends a lot of time repeating back to kids the stupid things they've just said. Tearaways: that's the word Mum would use. Boys like our brother Billy was for a while.

Not even if you just came for the weekend? he asks. For three days or something? The wedding is on Saturday. You can stay with me and Wendy and meet her daughters . . .

Well . . . will Mum be there?

Of course Mum will be there, Tina, it's my wedding!

I hear a splinter then, in his accent. Is it Dad I hear, in his voice? Dad was born on a farm just over the Suffolk border, and he was proud of that, of the Suffolk rather than the Cambridgeshire Fens in his accent. Suffolk he felt was the real thing: the first East Anglians, the originals. Not that anyone but a local would know the difference. Mum would tease him and say it was all poppycock anyway. Don't listen to a word he says — he was born right here, at Black Horse Drove! Whatever the truth, wherever he was from, I heard it then, fleetingly. My brother's "o'course" sounding just like an old Suffolk farmer.

Me, I'm standing in Merrill House, on the campus of Amherst College, Massachusetts. The apartment is pale, clean, unmistakably temporary. Behind me, Poppy lies full length on the cereal-coloured sofa, staring at the TV, a giant glass of kiwi juice balanced perilously beside her on a cushion. The windows and door to the campus are open and behind me an electric fan purrs; in front a sprinkler sends jets across the grass and the well-cared for pine trees, soaking the pine-needles so that their smell rises up under the coffee smell like green fingers.

There's a little crackle on the line and a cough.

OK, I tell Andrew. I suppose I can ask Yelena. My post-grad. She can feed him and keep notes for me. Hopefully he'll hold off with the babies till I get back. It's a shame they're so unpredictable . . . it's such a worry, I've never really entrusted them to a student before . . .

I'm sure your seahorses will manage perfectly well without you for three days, Andrew says. He hangs up.

Poppy darts me a look. She's attuned. She gets up, rescuing the glass of juice just in time and closes a couple of the windows, pulls the Venetian blinds to half-shut out the sun.

Would you like to confront the parent of a seriously obese child? Poppy says.

It's a catchphrase we like; it's from one of those *issue* programmes when "average Americans" get to discuss their problems with experts. We whisper it to one another whenever we pass people so fat that we cannot resist staring: a woman whose flabby feet overhang the edges of giant, specially constructed sandals; a man who needs a whole bench to himself in a restaurant. Poppy means, on this occasion, are you OK? There must be something in my face, my voice, perhaps my squinty eyes. I don't know what the clue is, what I'm giving away. I know I'm gazing at her, and I know she is a dark shape in front of me, I can make out perfectly well the bright red legs of her jeans; they look like two chilli peppers, but that's about all I can see. A shape, another shape of a fairer girl, an imprint, or blot, like a negative on a photograph, is struggling to form, right in front of her, right where my daughter's shape ought to be. And there's the smell, the familiar acrid burning smell from such a long time ago, and the sense of somewhere inside or beside me a giant shell cracking open.

From a long way off, down a well or a long tunnel, Poppy is shouting: Dad! Dad, come here!

Then the biscuit-coloured floor tiles are speeding towards me: I don't know if I'm staring at a screensaver, or a blizzard, or tiny pieces of my own smashed brain.

This is the resurgence that Dean is talking about. These are the freak symptoms. These, and Mandy, are why I need to rethink my medication.

The first time it happened I was about ten, in church with my brothers. It's a Baptist church a short walk from our house, on the straight boring road that drives right through the centre of our village, and I'm allowed to walk there on my own and take my brothers so that Mum can get on and cook the Sunday dinner and have five minutes peace. It's the only five minutes peace she gets all week, she says.

Dad has already left. He leaves before any of us are up. He's on a mission, he says, it's the Search for the Secret Pike-Perch. Last night he showed us a fishing magazine, smacking the page with his finger. *And then they came. Pike-perch from a fenland drain.* He cracked into one of his shot-gun laughs, so noisy we all jump as if jerked by a string.

Some bloody stupid River Board employee — can you imagine it! He's let them loose in the bloody Relief Channel!

Quickly, my brothers laughed too. They have church ready, their excuse if he ever asks them to come with him, makes them carry his nasty smelly bait, the swilling bucket full of chub and roach and rudd. But they needn't worry. It's only me he likes to come fishing with him; they're too rowdy, they can't sit still.

Our church has a Girls' Brigade; it involves wearing white gloves and a navy cap, and Andrew and Billy, being boys, aren't allowed to be in it. They don't get to have their own special bibles, with the lovely gold-edged pages.

Billy is a pest: the worst fidget. He likes to sing the words to the hymns all wrong, loudly, to annoy me. *Stuff him, stuff him!* he'll sing to the tune of *Praise him, praise him*, right here, in God's house, where God is not snoozing or out watching over other more important people, but listening intently to our prayers. Every time we are told to kneel on the little blue pillows on the floor in front of us, Andrew forces out a fart. Then the pair of them huddle together, convulsed in a scuffle of giggles and punches while I bat them as hard as I dare on their heads with my bible.

This day, there's a new minister. He is young, with black raisins for eyes, like the face in a gingerbread man, and an Adam's apple that bobs so much it makes me feel sick. He is wearing his long black robe over jeans, which I save up to tell Mum later, knowing how much it will insult her. He is telling us a story in his

22

own words, not using thees and thous: making Jesus sound very casual as well, like he is wearing jeans under his old-time robes too, in the story. I like to fiddle with my white gloves, smoothing them neatly down over each finger, and I'm constantly adjusting my hat with the two grips on either side. I know I look smart. In my white handbag with the hard clasp in the middle I have a tiny mirror in a pink plastic compact, with stars on it. I would like to check my hair again to see if my fringe is lying flat, but the minister is close to me and his voice has become louder, and I'm afraid to move my arms.

Then the story corkscrews. I missed a bit somehow when I was feeling for my pink compact, and suddenly the minister is talking about some man, found on the wayside, with a bullet in one arm. We can't possibly be in Bethlehem. Billy and Andrew perk up at the word bullet, like dogs, with their ears twitching. The minister steps forward from the pulpit, begins to walk amongst us. This church is small and airless. It smells of my brothers' socks and of leather and wood polish and women's hairspray. Jesus is pinned on the wall right behind him, a wooden, lanky figure, drops of wooden blood dripping from the crown on his head, his wooden pupil-less eyes boring into me. Some Pharisees are apparently passing the man, who is lying there half-dead, having been shot by members of a rival gang. My head is spinning with the idea that they had gangs in Jesus's time and bullets. I'd definitely thought bullets were modern things, like telephones or electric lights.

Now the minister is near our bench. He pauses right in front of us, the knees of his jeans level with my seat.

He's too close. I can smell smoky denim, just like Dad's coat. Think about it, he says. Are you going to be somebody who looks the other way? And his voice is sly, low; I see a tiny glob of spittle fly from his mouth to my gloves, but I daren't brush it off.

No, no, not me, I think, but I say nothing.

Thank God at least the Samaritan has come along now, he probably looks a bit like Cliff Richard, and now he is doing his bit. He's produced a knife, a red Swiss army knife with that little white cross on it and all the tools for cleaning your nails and getting stones out of donkeys' hooves, and begins digging at the bullet. It's curious how much time the minister gives to this description; he shows us with his hands how the Samaritan digs and twists with the knife, trying to dislodge the bullet. He is right in front of Billy and Andrew and they are eating out of his hand. Perhaps that's it, he can't resist the sense that he has them and has only to reel them in for two new fishermen to add to his boat. But it's way too vivid for me. I can smell the blood and see the white and pink textured flesh like the guts of a fish and somehow this must be Mandy. Is this what has happened to her, is this what they refuse to tell me? And then I smell burning, a sharp smell at the back of my throat, and a huge, spiralling fear is building up right under my nose, so that I have to flap my arms to press it down, as if it is a big bird, attacking me; then there is a white and grey feeling, like something tunnelling, like being overtaken, and I've been here before, too, twisting and turning and never getting out, something gripping me, holding me tight,

24

and it's not like pain but only fear and sickness and voices turning into slurry underwater sounds and then a great wash of navy caps and white gloves and crackles like small fireworks exploding. Then nothing.

Later, Mum blames Andrew. He's older than Billy. He should have seen what was happening. Look at her face! she shouts at him: she's white as a ghost. As the holy ghost, whispers Andrew in an aside to Billy. She was twitching! Billy agrees. Mum flicks the tea-towel at him to smack him round the head and misses.

She's cross again but none of us knows who with, or why. Dad is still not home. The meat is dried up and the roast potatoes hard and brown, and she's slamming his plate into the oven and kicking the oven door closed with a great big slam. The boys managed to get me out of the church and Mrs Richardson, a neighbour, brought us home. That must be the final straw, the Mrs Richardson bit, as when we arrive Mum has flour in her hair and a sweaty look, with red cheeks and steam filling the kitchen. She's flustered and not at all grateful and when Mrs Richardson says, oh Doreen, isn't it sad about the little Baker girl? Mum turns very red and nods her head towards us, frowning in a strange way, which Mrs Richardson doesn't seem to understand at all.

I feel I have done something disgusting, and this only adds to the already disgusted and fearful feelings I have about it. I know it's something to do with Jesus, and something to do with Mandy, and not listening enough and not paying enough attention. But also, it's to do with that bullet. With picturing it, picturing the flesh, the knife. For other people these things are happening somewhere else, somewhere the minister is describing. For me, it is right there under my nose, inside my own skin.

I'm nearly eleven now: it's one whole month since Mandy disappeared. No one has told me anything, given me any clues as to where she might be. The whole world has fallen eerily silent about Mandy Baker, a girl as real a month ago as my own fat freckled arm, now vanished in a puff of smoke, with no rabbits or bunches of flowers, nothing left in her place.

As for the fainting, no one takes me to the doctor. It was probably a bit airless in that church, Mrs Richardson says. I'm a silly girl with too much imagination and my mother has enough on her hands without *that*.

In my purple bedroom, in private, I like to dance myself into a frenzy. I wish we went to the kind of church where this was what we did, all together. I like to shake my hair until it whips my head, stomp my feet, shake shake shake myself, shake the evil out of me, shake my hands, feel tremors rise up from the floor, shimmy right through me, feel the blood rush in me: maybe it's only the holy spirit sneaking his way up inside me, isn't he rising up in me, up to my throat, my head, my eyes? I can really feel something, someone, something is definitely there, some power. I feel it as part of me but bigger than me, like I'm the centre of a web full of threads, fanning out to the whole world and me just one girl, one small silly, girl . . . Tina . . . Teenaaa . . . At the end of this dance routine I like to slump to the floor, *spent*. Our teacher used this word when two dancers from the Ballet Rambert did this. They came to our school.

Here's Mandy, here's what she looks like at seven years old, in our Musical Movement class. She's a well-built girl, her flesh so packed and creamy pale she seems juicy to me. I sometimes think of biting her, of what she would taste like. (But I'm seven now and I don't think I've bitten anyone since I was four.) Like all of us, she is wearing a white vest, slightly baggy, one pale pink nipple peeking out beneath a too-big armhole, and large navy blue cotton knickers, with grey bobbles of fabric across the bottom. Her feet are bare, her toes fat and well shaped and healthy. Mandy's hair is blonde, like mine, only hers is blonder and finer and is the sort of hair that swings back into place very easily, where mine is not. She smells like a Sherbert Dip Dab, which she was eating before it was confiscated. As it's the rule for Musical Movement, Mandy has her hair tied back in a band, the sort we call a bobble: two cherry-red plastic balls are attached to the elastic. There are other children, of course, a whole class of them, boys and girls, and no doubt noise and mayhem too, but I'm concentrating here on Mandy, she is the only one I can see. She is running along a narrow wooden upturned bench, and the teacher is plonking out notes on the piano, and we are in a primary school dining hall, serving as a part-time gym, in a Cambridgeshire village in the early nineteen seventies — see how much information I have, now it's coming to me, now I'm really trying! And now Mandy reaches the end of the bench and jumps to a blue mat, inelegantly. Her feet make a great thud. I can hear the thud perfectly. The rest might be inaccurate, an amalgam, concocted, something to picture; but not that thud of her feet landing, that splat of dusty bare soles on rubber. That I can hear. That, I'm sure is real.

This one is a few years later, late afternoon in May. Mum is at work, at Lipton's on the High Street. She finishes there at 6p.m. so I'm to get the boys' tea. Dad is at the British Sugar Social Club, where he is most nights, where he is most afternoons, while the factory is closed. I've grilled the fishfingers and peas and made them into a nice smiley face shape and called the boys down to eat them and upended the ketchup bottle so they can help themselves and poured them both a cup of Dandelion and Burdock, all so that I can sneak into the bathroom, lock the door, open my secret package.

After school today I bought this hair-dye from the chemist next to Burrows in Ely: Harmony Copper Gold, in a cardboard pyramid, something like a Toblerone. I had no idea Copper Gold would make such a mess. The sink, the towel, the bathroom lino — an autumnal flower pattern, thankfully, so the rust-coloured blobs blend into the leaves — all are splattered. Now I've slapped it on, my bare neck streams with red, drips sliding from my scalp down my face in bloody stripes, and the straps of my vest and the lace neckline are all stained too.

Half an hour later and my hair's rinsed, dried and sticking around my head like a golden dandelion, like the girl in the Flake advert: a fluffy auburn glow. The bathroom stinks of chemicals but is mostly mopped and shined. Our autumn-toned ceramic basin, toilet bowl and bath are like the floor, slightly more autumnal than they were, but I'm not sure anyone could tell, unless their face was up close. Only Billy would put his face to the bathroom floor and he would be looking for a hand grenade for Action Man, so I doubt he'd notice much else.

I have new clothes, bought yesterday in Peterborough, and I can't wait to wear them. A denim skirt, made of panels joined together, slightly stiff. A halter-neck top which, being ruched and gathered just under the bust-line, actually makes it look like I have breasts. Especially when I tie the neck really tightly.

I shouldn't go out when I'm in charge of my brothers but now I can hear the *Blue Peter* music so I know they're happily in front of the telly. I want to nip over the beet field to Jenny's house to show her my new clothes. Jenny lives less than half a mile away in a farmhouse up East Fen Lane. Between our little council street and her house is the field and after that a lane lined with high hedges where we pick blackberries and sloes in autumn and it will take about fifteen minutes to walk there, so I figure out that I can easily be there and back before Mum comes home, as long as I can bribe my brothers into not telling her.

I'm running over the field and it's sunny and windy, with the rich black lines of ploughed earth catching the light and almost shining. The rows make me think of melted chocolate, folded and ribbed, or the inside packaging of a box of Milk Tray, brown crinkled paper, corrugated. The wind flutters my chemical-scented hair around my face and out of the corner of one eye I can see Ely cathedral on the horizon, right behind the beet factory, rising up like a snail with horns and one smaller hump. It looks as if it's looking at me.

As I reach the high hedges of the lane, I glimpse two figures at the entrance and slow down. Boys, I think, at first. Then: men. They are standing together, one on either side, in silence, not smoking, not talking or laughing, just standing. One has very black hair that rises from his forehead in a jerk. The other is small and faint. I have never seen them before but they are looking at me expectantly, like they know me. Like they are waiting for me.

I pause for a second, not understanding why I am hesitant to walk between them. I secure a piece of hair behind my ear, a movement that flicks my wrist outwards, an appealing gesture, I think: kind of sexy. Yes, I definitely think I'm sexy. I hitch up the halter-top. The wind drops suddenly, away from the field. I can no longer smell the wind, or the hair-dye. Instead there is another smell, one so subtle I don't register it at first.

And a voice says, perfectly clearly: *Don't go down there*. And for the second time there is a burning smell.

What kind of voice? I don't know: a voice. Well, of course, I can't remember the voice itself, only what was

30

said, I'm listening and watching now from too far away. The boys — men — are very small, tiny in fact. It's me who is big, me who is watching, waiting for them. I am about to change their lives for ever. I am about to end their childhood.

But I really can see myself, this newly auburn-haired, leggy girl, in another time, and know what mattered, despite everything, what might have made a difference to me. There is study now, the *science* of memory; a friend of Dean's, a neurologist, is always talking about it. One time he says: of course, Tina, when one remembers something, this is happening in the present, not the past, so in fact it is not an old memory at all, trawled up from some place, but a new one, created afresh . . . Yes, yes, I say, irritated. I know this, surely everyone does, I mean, I'd expect a small child to know it, just through trial and error, just through trying to deliberately bring up a memory (bring it up, like a burp, like something that's good for you: better out than in) and finding out that it's not the same.

Every time we remember something, what we are remembering is actually only the last time we remembered it, he says, with such authority. This guy. This friend of Dean's.

So when new facts emerge, new details, how can I know if they were there at the time, or if I am embellishing? It's like looking at slices of film floating in a tank of chemicals and shifting some and moving others, and laying something new over them, and then removing it again; noting all the combinations, all the possibilities.

I'm thinking of that time and trying with all my might to tell it accurately and not cheat because this one really did happen and then suddenly, at the mouth of that lane when I walk myself there, what I remember, what I hear, is a voice. Someone saying, right inside me or perhaps beside me: *Don't go down there*. And there is the same burning smell. But it's even more confusing than that. I didn't hear it at the time, or didn't think I did: it has taken me nearly thirty years to hear it, to really take it in. What does that tell me about Mandy, about what I might be able to figure out, if I move the film about? I can hear the voice now, it's part of the memory when I replay it, that short walk made a difference in my life, both because of what happened, and because of what didn't. It shaped me. Without it, I would have been otherwise.

OK, so here I am, coming through Customs with my ears full of pressure from the flight, like the pressure from a dive. I ring Dean from Heathrow, a reverse charge call, just to tell him I'm here in London safely, but it's Poppy who answers. I'm here in England! I tell her, but either my ears or the line make her voice come back wobbly, with a delay.

Poppy, it's me, I say, is that you? There's something wrong with this phone. You're breaking up! Poppy, I can't really hear you. Tell Dad I arrived safely. I'll call later.

I hear my own voice in one ear, repeating this phrase, then a whoosh. A sound like wind rushing through a beet field, or a train tearing past.

32

Pulling my one small drag-along trolley of hand luggage, I hold my nose and blow out, the way we deal with the pressure underwater, but it doesn't work still, nothing works. There's no sense of pop, of release, of hearing normally again.

God, I'm probably going deaf, I think. These things happen once you hit forty, better be prepared. I mean, not to turn deaf, but for things you took for granted ceasing to work. Eardrums. Eyes. I should see a doctor while I'm here as, after all, I wouldn't have to pay for it. (Not that I do, anyway, my doctor being my next of kin but it's the principle of the thing: it's one of the few British things I'm still defensive about.)

I could do with Poppy right now. Her long-sightedness. I often simply ask her, delaying the moment when I need to take an eye test, what does that say? *Welcome to Heathrow Airport*. What about that one? Does that say Hertz? Or anything about Car Rental?

So, I find the counter for Hertz and wait in line (*queue up*, I think, now it's "queue up") only to discover there's some "unfortunate mix-up" and yes, there's the record of my telephone booking (the red-head has her name badge pinned on the very apex of one of her enormous breasts, so that it tilts forward and the name can't be read) but she's terribly sorry, madam, that car has "gone out already". She says this as if it took off somehow, and drove itself away. Mistakes happen, and normally I'm the world's coolest person, Poppy says it would take a sledge-hammer to the head to get me riled up, so I'm surprised, I'm really shocked, to see my hands on the counter in front of me, trembling. I hear myself saying, in a voice that sounds like a twanged violin string, that this REALLY ISN'T GOOD ENOUGH.

A spotty manager is called. He's younger than she is, but assesses the danger more rapidly. He's obsequious. Of course, of course, we're terribly sorry, madam, and as an expression of that, do let us upgrade you to our business-class vehicles. Yes, yes, no extra cost, of course.

While they photocopy my credit card, I turn the new key over in my hand, studying the blue BMW triangles at the centre and watching my hands to see if the trembling subsides. It does. The red-head nervously pushes a photocopied map of the carpark towards me, marking my car with the letter X in biro. Everything the young woman says to me sounds wavery: her repetition of my name and her instructions about Carpark B and full tanks and petrol; until I shift my bag behind me, turn towards her with my other ear and then she sounds fine again.

Enjoy your stay in England, she says tremulously.

I imagine Dad taking the piss out of her. It was his speciality: strangers. Nothing about them frightened him. He once ran up behind a man walking the tiniest, most ridiculous-sized dog and yelled at him: oh my God, you've forgotten your dog — you've brought a bloody mouse out with you!

How sorry I used to feel for shop assistants! Standing beside Dad, my eyes at ground level, or staring determinedly at his trouser leg, while he blasted someone about something. He would start with that deadly sarcasm. May I ask you something? Is somebody

34

paying you to be this — bloody — slow? And then he'd be off, like a rocket launch. I'd try not to stare at the scarlet-faced girl, her eyes glittery with tears, only whispering as loud as I dared: Dad, Dad, come on, here's the manager, let's go now.

I glance back at the red-head, an apology forming, but she's turned her shoulder towards me, determinedly engaged with another customer.

Andrew and Billy's worst insult for me was to call me a pig, but the word pig was banned in our family.

Pigs are smart, Dad says. Don't ever underestimate a pig.

Of course, Grandad had the pig farm. Dad likes pigs.

Even their tails squeak, Dad says, another time, and we don't understand this, or we wonder how the tails can squeak, but Mum says he's talking about the money, he's meaning that you can sell every last bit of a pig, it's all valuable. We used to race them, Dad says. We'd sit on the choice pigs, me and Danny Browne, I'd be astride our best porker, the prize-winner, the Large White; I'd be holding onto little old boy's ears, my spurs digging into his flanks, mud flying into our faces . . .

Don't listen to him, Mum says, with one of her huffing sounds. She always says this. Why do you say all that, Graham? You know they believe every word.

He just laughs. He gets hold of Billy's ear and says: I bet you can squeak like a pig, can't you, and Andrew is laughing too, but Billy's not, he's scowling and saying ow. We like Dad when he's in a good mood like this. He's noisy and he teases us and he knocks over all our toys, jumping about and play fighting; sometimes he roars at us, holding his fingers like claws in front of his face and saying: I'm a Fen Tiger, me!

They're not tigers, really, but people, Mum explains to me later. They were Dad's ancestors, or so he says: water people, the ones who lived by fishing and catching wildfowl and who resented the Dutch coming in the seventeenth century, the Adventurers, coming to drain their lands. But whatever she says, I picture a real tiger when he says this. I picture him riding on the back of a pig, digging his claws in, like the big cats in the nature programmes, their heads dipped under the throat of their victims, so that they seemed entwined, romantic even, but I knew the teeth were locked there, that's how they got them: the jugular.

I can't resist Dad's pig stories. He wants me to sit on his knee, even now I'm so big. He clamps his big arms around my folded ones and tells me again about the first gilt Grandad ever bought and how it was forty-five quid, a fortune, he says; would be even in decimal money! How he bought her "in pig" and he tells me what this means and how she had so many lovely babies that first year, and how sad he was the first time, when Grandad made him take them right off the teat at eight weeks to sell them.

Why did you have to?

Well a farm has to make money, you know. And we had a big prize boar to breed with my lovely Essex gilt to make the blue pigs that we could sell the best, but we had to castrate the others. The other little old boys. Do you know what castrating is?

I shake my head.

He laughs, rolling his eyes, making a movement with his fingers like scissors, and tickling me roughly.

We'd go *chunk*, he says, and cut them right off. Their little pig balls. No anaesthetic, nothing. They make the most terrible scream . . .

He's really laughing now, he says: your face, you should see your face!

Oh Graham, Mum says again. She's cross with him and so I think she means he is lying again, or it's make-believe. I hope that's true, I suddenly don't want to hear any more about the poor little pigs, so I put my hands over my ears, and sing Jesus loves me this I know, and Dad calls me his little piggy-wiggy, his honey-bun, and tickles me some more.

This hire-car smells like after-shave: it smells like a business man's car. I discover the air-freshening offender dangling from the rear-view mirror, an impregnated piece of cardboard from the Yankee Candle Company. The smell makes me think of Poppy again. That day we made a trip to the Heritage Candle Factory, a kind of joke. The smell smacked us, even from the highway. A day so hot it was a wonder the candle factory didn't melt into one giant wax mound in the vast parking lot. Lavender, vanilla, maple and wax, blended to the power of a small nuclear explosion. And even in mid-summer, there were giant Christmas tree candles, Santa-shaped candles that somehow looked like dildos to me. I wondered for a moment whether

Poppy thought this too, or whether she was too young to know what a dildo was.

Do you think you're up to going to your brother's wedding? Dean had asked, gently, lying in bed, back in Amherst. Do you want me to come with you?

I considered this, tempted. Of course, it would be easier if Dean and Poppy came with me. They'd seal up my edges, nothing would get inside. The family thing would just glide over me. I didn't really understand why, with all the misgivings I had, after all the years of avoidance, I wasn't taking this option.

I'll take my medication, I said.

That's not what I meant . . .

It'll be fine, I told him. It's only three days! It'll be a chance to see Mum and my brothers, maybe a few old friends.

You hate your old friends, Dean murmured. He didn't add: you hate your mother.

Maybe see a few old places then, I said.

What we were skirting around, what Dean was not saying was: you haven't been back since your dad died. I didn't even go for the funeral and I know Billy in particular has found it hard to forgive me for that. I was meant to be Dad's favourite. I was the one who enjoyed that privilege for all those years and I'm the one who, when it comes to it, says: this is too hard and I don't want to do it. Of course I gave them reasons. I had just submitted my PhD, I was waiting for a viva. But this was like speaking a foreign language anyway. PhD? All those years, and still just a student?

What I said to Andrew was this: look, he left us years ago. He made it clear he wasn't interested. God, even this, even what he did — it wasn't for us but for somebody else. A girl half his age. Why should he expect us to jump to it for him now? What did he ever do for us?

Andrew said: Christ, Tina, I'd no idea you were so bitter.

Driving into the village is like driving through a cloud of bees, through something heavy or choking, something you have to point the nose of the car towards and hope it can plough right through. The village — just some houses — falls either side of a road where every jolt and bump is remembered. A small improvement: the railway crossing is no longer manned. You could wait half an hour for Tom Lackersby to put out his pipe and bestir himself to open the gate. At the second crossing there is a bunch of white cars with phone numbers on the side, a taxi service, maybe that's even Billy's company, isn't that what he does now? Probably the lack of buses. I remember Mum saying it was appalling how this government has neglected the countryside; how the old people now have to use taxis all the time. As I wait at the crossing for the train to pass I notice an oversized goat, chewing intently, tethered to the fence of a newish-looking surburban house.

The beet factory closed down before I left. Now it's a haulage company. Still plenty of trucks. A new access bridge built over the river. There are giant warehouses where the factory was, meaning the view of the cathedral is still partly obscured. But it's all cleaner, quieter. The sickly burnt smell during the Campaign, the trundling night and day, the trail of filthy discarded beets on the road, the foul-smelling smoke from the chimneys: all gone. I wonder for a moment about the work they did here. The quarry they dug, I remember it suddenly, what year was that? There were danger signs up, we were never allowed to play there. Hundreds of men delivered beets to the factory. Scores more worked there. Did they search the quarry, the year Mandy went missing? Did anyone think to prevent them from filling it in?

The train crashes into my thoughts, passing swiftly, a green caterpillar, nothing like the old American trains I hear deep at night on campus, so slow and long, like an orgasm: rumbling in the distance for a good ten minutes before arriving and then crashing through my sleeping brain. This is slick and brief. The second it passes, the lights change and the barrier lifts.

And then suddenly I'm driving over the Fens proper, towards the fields again, the peaty earth, richer, darker than any I've ever seen. God's snooker table, Mum used to called it. Not for the green baize — there's none of that neatness, that trimmed golf-course look — but for the flatness, the sense that the buildings were just rolled out like balls until they came to a halt, and that's where they ended up. And that's me, too, I realise. Spooled out here, under this blue clear beloved sky, like an insect trapped beneath an enormous blue basin.

It's the sky, of course, that makes it so unlike anywhere else I've been. The car windscreen is just full of sky. All sky and hardly any earth, only a fine black skin capping the centuries of water, the secrets. It reminds me of the drawings I used to do when I was little: I'd crayon blue at the top in a strip and then a band of green or black at the bottom and it never seemed to occur to me that the middle bit, the bit I left white and put the people and the buildings in, just couldn't be accurate. Now that's where I am. I'm driving right into that white uncooked space, the page I left blank.

Mine is the only car on the road. The huge pylons lacing the landscape pass me, as wonky as ever, lurching. They look drunk. I'm doing sixty as I approach the village and I don't want to stop. Signs flash at me to slow to thirty but it's almost impossible: it's a typical Fen road, long, straight, going nowhere, a Roman afterthought, and like a million bad-boys on motorbikes, cursed by the villagers, I keep my foot on the accelerator, keep going.

And so our street looms up before I'm ready, I miss it the first time and have to drive as far as the river before I can reverse at Lark Bank, come back. Here the land is dry and from the road I see the faint shade of clay, a long striped sweep visible in the earth, where the old rivers used to run before they were diverted. The farmhouse on the right before you turn into our street is a couple of hundred years old and a fine example of how the peat is shrinking: the house has sunk a good few feet since it was built, and more still since I last saw it. It too is on a slant, "on the huh". Dad was always saying that it was the engineer, "bloody Vermuyden", that we had to thank if half the houses were sinking, since the more the Fen is drained, the more the peat contracts, something "those Dutch bastards" weren't expecting at all. That's why some of the rivers are higher than the land in places like Tongue End (a favourite fishing haunt of his). He'd forget himself, jab the ground with his fishing rod when he said this, then get mad in case he'd damaged it. It was the Fen Tiger in him again, resisting the "land-lubbers" with their fancy plans to triumph over the power of nature, or rather water, his preferred environment. (Never mind that it all happened hundreds of years before he was born.)

I don't need to ask Dad to know what he'd make of the new houses sprouting here: new-built fancy-pants modern ones, with their over-sized garages and gravel drives, replacing most of the council houses that used to make up this street. Council houses are another feature of English life I can't seem to convey to my American daughter. She thinks of The Projects, pictures the Bronx. Not these thirties redbrick houses, well-kept hedges. The same sort of house my mother grew up in, was born in. The sort of house I lived in for eighteen years.

I forgot how well I knew this street, with its houses on one side, fields on the other; this red post-box, this skewed telegraph pole. I forgot I knew all this, but here it was, waiting for me, stored up. I switch off the engine but stay inside the car, only loosening my seat-belt, making no move to get out.

When I was really little, I mean about seven, I suppose, or maybe eight, I had this thought that the

42

world didn't actually exist. None of it. It was one great black void, just like the bible says it was before God invented it. Not my bedroom, my house, my street, my fields, the Fens, the rest of England, the sea, the other countries, the world, the universe. What I thought happened was that I made it up. I used to close my eyes and for a moment, I really did believe it all dissolved. It was just happening in my head. And then I had this terrified understanding that if I didn't make an effort, if I didn't concentrate hard on imagining it all up, dreaming it up — the purple carpet of my bedroom, the white chest of drawers with the pink flower stencils, carefully applied by Mum, then the bedroom door, then the stairs beyond the door — then my world would also not exist, or exist only partially in the bits I'd imagined and beyond that would drop away into black nothingness. It was exhausting, this imagining. I had to keep it up at all times. I'd forgotten that peculiar way of thinking about the world, but here it is again. This place surely did not exist in all the years I was away. It's only here again in this shape because I'm here, thinking it.

I close my eyes, inhale the disgusting car air-freshener smell. Then I open them and blink and the speckled green fields, the pea crop, blurs into a Monet painting: a mass of yellow and green dots. A shadow swoops across the field, like the arc made by a compass moving across paper. My eyes fall on the square of rough land in front of me, the place where our house used to be. Now it's a knee-high tangle of grass and weeds, with a *Plot For Sale* sign and a straggle of poppies the colour of dried blood, heads dropping. Our garden merges into the fields now the fence has been taken down. Or rather the fields have finally crept right up to our garden and claimed it. There's no sign of my old swing.

I climb out of the car. I feel a pang of hurt that my brothers didn't think to tell me the council had demolished our house. But then, why would they? They probably neither know nor care. Neither of them has lived in the village since they were old enough to get a job, and Mum moved away soon after.

I can see my dad coming out of the shed, the place where the shed used to be. He's young, his hair is very dark and he has a beard, hair all around his face; I must be a tiny girl. It's cold, it's early morning, grey light, he's clapping his hands together then blowing on them to warm them, I can see his breath curling in front of him. I'm warm inside, someone is holding me while I watch him carrying stuff, rods and coats and folded chairs and wellies and stuffing them all into his white van, then slamming the doors once, twice, then kicking them, shouting, bloody damn things! and then going back to the shed, carefully locking it, putting the key in his pocket. Just as he's about to get in, he turns around, waves over at me; he's patting his pocket, checking for something. He touches his hand to his mouth, blowing me a kiss, then turns his back again, whistling.

I'm not the tearful sort any more than I'm usually angry. This is not like me at all.

Andrew's wedding is in two hours. I've just time to compose myself, gird my loins: that peculiar, old-fashioned phrase that's just slid into my head. What on earth is gird; why loins? Maybe it meant encase your loins in some kind of armour, bind them up in some way; an ancient equivalent of a cricketer's box. Protect your most vulnerable bits. Get ready. Yep, that feels about right.

Despite the warmth of the day, wind is scattering my hair around my face, fluttering a newspaper on the back seat of the car. We used to say that it was always windy here, no matter what the weather was elsewhere. Black dust blown from the fields lined the windowsills and ruined Mum's washing if she hung it outside, and occasionally it was worse: full-grown Fen Blows whipping up huge dustballs of earth, a black fog, like something you see on American westerns; they would roll over to our houses because there were no hedges, no windbreaks to deter them. When Dad lost his temper Mum called it a Fen Blow. (Watch out or your father'll have one of his Fen Blows.) When I was small I thought he had something to do with them, I thought that maybe he caused them by shouting too much.

The light is fantastically strong, painting a strip down half the buildings, making the green fields glitter; and that combined with the wind shaking the pea crop makes everything shimmer across the flatness. At the end of the field there is one flattened strip of black earth, the colour of burnt toast. I stare now in the direction of the cathedral, that view I've stared at a million times: big sky, blank field, long straight road. No beet factory but now this grey warehouse building, just in front of the cathedral. It's pale silver, the warehouse, like a giant reflective sheet, bouncing the light away from the glorious building, back over the fields.

The wind roars in my head like traffic, and again I wonder if it's the flight, and press a hand against one ear to dislodge it. This street was always a quiet one. There are a couple of parked cars, but no dogs barking, no children or adults walking. It's possible for me to walk back to the car and sit in it like this, at twelve midday on a Saturday, and hear and see nothing. If something happened to me, if the police were later to ask people, if they did a lackadaisical house to house search, as they did back then, as they did when Mandy went missing, it's perfectly possible. The field might be the only witness.

Sunny and windy, with the hedges high at the entrance to the lane. The first man, the pale one, shoves me. I'm so surprised I squeak: a weird sound, a stupid one. I turn my head to look at him, with the stark lucidity of a future recollection (you know — trying to see things as you remember having seen them): realising he has blocked my path and that I would have to push past him. Touch him. Another sound comes out of my mouth but is snuffed: the black-haired one has pressed his flat smoky hand over my face, his fingers digging into my cheekbones, and the fair one has my arms pinned behind me. The strangest thing is their silence, apart from their breathing, which reminds me of the breathing of a horse. They don't offer one another encouragements, comments of any sort. They aren't rowdy like my brothers, going for a head-lock; they're business-like, quick. My skirt is up in an instant. Their fingers, someone's fingers, are painful and scratchy. I am flooded with a deep, red-hot shame: to think that they will see my knickers, my new, blue, flower-sprigged, cotton-gusseted knickers.

I can feel *their* fear and panic and there's a smell that reminds me of something old but fresh like Brie, or mushrooms or boys' socks, and I can see the pus in a couple of red spots on the dark one's forehead and I can feel the desperation in his gesture, the unzipping, the producing of a ridiculous ugly thing, trying to leap out of his hand with its fierce livid head; but I've still no idea why a fair man and a dark man are pushing me so hard, why this prickly privet is piercing my neck like that, tearing at the skin on my back; why they are pushing at me, and one of them is making this terrible groaning, as if he is going to be sick, and my cheekbones feel like they will splinter under the weight of his fingers; and right in the centre of me I'm suddenly made of honeycomb. And I'm twelve, I'm two years older than Mandy was when she disappeared: I'm shaking, violently, head to toe, glimpsing the colour, the smell, or taste or texture of what might have happened to her, the thing itself, the thing no one ever talks to me about. Any minute now this man — this boy? — will burst through my skin and I will be over, finished, my body will crumble behind it; all of me, crumble to dust.

But that was nearly thirty years ago and now I can suddenly see the flaws, the inaccuracy. Because here I have arrived at last at a café in Ely, this little city that I know so well, after all, and so much is the same, so much so that my heart flickers with recognition every time someone comes in. This café — the name hasn't changed — is one that I never went in when I lived here. We thought of it as "posh": it serves something called Gentlemen's Relish on toast, which I'm eating. I've just told the waitress that the person at the table next to mine appears to have left their car keys, and in my purse when I open it (*handbag* now, of course, they don't call them purses here) there is a spattering of confetti, coloured paper hearts and flowers from the packet I'm hoarding for my brother's wedding. It's an hour until I'm supposed to meet them, I've told no one yet that I'm here, I just drove to the village and then sped back here, and here I am alone and it's all these incidentals — that single tulip in a wine bottle, bending its head towards me, that wooden chair with the yellow leather seats riveted to it, the memory of my father, his hand on my mother's backside, her standing at the sink — that allow me to admit: well, after all, I wasn't raped and I wasn't killed.

I didn't tell a soul either. I ran back over the fields, without looking behind me, the feel of those fingers still crawling up me and I thought it was no more than I deserved, probably, for deserting my brothers. I couldn't tell Mum when I should never have gone off on my own and there was another, more powerful reason for not telling her or Dad and that was a reason I couldn't admit to, or even allow to take shape. And in any case, I was fine. They didn't succeed in doing what they set out to do, or what they perhaps never knew they intended to do. A woman came along. A woman stood at the other end of the path. She looked intensely familiar, and I felt sure she recognised me; she was staring, craning her neck slightly. I saw her only partially, and the dark one with his hand over my mouth must have understood from my expression that someone was behind us. He hesitated, released his hand just enough for me to squeeze a scream through his fingers, and as I started screaming, he turned his head to see who I had seen. As he did this, I felt the other one release his grip a little — just enough — and I was quick and strong in the same way that even a baby can be strong sometimes, slipping through your hands like a fish, and I wriggled out from under them and dusted myself down and walked quickly (I knew instinctively that to run would be to invite them to chase me) in the direction of the field, and I didn't look back, and I didn't see where the woman — a pale, slim, smart-looking woman — went. When I reached the field, I bolted.

I thought I knew everyone in our village. It was odd though, I'd never seen her before, or I couldn't figure out who she was, why she looked at me the way she did, as if she couldn't quite see me, was trying to look beyond me, past the men in front of me, over my shoulder. I think she was wearing jeans and posh shoes, with heels, an unusual peach colour. That's what I remember. The wrong sort of shoes for the Fens. I couldn't somehow gauge how far away she was. She must have been quite close — the path is only short — but she seemed to be far, a long way off.

The men too, I had never seen them before, but I did see them once afterwards. They were drinking beer on the back of a truck, a truck piled with sugar-beet, trundling down a track across the fields. They were workers then, farm-hands, cheap labour. I felt reassured. After all, men from your own village can't be rapists or attackers. Only others. Outsiders.

The whole village changes during the Campaign. That's what they call it, the season for harvesting the beets, October until March. The whole place rattles and shakes with the lorries trundling through, lorries so full, they drag the road with their bellies as they go in.

The factory chimney steams and pumps and everywhere there's beets dropped beside the road, hard, covered in mud. The sign for the village is splattered in mud too: no one can read it. They used to bring them up the river by barge, Dad says, a huge pile of beets, boats nearly sinking under the weight. He says he can remember those days but Mum tells him off, says that's nonsense, that was in the thirties, before he was even born. He takes me to the factory, he likes to show me off to the other men. This is my little old mawther, my Tina, he says. He twirls me round and the women cluck at me like chickens. These women wear white caps over their hair and call me "my beauty" and lift me up over the huge vats, show me how the sugar-beet floats in the water, getting all the mud cleaned off; they tell me that's what the big clouds are, pumping up into the sky, it's just the steam from the cleaning. The vat is full of weeds and stones, all held in this enormous sieve, the

50

water brown and filthy beneath, but the beets at last coming clean.

Isn't she lovely, they say, what a little blondie, isn't she a cutie-pie?

I've got a big ribbon in my hair, red velvet, and a red and white check dress. My dad hugs me tight, he's proud of me. The lady with the curly ginger hair sticking out from under her cap is smiling at him and he's touching her head, he's telling her to straighten herself up, the cap's on the huh, but she's not cross at him for telling her off, she just laughs and makes big eyes at him. He carries me on his shoulders, shows me the giant slicing machines, making the cossettes ("You wouldn't want to put your fingers in that now, duckie," the curly lady says), then the giant brewing vat, like an enormous teapot, Dad says. The place smells like bad farts to me, sort of cabbagy and sweet at the same time. My daddy is a foreman in this factory, he's a big man, he's tall and he gets to see what all the women are doing, and tell them off about their hats. He prowls up and down round the giant metal tins, he plucks a cossette from the shoot to the cleaning vat, pops it on my tongue. Can you believe that's where the sugar is, he tells me. I spit it out, it tastes like nothing, it tastes hard, like soap. We stare into the swirling dark browny-yellow water of the vat with all the little cossettes twirling round in it. It's hot in here. The men shout things to Dad about his little girl. He smiles and waves to them and calls them Dirty Old Dogs. He tells them to get back to work.

At thirteen, it's boys, makeup, and the ouija board. We pronounce it Weejee board. It's not actually a board, but just some squares of paper, torn from our school exercise books, laid out on a formica-topped coffee table in Jenny's front room, with the letters of the alphabet written on each in red felt-tip. Then some extra pieces with *never* and *usually* and *maybe* on them, to save time spelling. Jenny dims the lights. This being a new house, a sort of temporary house, built by Jenny's father, the lights are dodgy. It has to be here, though. Jenny's mum and dad are the only ones who ever go out. They leave her older brother, Steve, in charge of us but he sits upstairs with his mates, smoking or else, like today, he goes off down the Dog and Duck. Cherry turns the frosted blue tumbler upside down and we sit on the carpet around the table, each resting one little finger on the glass. It has to be the little finger. Index fingers are cheating: they put pressure on.

It's Jenny's turn: she gets to ask the question. Sometimes we shout them out, in the beginning we shout, when we're lively. Later, nails bitten, hair twisted into corkscrews around our fingers, we whisper into the glass, steaming it up. You must never ask if God exists. That would make the glass shatter. We know it is the Devil, or one of his servants, pushing the glass around the table, spelling out the words, and bad though he is, the Devil is like George Washington: he cannot tell a lie. So Jenny asks, loudly, confidently: does Brian Jackson fancy me? Cherry giggles and her breath blows several of the letters off the table — *sorry sorry!* Once she's rescued them, we solemnly return our fingers to the glass. We wait, shifting our crossed legs under the table. Nothing happens. Fingers tremble. Cherry coughs, turning her head to one side, cupping her hand. Three pairs of eyes stare at the upturned tumbler.

It begins to tip. It always begins with a tip. Then a sticky, jerky kind of shift, then a smooth slide towards a letter. Sometimes, terrifyingly, it hovers between the *yes* and *no* place, a struggle for power seems to be taking place, long enough for us to really worry. Its route is often circuitous, refusing to spell out. Answers rarely make sense. Does Brian Jackson fancy me? Frgki. *Frgki?* Frigid! Cherry shouts. He thinks you're frigid! She's giggling, coughing again. Sometimes bits of phrases are spelled out. We repeat them, hopefully. Y-O-U — you! M-U-S-T — must! G-R-O-W-N — grown! You must grown? You must . . . *You must grown over the tires.*

Disappointed, we lift our fingers off. Removing fingers breaks the spell.

You must grow tired of him, Jenny translates. She's sure that's what it means. That's her answer. She sits back, nods sagely.

Jenny is always the translator. She's thirteen too but unlike me she already has her periods and a bra with detachable half-moons of padded fabric. She showed us one time, and then slotted them back in, digging her hands right down her blouse, rooting about like Mum does when she's finding potatoes at the bottom of the sack, elbows jabbing. Jenny does this funny thing with her fingers, too. I love to watch her, in class, unzipping her pencil case. She holds her fingers slightly bent at the ends, prissy, delicate, as if the pencil shavings and broken nibs of pens are too dirty for her. The last inch of fingertip seems to tilt up slightly, although I am sure this can't be possible. But they're definitely different fingers from ours. Older. Remarkably bendy. Supernatural fingers.

It's my turn and I feel stupid. There isn't a boy I fancy and I asked last week if I'll ever marry David Soul. (I will.) Jenny is impatient. If you dither too long she gives this long drawn-out sigh and snatches the glass and moves it towards Cherry. I keep my hand over it, like a claw.

So I whisper, lifting the glass to my face, but Jenny looks at me, and I feel she somehow managed to hear me. *Is Mandy Baker dead?* I put the glass down hurriedly. It's three years ago. Time enough for an answer.

Fingers to the glass. Let us begin, says Jenny. Her priest's voice. Nothing happens. Is anybody there? Jenny booms. Cherry giggles.

If you are there, make the lights flicker! Jenny commands.

The hall light splutters, almost goes out. Cherry gives a startled whine, like the sound a dog makes dreaming. Jenny stares at the curtains, which do not twitch. My fingertip aches, all attention focused on it. The glass tilts, tips, starts jerkily moving. It's heading towards the Y.

Yes.

No hesitation. It simply moves to the paper with Jenny's writing, red letters; small, round. The Y curly, with a little loop. The capital E. The swirly S. Yes.

What did you ask? Jenny wants to know. She's staring at me.

The lights are perfectly fine: it's Jenny's voice that makes me hesitate, that makes my heart punch at my chest.

And then suddenly, the family dog, a massive black Doberman that stays tied up out front, starts barking and all three of us jump out of our skins.

She asked about some missing girl from our old school! She asked a spooky question! Cherry shrieks.

You moved it. You pushed it! Jenny accuses.

Ssssh, that must be your brother coming back —

I'm glad really. I don't like it when we call up the spirits and Stephen isn't home. I'm always worried that one of us will be entered, if we're not careful, possessed by an evil spirit that commands us to do filthy deeds (mostly sexual, rubbing yourself in rude places with a crucifix, that sort of thing; or screaming obscenities at the Maths teacher; or ripping off our aertex vests and showing the entire class our pink chewing-gum nipples).

Jenny is sweeping the letters into a plastic Lipton's carrier; she throws the tumbler in too, shoves the bag under the table just as Steve barges in. A pack of cards, appears, Jenny is dealing, smoothly, head bent, she doesn't look up or acknowledge her brother's grunt.

When Steve has slid past us into the kitchen in a cloud of stale smoke and we can hear the fridge door opening, Jenny hisses:

Mandy Baker. That girl who used to live over by Burnt Fen, all alone with her dad? He did away with her. I heard my mum saying it to one of her friends. He was a bit, you know.

She taps her head with one finger.

But he's not in prison. He's still living there! I see him all the time, I hiss back, incredulous.

They never *proved* it, idiot . . .

Her brother comes back in, flings himself heavily onto the nearest chair, turns the telly on with his socked foot on the dial. (I wish I could do that.) This is our signal to pack up and go. It's the *Dick Emery Show* — *oooh you are awful, but I like you* — Dad's favourite. Dad sometimes does his own version of one of the characters in it: the priest. He sticks this old pair of false teeth on top of his own and then puts his face really close and grins at me, so that he looks like a Halloween pumpkin.

Cherry and I always run home. I've never told Cherry about what happened once on my way to Jenny's house, but I don't take the short-cut over the fields any more, and I always call for Cherry first. My hair is blonde again, I let the red grow out. I didn't much want to be a red-head any more.

It's Jenny's dog that scares us most. It's so black it blends into the darkness with only the little chips of its eyes on show. In the front garden we have to run past it, barking and stretching to the edge of its rope. Jenny laughs at us. She'll come to the front door and stand stroking its head — the dog becomes a pet again, nestling against her, its tongue drooping.

56

Come on, Black Shuck, Jenny says, laughing, doing her spooky voice: come on, Prince of Darkness, the Evil One.

Its real name is Prince. It's a watchdog because Steve sells used things, pieces for cars and motorbikes, and some of it's kept in their back garden and somebody might try and nick it. One time, Stephen put up a sign that said *Keep Out Private Property* and he nailed four dead moles to it by their tails but Jenny's mum told him off, she said he was giving their house a bad look, it's bad enough that the house is only half-finished with great piles of bricks in the front and now tyres and gear-boxes with grass growing over them. She said that sign was giving her the creeps, so Steve had to take it down.

Black Shuck is a local story. It's just made up to try and scare you, my dad told me it. If you see Black Shuck, he says, if you sense a dog beside you; if you can hear it breathing or see the bright red splinters of its eyes or maybe a little spiral of steam rising from its breath when you're out all alone on the droves or in the middle of a Fen Blow, it's a signal. It means you're going to die.

I like to be scared, but I prefer real things, things like that girl whose head spins around in *The Exorcist*, or the ouija board. I don't really believe in Black Shuck because I found copies of *News of the World* stuffed down the arm of the sofa at Grandad's house and I read them and I know they are exactly what Mum is trying to keep me from knowing about. It's the same reason she switches off *Monty Python's Flying Circus* if

I come into the room. Men who like to dress up as women in stockings and suspenders; evil lesbians who have butch haircuts and try to be men; devil-worshippers who pretend to be priests and then rape the old ladies who look after the church silver and do the dusting; nymphomaniacs who murder babies where they work in hospitals. They're everywhere, they're even in ordinary-sounding places like Bury St Edmunds. They're much scarier than a stupid black dog with red eyes, because they're real.

Still, I can't quite imagine any of them coming to our village, coming to Burnt Fen to do away with Mandy Baker, any more than I can imagine Mandy's own dad doing anything so nasty. Despite my question to the ouija board, despite its answer, I don't believe it for a minute. Mandy is out there somewhere, on a train or in a new house, in a new place, somewhere like London. I still chat to her, in my head. I feel her beside me sometimes in the playground, hanging monkey-style by her bent knees on the bar, her skirt over her head, her eyes all weird and upside down. She's wondering why her mother left, and saying she's going to Ely to live with her. She's no better than she should be, Mum says. But she's definitely alive.

Here's another one. In this one, I'm swinging on an old metal-framed swing, I'm in a garden, it must be our back garden. It's summer and late; the crop is high and green in the field in front of me. Billy lobbed my shoes over there a week ago and this year the field has been planted with corn, not beet, and it's tall now and

58

scratchy and the farmer shouts if you go in there, damaging his crop, so we haven't yet found them. This swing is creaking and jerking, giving me a tiny thrill at each point where I fear that it might release me suddenly, the old rusty chains unlinking as it dashes me into a heap on the lawn. I don't know who has taught me to swing. I can remember the feeling of being pushed not so long ago, how it irritated me, with the rhythm broken every time I returned to Mum's rough push and the little judder and jerk before swinging again. I'm singing at the top of my voice. *Swing low, sweet chariot.* (I have to bury my chin in my neck to try to push out the notes.) *Jesus Christ, Superstar! Do you think you're/ who they say you are?*

Beneath me is a scuffed patch of earth. Brown puddle in the green. I could swing all day and all night. I can hear Mum calling, I know it's late, my brothers are already ready for bed, my legs are out in front of me, white socks stretched right up to my knees, knees with a smattering of freckles right in the middle of the knee-cap. I'm not a good singer, but I love it. Singing gets me high. High is not a word I know. Singing makes me feel special, like Jesus's sunbeam. I throw my head back until I feel sick, I stare at the big, big sky, at the crows, massing on the telegraph poles over my head, I picture all the other girls in their gardens, swinging on their own swings, happy, happily, like me. *Jesus loves me this I know/ cos the Bible tells me so.*

And then Dad is there. What a beautiful singing voice, he tells me. I'm startled. I'm the apple of his eye. He has told me it many times. I've looked for the apple in his bright blue eyes, but instead all I can see is the little dark figure of myself, looming bigger. My brothers are not the apples of his eye and I know that makes them hate me.

He has this game he plays, when he puts me on his knee. I mean, not now, not now that I'm ten, but before. He holds his hand in front of my face and says: see my finger? See my thumb? See my fist? Now here it comes . . . And then he curls his fist and pretends to zoom it at me. He doesn't play this game with my brothers. With them, it's just the fist, not the rhyme.

Is that you singing, Tina? What a beautiful singing voice . . . he says. Tina can do no wrong as far as Graham is concerned, my mother says. She says it in a tone of voice that makes me stare at her, she says it to her mother and her friends, she says it when my brothers are in the room so that Billy will sneak up beside me with his spoon, hot from dipping in his tea, and hold it against my bare leg until I have to snatch it away from him. But I never scream.

It's dusk now, there's a pink sun over towards the Colsons' farm; long fanning lines of pink streaking through the cathedral. Dad is smoking, wearing that big rough cardigan he has with the pockets for keeping his tobacco and his papers. He stands by the kitchen door, pausing to roll the paper, now licking the paper, holding both sides up to his mouth; he has been sent out by Mum to fetch me. The cigarette tip glitters red. A red spot in the dusk. I hear his intake of breath, I close my eyes and open them again quickly and he is just a shape, he might be a really big Labrador dog. He

60

takes deep drags on his cigarette and then he is singing, really softly.

Green grows the laurel, soft falls the dew/ Sorry was I, love, when parting from you . . .

He pauses to puff again on the roll-up. It's a surprise to me to hear him do anything softly, or to pause. I didn't even know he could sing like that, one of those really sad, Irish songs. It's him who has the singing voice. I bet he wishes I'd inherited it, but I haven't. His is lilting, sort of painful, cracking in places, in others — when it needs to be — smooth and plain as the plainest chocolate.

My legs poke out in front of me. My throat is to the sky, neck aching with the weight of my head, with the weight of my dad's song in my ears. My hair whips behind me, my voice wobbles, fails the notes. My heart flies up, arcs and plummets in a great leap, with the rest of me.

But at our next meeting I hope you'll prove true/ And we'll join the green laurel and the violets so blue . . .

I try to sing along with him, but he hits the notes so easily he slips away from me. As he is walking towards me I swing away from him, flying up, up to the highest, most dangerous point yet, wavering there, and I'm gripping the chains, they're cutting into my hands, I'm suspended, balanced on this flat block of red-painted wood, skirt billowing; in a garden of a house that no longer exists, in a village in a country, looking down with a giddy tug, at my own tiny house, my own tiny father, *a man too who no longer exists*, and then I really do flip, far away, into this now that I'm describing: further than I'd dreamed possible. I'm so far that I can look right down at that long ago man, singing his doleful green laurel song and barely hear it: *I once had a sweetheart, but now I have none . . . she's gone and she's left me, to weep and to mourn . . .*

I haven't yet come into the house, I haven't yet been told that Mandy is missing. I've lived ten years already, but I haven't known anyone who is dead.

The police are in our kitchen. I saw the car about ten minutes ago but I thought it went further on up the street. I didn't realise it had stopped right outside our house because on the swing, my back was to the road. Dad and Mum have been inside talking to the old policeman and the young one and now they think they should call me in and tell me something about it.

It's Monday night now and Mandy's father reported her missing yesterday at seven-thirty, having last seen her at 2p.m. on Sunday afternoon when she went out on her bike to play. She was on her own. She didn't say where she was going. The bike has been found, down by the River Ouse, around the bend at the top end of the village — halfway between Mandy's house and the village proper — a bend that slightly hides it from the bridge. It is definitely Mandy's bike. It is lilac, with a white basket, which contained an ice lolly wrapper from a Fab and her pink sunglasses with the sparkly bits in the frames, and has handlebars with *I Love Donny* stickers, one with Donny's face scrawled with biro.

Yes, Alf, Mandy's Dad, he phoned us about six, Mum says. I knew there must be something wrong when I heard his voice. He never uses that phone —

Six?

Yes, it must have been six. Six when we got back. We'd been at church, well, not our Graham, he never comes to church with us —

Better things to do, Dad cuts in. You've heard about the pike-perch some idiot let loose in the Relief Channel? They're snaffling up the bream! They'll be on the banks next, taking a chunk out of someone's leg! Too good to miss, if you ask me . . .

He knows this policeman; he drinks at the Social Club. Dad calls him Crisp, for his curly hair, he says, laughing.

No, it was just me and the boys and Tina, Mum says, ignoring him, and then after that we went to the coast on a special trip, on a bus, with the church. A picnic and a run around on the beach. I don't know why she didn't come with us. Mandy. I did ask you to ask her, didn't I, Tina?

I had forgotten to ask her. Worse than that, I had "forgotten" because I didn't really want her to come. I was sulking, we'd had an argument. Mandy had told Alison Medd not to talk to me for no reason at all. For three whole days the two of them had been sitting next to each other in class, giggling and passing each other drawings of me, ones of me in my Girls' Brigade uniform. She thought our church was funny. I would have asked her to come to the seaside with us, but I was scared to ask when she was in one of those moods. I usually waited for them to blow over and for Mandy to suddenly smile and offer me a lemon-flavoured Flying Saucer, but this time I'd waited and then it was too late. Sunday came and I just hoped Mum wouldn't ask for a proper explanation.

She didn't want to come to the seaside, I tell the policeman called Crisp. I watch him, to see if he writes it down, but he doesn't. I glance at Mum to see if she sees through the lie, but she is busily pouring tea for the policemen and fussing over two sugars or one and saying: poor Alf, he was in such a state, I could hardly understand a word he said. I thought she'd been at yours all afternoon! he kept saying, as if it was my fault. I mean, that man lets his ten-year-old daughter bike from one end of the Fen to another and then acts like that when something happens . . . I sent Graham over. Graham was there, oh, by about eight, maybe eight-thirty. He told Alf she'd turn up, but I think Alf had reported her missing by then.

You know his old girl the hairdresser's left him? Dad says, and Crisp nods. He does know this.

Alf phoned about six, Dad went over . . . about eight. I'm replaying it all, furious that they can have kept this important stuff from me, kept it secret for a whole day! No wonder she wasn't at school today. I just thought she was sick. Sunday night we always have our hair washed and eat banana sandwiches in front of *Stars on Sunday*. None of us likes *Stars on Sunday* of course, but Mum insists. For the singing. I'd heard the phone and it was the phone in the living room, Mum opening the sliding doors, the doors made of orange bubbled glass, and standing there holding the green phone to her ear and tapping her fingernails on a coaster, a white round coaster with orange daisies that she's turning over and then tapping and tapping as she talks.

Mum hadn't said a word to me about that phone call. What she did was, she went to the shed to find Dad. And then she came in and started buttering more bread for some extra sandwiches for Billy (always the hungriest) and when Dad came in later she phoned again (Mandy's dad, I suppose) and it was all hush-hush and sort of closing the glass doors and murmuring to Dad and then finally, when we were brushing our teeth, the kitchen door banged and Dad went out. I heard the metallic sound of the door of his van slamming and the engine chicker-chick into life and then growl off down the road.

Eight o'clock Mum says it was. Even eight-thirty. But it couldn't be that because *Stars on Sunday* finishes well before eight. It must have been earlier. Closer to seven-thirty, when Dad went out.

I know you have to tell the truth, be careful to be accurate and tell the truth to policemen because they write it down and check it later. I'm worrying about the bit about "forgetting" to ask Mandy to come on the church trip with us. If I tell him why, tell him we had an argument, tell him that in fact — as was often the case — my very best friend was not actually talking to me, hadn't been since Wednesday morning at school, what would he think? I know he won't think I've done anything to Mandy, I'm not stupid enough to think that policemen believe little girls kidnap one another, or any such thing, but, well, it wouldn't look good. I'm supposed to be her friend.

The policeman with a notebook open has a round head under his cap, which he takes off to make Billy laugh. He doesn't have curly hair at all! He's just as bald as a boiled egg. I don't understand what Dad means about his name. Crisp is always a nickname for boys with curls round here.

You lads haven't seen this girl Mandy anywhere since yesterday afternoon, have you? Policeman Crisp asks, and my brothers, lined up in their pyjamas, shake their heads solemnly. His head is quite smooth, with a red ring pressed into it where the hat has been. Billy's hand twitches and for a second I think he is going to reach out and touch that head. The policeman puts his cap back on, with a funny movement, tilting it from one point at the back. I think of the top of a toilet seat, lifting and sitting back down again.

He is drinking an instant coffee from a cup that has a cartoon man on it with a fishing rod and the words World's Greatest Fisherman. Dad's cup. The coffee smells strongly of evaporated milk, evap, Mum calls it, her emergency milk for when we've run out. She had not expected visitors at this time on a weekday evening.

Live-bait is it, Graham? What do you use to catch these giants, zanders — is that what they are?

You mean pike-perch? Oh yeah, they need something special, Dad says. Dace, rudd, whatever I can get. Skimmer bream if I'm desperate. I'd left a net-full overnight down at the reed beds and the bloody eels had half of them. Took their heads right off.

So you were fishing most of Sunday were you, Mr Humber? the young policeman says, politely. Everyone looks at him, as if they're surprised that he can talk. His ears turn red. Crisp nods towards Dad's mug, answers the question for him.

Mr Humber is a star fisherman around these parts, Marcus. One time Nene carp record holder, isn't that right, Graham?

Dad tries not to smile but I can tell he's pleased. He's fiddling with his papers and tobacco tin, rolling another one.

Well, tide is turning against live-bait, you know, Dad says. Already some of the little old boys won't do it. But I always think to catch the big fish you've got to have something to really tempt them, you know, make its fat old mouth water. You'd know about that now, wouldn't you, Crisp?

Crisp laughs and flips his notebook shut.

Sure do, he says, nodding his head towards the younger policeman, who stands up so suddenly that our kitchen chair falls over. Mum is right behind him, picks it up, tells him not to worry, and begins gathering up the cups. I know she wants to get my brothers off to bed.

Well, I'm sure she'll turn up. She'll get a good hiding from her dad when she does, that's for sure, Crisp says.

Mum goes to the front door with them and I know she is murmuring something about Mandy's mum, Sandy, and I can tell from her tone, not the words, how disapproving she is; any woman who leaves her own child, even for a while, even if she now claims she was going to come back, a woman like that . . . well.

I want to say to them: Mandy picks her nose. I know already that this truthful statement would not be welcome and it wouldn't be written down, either. It would put me in a bad light, as much as Mandy. Nose-picking is neither to be done, nor spoken of, in front of adults. Neither a nose-picker nor a tell-tale be. But whenever Mandy's name is mentioned, I want to say things like this. I hate the way they make her sound so sweet, so goody-goody. It's not Mandy at all. When I think of her, that's what I picture. The slow-turning finger, disappearing.

Dad watches them leave, his back to me, whistling. He has forgotten my brothers, who are hanging about the corridor in their pale pyjamas like ghosts, hoping to remain invisible. Now he spots them and roars at them to get upstairs to bed. He stops suddenly, turning to me. My heart is speeding, it's like footsteps running up a stairway. My heart always bumps around when he shouts, even if it's playful: I'm just never sure. He turns around to face me but his face has changed, melted, his blue eyes all crinkly at the edges: now come on, he says, don't you worry about that little friend of yours, she'll get what for, just like he says, when she does turn up (running his hand through his thick black hair, making it stand up in a funny way at the front). He seems worried himself. All the adults seem worried. Mum comes back and ties on a pinny, a pinny covered in orange and brown flowers, round petals, the same kind of flowers on our patterned wallpaper. She ties it with a ribbon at the back and puts the cups into the sink and says she'll pick me up from school tomorrow. I'm not to go out, on my own, on my bike, *at all*. Do you hear me? she says and she says it sharply, her grey eyes narrowing.

I say that I do.

Mandy's eleventh birthday is in three days' time. I already bought and wrapped her present last Saturday: a one-year diary, turquoise, fat, with a little lock and a girl shown in profile on the front with long blonde hair like Mandy's and one giant, eye-lashed eye.

I've wrapped it with this nice pink and lilac paper and also bought her a bar of Bournville chocolate and a card with a girl with roses on it and a yellow halo round her head. The card is already signed: To Mandy, Happy Birthday!! Love from Tina! When the policeman leaves, I get the present out from under my bed and unwrap it. I turn the diary over and read on the back: Forget me not. There are spaces for addresses, birthdays and anniversaries. As it is long past January, the month when diaries sell, it only cost me 25 pence. I take the key, which is attached by a piece of ribbon and unlock it with a satisfying click. Inside it has lists of birthstones. Mandy's, being June, is Pearl, which means long life. Her flower (from another list) is Rose or Honeysuckle. Mine is Calendula, which I've never heard of: not nearly as nice as Rose. For my birthday I want a mini-printer, the kind that presses white letters onto blue sticky strips; so that I can stick names and slogans on all my things.

What if Mandy doesn't come back before her birthday? Well, if she does, since I bought this in the bookshop on Fore Hill, it will be all right, I can easily get her another. With my felt-tip pens, I draw a girl's face on the first page of the diary, a face carefully copied from the girl on the cover. In the space where it says, *This Book Belongs To*: I write, Tina Humber, aged 10 and three quarters.

Mandy is sparkly. She likes to wear those painful plastic hair-bands in glittery colours, the sort that burrow into your scalp with sharp teeth. (I can never wear them: they give me a headache.) Her neat fringe is always pressed flat on her forehead and she has a nose as neat as the tip of a pencil-rubber and thick matted lashes (thicker than mine) that make her look older than she is. She is a quick talker and top of the class in spelling. When she's writing, she twists the pencil in her hair, or parks it behind her ear, or sometimes, when she thinks no one is looking at her, she pushes the blunt end up her nose too, and twists. Last year, egged on by Jonathon Drayfield, the boys in our class voted Mandy Baker the prettiest in the class. I was voted the second prettiest. My hair is a kind of rat-tailed blonde and I don't wear the hair-bands.

So on Tuesday, Mum walks to school with us, instead of my usual walk through the village trailing my brothers, and for the second day, Mandy isn't there. She isn't sitting next to me on the polished floor in assembly, so we can't flick crumbs from yesterday's dinner towards each other. Miss Hazlehurst reads the register and she doesn't do what she normally does when people are absent, she doesn't say *Mandee! Ba-ker! Abb-sent!* in that heel-clicking voice she has, instead she just skips right over, hopping right from Susan Babcock to Janet Clarke without a breath.

And when I leave school there's a police car parked where the ice-cream van usually is, and the old policeman with the toilet-bowl head is standing beside the open door with the radio sizzling inside. A whole muddle and straggle of mothers and aunties are waiting for us, where normally there would be only one bus, the one to take the children like Mandy to the faraway places like Burnt Fen, or Black Horse Drove, for the children who live in farms, far from a school, and so come to ours. The band of mothers startles us. It's then that we know how wrong things are.

That night there is a picture of Mandy on the local news. It's Mandy with her pressed fringe, a school photo, hair pushed back behind her ears, wearing a smock dress that I know she hated: turquoise, with a floppy broderie-anglaise collar. Her mum made it, weeks before she left. And now everyone is going to think she looks cute but Mandy won't be able to pull that face, the cross-eyed one that means: *this rotten dress!* All her anger, her fury at her mum for going, is soaked into loathing for her dress. On the photo she is not quite smiling but her mouth is naturally turned up at the corners, shiny with some Coca-Cola-flavoured lip gloss; the shape of a paper boat. She is looking straight out at me from the TV set, that half-smile, those wide-apart, clever eyes, making me shiver. She is a blonde girl, ten years old (days away from her eleventh birthday), missing for two days in a Cambridgeshire village. Height four feet two inches. Build: medium. Last seen wearing a purple and lilac print dress, purple beads, white socks, purple leather sandals, leaving her home on her bicycle on Sunday June 9th at 2p.m. It is believed she cycled towards Ely, in the direction of the River Ouse. Police are appealing for witnesses.

That word leaps from the TV set. Appealing. I hear it in rainbow-colours, sparkly, like Mandy. They're *appealing* for witnesses, what can that mean? Why aren't they just *asking* for them? Appealing is a word I heard my mother use yesterday, and funnily enough she was talking about Mandy. She's such an appealing little thing, Mum said, in a phoney sort of hushed voice, talking to one of the other mothers. It seems to be Mandy's word, now. She's stuck with it.

Teeny Tiny Tina. I had a doll called Teeny Tiny Tears. I feel tiny again, getting out of the car, parking at an angle between the white lines in Ely registry office carpark, crunching the gears as I try to reverse and straighten up; narrowly missing an enormous yellow crate with the words Grit and Salt on it.

All this is witnessed by the small group I now recognise is my brother Billy and his wife and kids. Here's our Tina, he says, as I climb out. He's standing beside the squat school-like building of the registry office in a dark suit; the trousers flared, the jacket tight across the back: he hasn't worn that suit for years. It

72

gives me a jolt, seeing him with his tin of tobacco balanced on the low windowsill behind him, rolling a cigarette, using exactly the same gesture that Dad always used, and to see that Billy's hair is receding in a neat circle at the top, his face is flabby at the jowls. I realise I have been picturing Billy with that habit he used to have of walking everywhere on his hands, back arching, his feet with their dirty soles upwards, his t-shirt falling down over his face.

Being so early, I thought I'd be the first here. Thought I'd have time to gather myself, to shake out this odd whistling pressure that still sneaks through one ear. But no, I hadn't counted on my brother's impatience, his chronic punctuality. I'm so unused to wearing a skirt and heels that I struggle to get out of the car with any dignity. Probably flash my knickers at them. Billy hasn't seen me in fifteen years and here I am in all my glory as Mum would say. The further I walk from the car, the smaller I feel. He towers above me, this middle-aged kid brother, our Billy; only I haven't called him that for twenty years. The hug he gives me is fierce, grisly. Gaynor and I kiss each other on the cheeks: a gust of something chemical and flowery, like walking past the perfume counter in Selfridges. I sense she is not comfortable with this cheek-kissing: I guess she finds it "posh". I haven't seen Gaynor for nearly ten years but I'm pretty sure there was about fifty pounds less of her in those days. Strangely, though, she looks better this way. She's poured herself into white cotton trousers: she doesn't seem the least bit self-conscious, judging from the sparkly flip-flops and the silver and blue flower in her hair. Easy to see why she and Mum have always got along just fine.

There is a white sign on the wall behind Billy's head and on it an enamelled black finger pointing: Register Office. Not registry, then. That must be old-fashioned: it's also a while since I've been to a wedding. Beside that notice is a photocopied poster. A fair girl and a dark girl. Missing.

How are you all? I ask. I remember to smile.

Two girls stand next to Gaynor, gazing blankly at me: my nieces. Kylie must be the younger one, I think she's probably nine now, but this blonde girl is small for her age; pretty, except for a mouthful of teeth so higgledy piggledy that one of the top eye teeth is practically facing outwards at a dagger-like angle. I don't know why I'm so surprised to see that she looks like Billy. And, since Billy and I are the ones who had the same colouring and the same soap-on-a rope kind of bodies, always dangling ourselves, floppy-limbed, monkey-style, leaning or hanging from any available banister or bar, that she also looks like me.

Charlene, thirteen, is wearing bright pink jersey trousers, with the word *sexy* across her bum. She's acting bored, flicking through a magazine, though she accepts my hug and warms up when she discovers I know who Peaches Geldof is and even went to a Boomtown Rats concert, once, when I was eighteen.

Look at you! I say, feeling no connection at all to these two girls with their appraising stares, their very English teeth. Poppy has a mouthful of metal, as does

74

every other girl in her class. Like all of them, last year she chose the colours red white and blue for the plastic bits between the braces. This I permitted, since I felt guilty that she was the only one in her class whose Mom refused the car bumper sticker with the stars and stripes on it.

Well, where are you hiding Dean and Poppy? Billy says.

This irritates me, as he knew it would. Andrew, Billy, their various spouses (Andrew's first wife, Jenny, is my ouija board friend from school, though we haven't spoken for years) and kids weren't invited to our wedding. They didn't accept my argument that the ceremony was merely a practicality to sort out the green card issue, making it easier for me to work in the States, and have acted ever since like Dean doesn't really exist. Is perhaps, like a lot of things, a figment of my imagination. They've been to visit me once, in Amherst. Poppy would have been about one, Charlene four, Kylie newborn. That's all I remember: the ages of the children. The cups of juice; the bibs drying on the radiators; the piles of folded washing. One of them was always wailing. I used to escape down to the basement, to the comforting throbbing noise from the huge communal washing machines.

I stare into the window of the registry office ("register" just doesn't sound right) at the little white pot of plastic poppies, the signs asking: *Have you seen these girls?* and urging citizens to call a help line. There is a silence; I think they are waiting for something.

Weird as you ever were, I see, Billy finally says, trying to make it sound playful. He finishes his cigarette, throwing it towards a clump of dandelions growing out of the walls of the building in front of us. We all turn our heads at the sound of another car approaching, tyres creaking as it drives over a man-hole cover. It's a couple I don't recognise; a man, a woman and a tiny version of the father, complete with denim jacket, denim cap.

That's Eddy. Doesn't he look cute in that cap? Can't remember his girlfriend's name. Gaynor nods towards the miniature adult.

Wow, Ely, I say. So busy! So many new houses.

Have you seen that big Tesco's at Angel Drove? That's new since you were here last, isn't it? Gaynor asks. The shops are always changing. It's all card shops and charity shops. Cutlacks is still here. But it's on its last legs.

She grew up in a village the other side of Ely to ours, and went to a different school, but she's lived here her whole life (a life she seems to have spent cataloguing shops and their demise). Lipton's, she says, isn't that where Doreen worked? Ah, that's gone. Did you see the Rex closed down? We have to go to Cambridge now if we want to go the pictures. That was after you left, wasn't it? And Newday, the furniture shop, near the old Scotch Bakery, remember that? They're both gone.

Was the cathedral here when you lived here, Auntie Tina? Kylie asks me.

We all turn to look at the cathedral. The bottom half is obscured by a shop-front — a wide building hosting two shops in one. I'm not sure it had the same name, but it's surely the exact same shop. Angela's Ladies Fashions — in fact I think it's the same two neat dummies tilted conversationally towards each other, one in a turquoise house dress, the other in red slacks and a tucked-in floral print blouse. They share their shop space with Fenland Music, violins, sheet-music, bows and notices about chamber sessions, that kind of thing. Behind all that the cathedral suddenly rears up, a great grey robot against the blue crayoned sky of a child's drawing: its twin pillars held rigid against its body, like raised arms.

Our Kylie's not the brightest spanner in the tool box, Billy says, ruffling her hair. Of course the cathedral was there, you dippy cow. Your auntie might be old but she's not older than the bloody Fens!

I fiddle with the buttons on my jacket. This sounds just like Dad. Billy doesn't notice and Gaynor doesn't admonish him, either, so I guess they find it harmless enough.

Isn't it terrible? Gaynor nods towards the poster of the missing girls outside the registry office. I notice that Charlene and Kylie immediately jerk their heads towards her. Listening, suddenly.

Been on the news night and day since last week, Gaynor says. The fields around here are crawling with them. Helicopters, everything. Half of England's out looking for them.

Which half?

What?

Well, half of England is out looking for them, you said. It makes me think: what's the other half doing? Are they the abductors and paedophiles?

What???

Gaynor adjusts the flower in her hair, eyes me carefully. She glances once at my brother and there is a pause when I think she might actually answer my question.

Andy's bringing your mum, she announces, finally. The girls go back to their chattering, realising that nothing of importance is going to accidentally be revealed.

(Don't rise to her bait, I can imagine Billy saying. She's always doing that, Tina. Picking holes in what people say. She's weird. Pretends to take things really literally, you know, just to get a rise out of you.)

He's got a new car, Gaynor adds. Pillar-box red, I think.

Ours is a family estrangement that no one acknowledges. A sort of drifting estrangement. Mum's also only been to Amherst just the once, when Poppy was first born. I have photos of her pushing Poppy in her stroller around the obvious tourist spots: Emily Dickinson's house, the Observatory, the Johnson's Building on campus. I remember she was astonished that American mothers didn't possess those complicated transparent plastic covers for their *pushchairs*, as she insisted on calling them. Why, doesn't it rain here? she asked. I hadn't really noticed this absence but offered the explanation that if it rained, Americans would put the baby in the car. She was shocked at their laziness and profligate use of petrol. No wonder there's a bloody hole in the ozone, she muttered.

Other guests are arriving, bustling past us into the registry office in a fugue of perfume and hairspray. Billy and Gaynor introduce me when they remember but their names immediately desert me. I'm thankful that I don't seem to know anybody. There's one cousin I recognise in the faintest possible way: only her retroussé nose remains in her grown-up face to suggest the pug-faced seven-year-old I remember. Her name has flown off, so I keep my smile on but let my eyes drift a little. I wish I wore glasses; I could take them off and be miraculously unable to recognise anyone.

At last, here they are, Andrew and Mum. And a woman, Andrew's bride, presumably. Wendy. She is sitting in the back with Mum, and she is unstrapping her seat-belt and then leaning over to help Mum with hers; Mum's arthritis must be playing up. But Mum isn't that old. She is not even sixty yet. She's heavier than she was, and she's done something new with her hair: a kind of silver bob. It's a young style: I'm not sure about it. I'm surprised that Mum isn't wearing a hat and seems to have on a subdued navy jacket, but when she opens the car door to smile at me I see the crimson blouse, with the huge floppy bow at the throat, spotty navy tights and her shoes — navy courts, with kitten heels and crimson bows — and I know at once that she is excited, she has been looking forward to this.

Here she is, here's Tina!

Like Billy, Mum speaks to me in the third person, a habit they always had. And Mum's hug is even harder than Billy's, containing somehow all the admonishment for the years gone by, for not keeping in touch: she practically cracks three ribs. A great puff of lilac perfume and choking emotion. I wriggle out from under it eventually. I try not to be too obvious about dusting down my linen jacket, my "blush" pink linen jacket, the woman in the store called it: a ridiculous misnomer I now realise — blushing is surely the most inflamed red there is. We break apart and stare at one another, adjusting our clothes.

Doesn't she look marvellous? Mum says, her voice quavery. My little Tina. Would you look at that tan!

Andrew comes round from his side of the car to kiss me and introduces me to his wife-to-be as his "glamorous sister from over the pond". I try not to notice how bald Andrew is now, in case the thought shows on my face. Wendy links her arm in mine and murmurs something about being really excited to meet me at long last and she's heard so much about me from Andrew. It strikes me that she means this. I almost pull away from her linked arm to take a better look at her.

She's a tall red-head, almost as tall as my brother, with a horsy gait and a square jaw, wearing a coral skirt suit that might have come straight from Angela's Fashions. She looks about as at home in it as I do in mine. Her eyelids are shaded with some strange blue powder and I know at once from the misapplication of it that, like me, she doesn't normally wear makeup. She must have let some misguided friend do this to her for today. Her two little girls are indeed cute, but perhaps not quite in the way Andrew meant. I think of them and hear the word how Poppy uses it, to mean snappy, or clever. Don't be cute, Dean says, where my mum would have used the word cheeky. Like their mother, these girls have a horsy, coltish quality, and look wrong in their matching lilac dresses with sparkles at the bodice and the word *angel* written in silver across their chests. Rose and Chloe. They seem old for their age, shaking my hand and speaking up clearly; even Rose, at five, is able to say confidently that she is very pleased to meet me and to give me an appraising stare.

There is now a small cluster of us. Mum is standing behind Andrew, fiddling in her navy clutch-bag for a handkerchief. Come on, let's get a photo then, says Billy, and we're herded together, Andrew and Wendy at the centre; Mum with her arm around my waist, Gaynor and the four girls shrieking and giggling, trying to get the heights right; floating like bubbles in a glass, up, down, randomly, before settling.

Cheese, Billy says. Come on . . . Gorgonzola!

We all smile. He clicks his tiny silver camera and we crowd round to consider the result in the little screen.

So many girls . . . Dad would have had a field-day! Andrew says.

His words catch at me: something small unravels. The photo is a riot of girlish shapes and colours: coral, lilac, blush-pink, crimson. I stare at him, but he's laughing with Wendy, he has his arm around her; I can't really see his eyes. And my ear hurts again with a piercing jab. *What do you mean, what do you mean, about Dad?* But now Andrew's moved away from our group, someone is congratulating him; his back is to me. The set of his shoulders and the back of his ears give nothing away.

Mandy's mother works at the hairdresser's, Zara's Hair. Her name is Sandy, not Zara, but whenever I see that green swirly sign, with its silhouette of a lady with flowing tresses, I think that it's a rubbish name for a hairdresser's, because it sounds as if Zara's hair is the only hair they can do. The place stinks of perm solution, a disgusting smell, but I secretly like it. Three hard-headed old ladies always line the back wall beneath the mirrors, like giant insects, their pastel-coloured netted hair under huge helmet-dryers.

Four days after Mandy goes missing I cycle past the shop. I want to talk to Mrs Baker, to ask her if there is any news. Part of me expects her not to be there — perhaps you don't go to work when your daughter is missing. What I don't expect at all is what happens: Mrs Baker, wearing a stained peach-coloured blouse with floppy lace sleeves, comes tearing out of the shop, screaming Mandy! Mandy! in a voice cracked right down the middle like a paving stone, and tries to grab the handlebars of my bike.

It's me, Tina! I choke out, the bike falling to the pavement with a crash, me still awkwardly astride it. Ladies from the hairdresser's are now surrounding Mrs Baker, hushing her and steering her back towards the shop. What are you thinking of, Tina Humber, how could you? a lilac-netted beetle yells at me, over her shoulder, as I try to climb back up and put the bike right. But these are the same women who days ago were murmuring that any woman who leaves her husband and child to live with her fancy man . . . well, I don't think I heard any of them actually say that Mandy's mum *deserved* for Mandy to go missing, but the idea formed in the air around me and it must have come from somewhere. Mandy is the only girl any of us knows whose mum and dad don't live together. We all know mums and dads who hate each other, but we don't know any who have split up. It's a double first for Mandy. The first girl to have a mum who leaves and the first girl to go missing. I wish she was here for me to say this to her because I know she'd be proud and it would be a way to cheer her up, a way to make her feel better about her mum and all that. It might be bad but at least it makes her special.

Now from Mandy's mother I can hear sobbing and the ladies spreading a soothing coat of words over her, murmuring *there there, Sandy* and in hotter, more indignant tones: *heartless, thoughtless girl!* and then light again, sugar-fine like that strange-smelling burnt white stuff that coats the air around the beet factory from October to March: *it'll be all right, Sandy, she'll turn up.*

So I think that this is somehow connected, this mistake is how the police come up with the idea of the re-enactment. To punish me. After school the following day, their car is outside our house again. Mum is in the kitchen, leaning her back against the cooker, and a different policeman, an older one, with a crumpled face like a deflated balloon, and pale eyebrows with hairs that twirl right out in front of his head, is drinking tea at our table. Three bags of British Sugar stand proudly on the table. I know at once that Mum will be trying to give them to the policewoman (she's always complaining that Dad's "allowance" from the beet factory takes up too much space in our larder) and as I come in the door I hear Mum saying huffily: surely it couldn't be seen like that, a little bag of sugar? He gets them perfectly legitimately, you know . . .

They all go silent as I walk in.

The policewoman turns to face me. Hello there, Tina! Hello.

Mum lets them suggest it to me, but she's biting the skin at the edge of her nails, her head to one side like a bird, watching. The policeman talks about how much help it would be to Mandy's parents and how often the general public has their memory jogged by these things, far more than you or I might think, you know; by the sight of a girl in a lilac dress on a bike, and how much I would be helping my "poor" friend Mandy, and her parents. No one can possibly know what they're going through, he adds, in a very deep voice, as if this sentence is important.

But I don't even look like her!

We know you don't, he says hastily, glancing over my head at Mum, but you are about the same size and your hair's about the right colour —

It's not! Mandy is much blonder than I am . . .

They don't listen to me. That is, they mutter and murmur and they tell me what a brave kind thing it would be and assure me that if I'm not certain, they can ask another girl from our school. But then they go

84

away and Saturday comes around and Mum has these things, these carrier bags, and she comes into my bedroom and opens the window really wide so that I can smell the lilac buds from the tree outside, and without a word, she tips the contents onto the bed. A purple cotton and poly sleeveless dress, with a print of forget-me-nots in a lighter lilac colour. A circle of large plastic purple beads. White ankle socks, also cotton-poly. Purple leather sandals with a silver buckle, tulip shapes cut into the toe. I've forgotten about the policeman's visit: I think they're all for me: a present. I pick up one shoe, size I, and stroke the leather toe.

Billy says: ugggh, spazzy shoes!

Mum slaps him, hard, aiming for his face, but missing and catching his shoulder instead, and then plonks down on my candlewick bedspread and bursts into tears. Billy runs wailing from the room. Andrew loiters in the doorway, his eyes on Mum.

They're not even *her* things, anyway.

Andrew's voice is accusing. He thought they would be. He thought they'd somehow get hold of Mandy's actual clothes (forgetting that this would mean they had found her) and I would wear them and parade in them and the photographers who have been lurking everywhere in the village — leaking out of every telephone box, propping up notebooks against their cars, smoking their cigarettes, just outside the school gates — would suddenly thrust their cameras at me, and Mandy's mystery would be solved.

None of us can understand why Mum is crying. Dad wanders in from their bedroom, taking his cigarette papers from his dressing gown pocket, and saying: now, what's all this then?

He looks at the things on the bed and he looks at Mum, but he doesn't cry, he just picks up the beads, which make a rattly noise, and then puts them down again, gently, on top of the dress. He puts them sort of in the right place, where her throat would be (if the dress was a person). I don't like him doing this. I don't know why he does it and I think for a moment he has forgotten himself, it wasn't really a good thing to do.

Mum is staring at him too.

Not in here, Graham, I've told you! she suddenly shrieks, her sobs forgotten, as he puts the rolled up cigarette to his mouth and feels for his lighter. She hates it if he smokes in our bedrooms. She tries to make it a rule but she says that rules and your father are like salad cream and red cabbage. They just don't go together.

Still, today he goes out. I hear him light up on the landing, hear his little intake of breath.

Will Mandy's mum be there? I want to know.

These are just some shop-bought clothes. The re-enactment is tomorrow at the same time that Mandy went missing. They will fetch me her bike and I am to ride it along the route they've circled in blue biro on a one-page map of our High Street and the river path and then stop at the point where what they know about Mandy's "last known movements" runs out.

In my mind, I'll be cycling down from Burnt Fen and then on towards the bridge over the river and past a row of parked cars: the newspaper men, lined up like pigs at a trough. But then chasing me, running, flapping her peachy, perm-solution-scented sleeves, will be Sandy Baker, tearing the air with her screams and calling out Mandy's name.

This is us playing. Playing with our dolls, a few days before Mandy goes missing.

Your lady goes to the shops and my lady's got a headache and my lady is lying in bed and pretend your lady comes back from the shops and she has a phone call from her boyfriend and he's saying Hey come on a picnic girls, and my one, my lady says I've got a headache, what will I wear? And your one says, let's go shopping again, in the car and buy some beach towels and sunglasses . . . and my lady, pretend my one says . . .

Our ladies. Our Sindy and Ken dolls, me and Mandy. Mandy's Sindy is blonde like we are; mine is dark. I always like the dark dolls, dark girls. Not Snow White but Rose Red, with white cheeks and scarlet lips. My Sindy has this fantastic little hairbrush, Mum bought me it last birthday, it's lilac with a tiny silver circle and tiny lilac teeth that tickle when you run them over your thumb. Mandy loves my Sindy hairbrush and she's asked me to swap it for some hot-pink Sindy mules but I say no, so then she offers her Sindy sunglasses, black with green lenses. She knows how much I love them, and I'm tempted, but I still say no. The lilac hairbrush came on a card as a boudouir set with fluffy mules and a nylon negligee also in lilac flimsy stuff and to replace the brush I'd have to buy the whole set again all over and they probably haven't even got it any longer in Woolworths so that's why I'm saying no. So then Mandy starts crying and tells me how mean I am and her mum has left her and don't I feel sorry for her and I offer her the lilac negligee instead but she says she doesn't want that rotten thing.

So then she's in a bad mood and when Mandy is in a bad mood, it's hard to win her over. Normally I would, I would give in and give up the hairbrush. I'd do anything to keep Mandy sweet, to make Mandy like me, and I do feel sorry for her about her mum going, in fact I'm really surprised at myself for being so tough, but it's the Sindy hairbrush, I just love it so much. When Mum comes into our room to tell us that Mandy's dad is here to pick her up, we are backed into our different corners of the room, arms locked around our knees, Mandy's face wet from crying, my bottom jaw stuck and stubborn.

Mum never notices our bad moods, she's always telling me she's not going to "indulge" me when I'm grumpy or crying, so Mandy is told to go downstairs and get her shoes on and I'm told to wash my hands because my tea's on the table. It's all done quickly and with my eyes squinting from being in a temper and so I can't really say how it happens, or if I'm right. But when I come to look for it, a few days later, the Sindy hairbrush isn't in its place, in the white tiny drawer of the Sindy dressing-table.

I don't know for sure. Maybe it just got lost. Maybe Billy hid it. But it explains why Mandy was horrid to me for the next few days. It even explains why she's gone. I think she nicked my Sindy hairbrush.

They say Mandy is missing, but I think of it as *hiding*. Missing for twenty-four hours. Missing for two days. Fears Grow for Missing Girl. I picture her crouching behind a hay-stack, her hair and jumper all sticks of straw, looking like a ball of wool with knitting needles sticking out of her, her hand cupped over her mouth. She's giggling. Or sometimes, I see her in a cupboard, the dark one under our stairs, with the Hoover pressing in front of her and Dad's green fishing wellies with their grassy wet rubber smell nearly choking her.

Hide and seek. Waiting for me to find her. *Five, ten, fifteen, twenty, twenty-five, thirty: ready or not, here I come!* We love to play it in her house. Hers has much the best places. Mandy is good at hiding, I'm rotten at it. It scares me, or else I get impatient, or want to sneeze, or shout: here I am, over here! But I'm loads better at seeking than she is. So maybe that's what she hopes of me. Maybe it's up to me.

Of course, I have some idea that other people do not picture her deliberately hiding. I am not so stupid that I can't feel the cloud that enters the room when the head teacher comes in in the middle of class or when a policeman comes to talk to us about Public Safety and Not Being Afraid. What I can't get hold of is the pictures, the things they won't tell me: what's inside this cloud.

Like them, I keep coming back to Mandy's bike, tipped on its side like that, one handle sticking up, the other digging into the earth of the river bank. In my picture (though I didn't see the bike of course, all I have to go on is what I heard and read) the pedal is still spinning, as if she sprang off suddenly, turned around, and let the bike fall. She wouldn't have left her bike behind although, despite what her mother said to the police, she didn't love it. Mandy wanted the same bike as mine, which is actually Andrew's. My bike is a boy's, with a cross-bar that you can cheese-wire yourself on and big wheels and it goes faster. Mandy's bike is especially for girls so it's called a Shopper, but even though it has small wheels it's not as good as a Chopper, because it has a silly basket at the front, and when we pedal side by side it's tough for her to keep up with me. Her wheels go round twice for every once of mine, and her bike only has three gears. Whenever the bike is mentioned, Mum's eyes fill up with tears, which to me is a waste. Mandy, wherever she is, won't be shedding any over her bike.

The first time I led a dive I couldn't find a single seahorse. I was down there for six hours in total, off the coast of Florida, with a small team of five. I was the divemaster, and though I knew we were in the right area, though we kept coming up and going back down again, I just couldn't see them. We'd float out over this ghostly set of sea-grass meadows, looking for a tiny tail tip. Like I said, they are absurdly good at camouflage. Changing colour, blending with the murky mud-green of the sea-grass. Just to really do your head in, they grow long skin appendages too, to look like algae. Then occasionally they're even barnacled, like rocks, and of course they don't move that much either, just hooking their tail around some grass and floating where they are, feeding and nodding their heads. Still, it was infuriating! It was embarrassing. To know they were there, possibly right in front of me. Straining and straining — is that a tiny coronet? Is that an eye? I felt — you would, after so many dives — convinced they were playing with me. Tricks. Or that they really could make themselves invisible, and that I was the first person to discover this phenomenon in the natural world.

The second day I didn't feel optimistic. I remember zipping up my wetsuit with a gloomy feeling, strapping the weights on, and thinking as I hit the water that I'd give it an hour, I wouldn't waste a lot of time. Then suddenly, I found a pair — in exactly the spot we had searched in the sea-grasses for so long the day before. And then the other divers were circling round me, and I was writing on the clipboard and pointing and all the others were giving the "OK" sign and the one for "cool", and I could hear my own breathing rasping excitedly in the regulator, as I saw dozens and dozens of them, nodding and pointing their beak-like noses, so transparent and fragile at the head they could almost be paper lanterns, but so strong really, so resilient, so rooted at the tail. Once I could see them, I couldn't un-see them. Later, one of the other divers described it as "getting your eye in". That's exactly right. I was amazed too, the first time I saw fishermen in the Philippines — on a campaign trip: we were trying to negotiate some restrictions on the amount they can fish — haul them up by the bucket-load, with no difficulty at all; even the children would point them out to me, in places where I'd been looking for hours.

It's partly about knowing *where* to look. And training the eye; being persistent and patient. Not blinking, not looking away. But mostly it seems to be about the determination, the effort. I've no doubt the seahorses still use all their powers on me, growing barnacles, changing colour, developing growths, swallowing the light. But I've got better at it, over the years. If you allow them to, facts do sometimes rearrange themselves, right in front of your eyes. You can look at the same thing, and it's as if a light comes on; or the old lens you've been peering through shifts away.

Wendy is shrieking and ducking as she stands in the garden of the restaurant with a shower of confetti flung at her hair by her own mother and mine, with Chloe and Rose on either side of her, clinging to her legs, Andrew slightly to one side. The positioning reassures me somehow; it's obvious that the girls have not been pushed out and that Andrew, shiny and pretty in his new suit and white buttonhole, is actually the new addition, the extra. There's no firm arm around her waist, claiming. I stand watching, a little back from the rest, sipping from my glass of champagne, while a semi-circle of friends point cameras at them and shout instructions. When Mum's film has run out, she turns to me.

So how are the miniature seahorses? she says, taking my arm and marching me towards the table, where the flutes of champagne are arrayed on a white paper tablecloth. A line of girls stand behind the table, lace aprons over their jeans, handing drinks to the guests.

Dwarves, I say, not miniature. Dwarf seahorses.

I thought you couldn't say dwarves these days? Especially in America. They're hot on that kind of thing, aren't they?

I sip the champagne.

(It's aggressive, her line of small talk. It's weighted with her disapproval, accusation. You went to that foreign country. You deserted.)

They're fine, I answer. Then, after a pause: it's quite hard to be away from them right now, they're all at crucial points in a reproductive cycle. You remember it's the males who give birth? I'm writing a paper about their survival techniques, their ability to colour change . . .

She drinks her champagne, bats away flies, twirls around as one of my nieces races past her.

Oh, still just that? I thought that's what you were studying years ago? When you first went to Amherst —

Yes. Still just that.

She's combing her hair, folding the comb, flipping it back into her bag, shutting it with a loud *snip!* and then cocking her head on one side, looking at me as if she expects me to carry on, as if what she just said was a chirpy comment, a murmur of encouragement, rather than what it felt like. A bucket of ice-cold water.

For God's sake, I tell myself.

Yes, I try again. I'm presenting a paper at U-Mass — the University of Massachusetts next week. I've left Yelena, my post-grad, in charge, and anyway these days a lot of the research is video taped —

Mum's looking over her shoulder at Wendy.

I don't think much of that suit, do you? I mean, I know girls don't wear white these days — and she's in no position to, either, you know she wasn't married before, don't you, those poor little girls — but well, you'd think, wouldn't you, she'd make a bit more effort. For her own special day. And that eye-makeup! Who did that for her, I wonder, Coco the Clown?

Mum fluffs up her crimson scarf, swipes at another glass of champagne gliding by on a tray.

She gives me a quick glance: a brushstroke, head to toe. A thorough lick of paint.

You look lovely, though! And proper shoes, too! I don't think I've ever seen you without your jeans and trainers. Not that it would have mattered, in any case; it's a bit casual, isn't it? I mean, it's nice and all that, but — my legs are killing me. Some of us need to sit down to eat. And she's obviously got money. Never want for anything, those two. Ballet lessons, piano. The little one, though. Rosie, is it? She's a handful. Right little madam.

She rolls her eyes and makes a sound with her mouth, like a horse expiring. I stare at her. I'd forgotten this gesture but that's it — I'm right back there, eight years old and terrified. I hate it when you make those noises, I dared to say to her once. What noises? I realise now what I didn't then: she has no idea she's doing it. So much disapproval — is that it? Or what, despair? Or is it envy, envy that others allow themselves the freedoms, the luxuries she never allowed herself. Anyhow, whatever it is, it's packed in that one breath and it's forceful, when she lets it out, you feel it as if she punched you.

Well, though. Andrew seems very happy, I say, lamely.

It's an old pattern. She predicts relationship meltdown, children going off the rails: my weapon is optimism, trying to be nice.

So how's Poppy? she starts, brightly. Interesting that she asked first about the seahorses. I didn't notice at the time but now it strikes me that she had to work up to Poppy and Dean.

She says something else but I turn my dodgy ear towards her and instead of her voice, there's only a wheezing sound, like an old man breathing. Maybe it's tinnitus, rather than pressure from the flight? I must ask Dean about it. Could that be a side-effect of my medication, too?

I move slightly away from her as she spots Wendy's mother and opens with a remark about the service and how short they are these days and fancy having a woman doing it, it doesn't feel quite right, does it? I shift towards another of the outdoor tables, manned by another row of pretty blondes in midriff tops and low-waisted jeans, worn so long that they trail on the grass, hems curling up at the edges, green and rough. The expanse of flesh in the middle of these girls (sometimes seeded with a pierced navel) draws my eyes. It was an area we despised when I was a teenager. We wanted it as flat and undeclared as the plainest landscape and we especially hated it if people (boys) touched it. These girls chat in sunny voices, their confident white bellies rising and falling, some firm, some wobbling, as they lift the plates, raise the spoons, offer me a dish of food. It's a buffet affair, rolled up colourful things on sticks, high-class salty things, not vol-au-vents or sausage rolls; other more exotic things which must be fashionable in England just now. (Billy is holding one tiny green-and peach-coloured roll out in front of him, between two fingers, twirling it slightly, like a jeweller examining a diamond). I stand near the table and load my plate.

Such a shame your dad can't be here . . . Wendy says, suddenly, a little voice in my ear.

And as she says it, mentions Dad again, I have the same feeling from a moment ago, standing outside the registry office, clustered around Billy's camera.

You know about my dad?

I'm sure my answer sounds rude. I don't know how else to put it. What if Andrew hasn't told her? Or told her a half-version, a fairy tale?

His suicide? Oh, yes. My God. He told me when we first met. God, awful. Bereavement counselling. It's my field, you know.

I picture a field: flat, extraordinary, like the Fens: the rich, purple-black soil, the strip line of golden sedge at the centre. They say it about me, sometimes. One of very few women in her field. It always brings a picture of myself with Jenny, aged thirteen, in a field of hulking boys, cabbage-picking. The stink of the cabbages, and the calluses on our hands; how we had to push back all the tough outer leaves before hacking them with a scythe that Mum was convinced would slice half my fingers. When we needed to pee we didn't dare to just

96

turn slightly away from the crop, like the boys did, periodically turning like sundials, to pee where they stood. We had to traipse to the furthermost hedges, as well hidden as we could, bunching up our denim skirts; keeping a vigilant eye on the skinny sun-burnt figures in the field, whose laughter and jeers still reached us, like balls tossed deliberately our way.

The only girl in the field. Gifted, Dean says, stroking my hair. You were obviously gifted. They are not afraid of gifted children in America. Impossible for me to imagine any response other than the one I always had: embarrassment. Poppy is already in a class for TAG (Talented and Gifted). She shines in the sciences, like me. Unlike me, there are more than two girls in her physics class. In our sixth form the physics teacher, Mr Hanson, called us Busty and Tiny. Busty — her name was Betty — laughed when I told her I minded. It got so that I would never put my hand up to answer a question so that I didn't have to hear that sarcastic: so, Tiny, what little gem, what pearl of wisdom, do you have to offer us? I once mentioned this to Yelena, in the lab. Instead of laughing, she listened to my story, blinked several times and then said: if he did that today in America, we could take him out. You know, like Thelma and Louise? With a gun.

There was a long pause, while I stared at her, with only the bubbling of the air flowing through the airline tubes to fill it.

Or at least get my dad to sue his ass, she added, more quietly.

Her dad is an East Coast lawyer. I couldn't tell if it was meant to be a joke. Envy always crackles under my skin around such girls, American girls raised on assertiveness and creative writing classes, expressing themselves all over the place. But beneath my envy is something else: I just don't know whether to believe them. Girls have always been skilled at forming the shapes expected of them. Even Poppy says with confidence that when she grows up she is going to be a marine biologist, like Mommy. She says it to please me and because she is attuned. Taking up a baton perhaps. Or maybe these girls blame us, feel they are living on an entirely new planet. The stupid mothers from light years ago, the victims.

Isn't that what I thought, too? About my mother, married for years to a nightmare. I asked her once. I think it was just before I left. What on earth was she thinking, marrying someone like Dad, chronically unfaithful? She was livid of course. She was loading washing into the machine and she had her back to me but as I said it she leapt up and whirled around and I really thought she was going to hit me. You didn't know him! she screamed at me. You don't know the man I married! And then, as always in our fights, she won by collapsing like a pile of washing onto the lino. Through tears she kept saying, it was the accident, that's what you don't realise. That changed him.

I'd heard the story before and by then I didn't buy it. According to her, he was a model boyfriend for the first year she knew him, when they were both sixteen, and they married a year later, when she was pregnant with me. But that year, 1962, the winter was bad, really bad, and he had a serious accident on his motorbike, out near Black Horse Drove, skidding on some ice on that treacherous road: a head injury. He was in hospital for months and the pig farm went to rack and ruin while his father had no one to work it for him. That's what lost them the farm, that's how Dad ended up working at the factory. It turned his head, she said, he was never the same after that.

It turned his head. Of course, that's exactly how I pictured it. Dad lying on the road, the motorbike beside him, his head turned, staring out at the frost and ice, his head all wrong, all alone somehow. Separated from his body.

It doesn't fit with the story he told. When Andrew asked Dad about the farm, Dad said those bloody porkers couldn't keep you in eggs and bacon. That after James Wicken of Soham beat him and Danny at the fatstock show, Grandad decided to throw in the towel. If you couldn't be the best, why bother?

At the time, I wanted this to be the explanation for the loss of the farm. I preferred it to the turned head/motorbike explanation. Dad had his pride, I knew that much. Fen Tigers were fierce, like all the big cats, they were magnificent.

Anyway, would that really do it, a head injury, turn a nice young boyfriend into a womanising bastard; turn the summer lands — his charming holiday mood — into a fullscale Fen Blow? I didn't think so. It was a version she told herself to get herself off the hook, that's what I thought. She had a blonde bee-hive hairdo in those days. (That's a photograph, surely? Black and white. She's wearing a miniskirt in a dogtooth check. Beside her, a really young man, a boy. Slicked dark hair, no sideburns but that unmistakable height and the beakish nose, a handsome nose for all its size. The beaming smile for the camera. He is leaning against a motorbike, she is leaning against him. So this must have been before his accident?)

Could it be true that he was so different? Took my breath away — that's how she described him once. Oh, you don't realise, she said, how handsome he was then, your dad, how young, with his blue eyes, so startling amongst all that dark skin and hair. And that hair! How thick, how curly it was. I bought him a watch once, just a cheap one, you know, for his birthday, and I remember it used to give me such a thrill to see him strap that watch on; that was my favourite thing to see him first thing in the morning, with his arms — muscled they were, you know, and always brown from being outdoors — she said, that used to send a shiver down me, and then she laughed, embarrassed. Your dad strapping his leather watch on his wide strong wrist. Those big fingers, to see them so gentle and careful like that, winding the watch. That was as close as she ever came to an explanation, to telling me what it was between them. Why she put up with him for so long.

Here she is again, thirty years later, triumphant in her crimson and navy, her flamboyant blouse. My father is dead and she is offering me a glimpse of her only strength, the only power she ever had: her viperous tongue. She's still talented, still capable of a deadly strike. Perhaps it's time to call a truce, maybe I should admire her now, after all?

Mum never likes it if Mandy calls round on her bike uninvited.

Tell her to ring you first: we might not be home, Mum tells me.

I don't understand what the problem is. Mandy's house is about half a mile up the hill from ours. If she's free-wheeled her bike down the road and we're not home, well, it's her own fault and the punishment is she'll have to lift her bum off the saddle and cycle fast to get up the hill, which is not really hard work, since it isn't a hill exactly, more a gentle rise.

I just don't like it, Mum insists. And don't be always answering back!

One time Mandy does come round when we were out. When we come back, there she is on the sofa in the sitting room eating an ice lolly.

Who gave you that?

Mandy looks as shocked as I am at the rudeness of Mum's tone.

I bought it with my pocket money, she pouts, with as much cheek in her voice as she dares with my mother.

Dad comes out of the kitchen, drying his hands on a towel, and smiles at us all. He glances from me to my brothers and back to Mandy on the sofa, but he doesn't look at Mum.

Mandy's come to call for Tina, he says.

Mandy bites off the red part of her Zoom lolly and tries to chew it. She makes little mewing sounds, as if the ice was burning her, covering her mouth with her palm. She is wearing a blue denim hat, a badge pinned on it with a yellow smiley face. I can't quite see her eyes from under it, but some strands of hair are sticking to her chin, all damp and streaked with pink from the coloured ice. She's brought the latest copy of *Melanie* to show me. We both look expectantly at Mum, waiting to be dismissed. After a second, Mum sweeps out, slamming the door to the kitchen so hard that the whole house trembles.

Trotting up the stairs to my bedroom, I hear raised voices in the kitchen. Dad's tone is sugary. Have a heart, Doreen, I hear him saying. The poor little mawther . . . I know they are talking about Mandy, about her mother leaving, moving in with that brickie from Chatteris. Well, I know what Mum thinks about that. But then she suddenly shouts, screeches even, and both of us hear it clearly: I'm not a bloody fool, Graham! I've got eyes in my head!

It's curious, this "eyes in my head". Surely eyes are on your face, not in your head? The phrase strikes me as funny.

I've got eyes in my head! I've got eyes in my head! I say to Mandy. I make the shape of balled fists on the top of my head, like an alien. We fall on the bed, giggling.

All these girls, Andrew said. Dad would have had a field-day.

Wendy has moved away, is talking to the best man, seems not to have registered my confusion. Or perhaps she did, perhaps my face was all too readable. Perhaps

102

she too has eyes in her head? What was it that Mum saw, that we didn't? Eyes that move independently, that's what I picture, the eyes of seahorses, able to swivel in two directions at once: one eye on the prey, another on the lookout for a predator. When we were really little, she'd say she had eyes in the *back* of her head, too. This was if we were pinching a chocolate crispy cake from the kitchen table and that phrase worried me as well, wondering about all the ways in which her eyes were different from other people's. So often she did seem to know exactly what we'd been up to and she could certainly tell if we were doing anything sneaky or sometimes even just thinking about it.

Andrew didn't mean anything, I tell myself. He was just talking about these four girls — Chloe and Rose and Charlene and Kylie — with flowers now slipping from mussed-up hair, broken daisy chains from the garden dangling round their necks, grass stains streaking their clothes. (A blob of chocolate ice-cream has obscured the word *angel* on Rose's dress, although someone has scrubbed at it with a tissue, making it worse.) Somehow, by implication, Poppy is included in his remark, being part of our family, being one of the five daughters we've had between us; but in my mind she is strangely big, bigger than them, towering over them in fact, with her long brown American limbs, healthy and intractable as shoots of maize, with her frank black eyes, so like Dean's, her dark glossy hair; and she seems bigger and tougher; squarer of jaw, more definite, less glittery, something else: a newer model.

But he didn't just say: we have a lot of girls. Replaying what he said makes my skin icily cold, my stomach twist. Was it an acknowledgment? Or is it just me? My new uncertainty with words: where familiar phrases suddenly loom up, misshapen or peculiar.

Field-day. The field again, but a different time. The beet crop, a different season. The land all burnt and flattened, every beet harvested; every stray plucked and flung by hand onto the back of the truck. It's early November with that low sunlight, the fierce kind of light that makes the colours truer: the green electric, the sky the deep blue of a mussel shell. I'm with my boyfriend, Russell. I'm thirteen.

Up ahead of us on the drove is a woman with a red coat, walking her dog.

The drove is a bank: higher than the road, part of the system of built waterways criss-crossing the landscape. The woman heads off towards a farmhouse and is replaced by two other figures, emerging from a barn. I hear her dog barking at them and then her red coat disappears and it is these two figures who are up ahead of us. A man and a woman. Actually, a girl: I know she's young by the way the ponytail leaps. She leans against him. She wears tight jeans and a white blouson jacket. I watch them for a long time, my heart scuttering like a rabbit. The white and the caramel jacket. That's the trick out here, the wide open landscape. Nowhere to hide.

That looks like my dad, I say to Russell. That man up there. Up ahead.

Russell draws on his cigarette. I like his eyes when he does that, how they narrow, become serious. He slips an arm around me, nestles into my neck.

Cradle-snatcher, he whispers.

It's his favourite jibe. His mates say the same about him.

Russell works at the beet factory too. He's the one who drives the scooper (he doesn't call it this, he calls it a truck, or the Baby) which shovels the beets into one big pile after they've been dumped by the lorries. He doesn't go inside much, or have a lot to do with my dad, who's on the distillation side of things. But he knows who he is.

She's not the first, Russell says. Your dad's a right one. There was nearly a riot one day when one of the women said he'd been messing with her daughter. Her old boy threatened to smack him. But he's got the gift of the gab, your dad has. Managed to worm his way out of it. Told them the girl was making it up to get them in a lather.

I don't know what to make of this. Mum and Dad have been having some ferocious rows lately, so it would fit. One was so bad that Mum tried to get out of the van as it was going along, and Dad dragged her back in and she was screaming, the passenger door open and her half-hanging out and my brothers crying and screaming too in the back. I was too startled to say anything. He screeched to a stop suddenly, sort of tipping her right out onto the roadside, like she was a load of dropped beets. There, you can walk, he says, if my company is so — *distasteful* to ya!

Mum picked herself up like nothing at all was wrong, looked around her, smoothed down her coat. Started walking up the Great Fen Road.

And then walking back with Russell, thinking about all of this, I recognise her. Dawn. Our babysitter. A girl in the fourth form. Mum sometimes asked her to babysit us when we were younger, before she thought I was old enough to do it. Dawn Staples. She has buck teeth and she isn't even pretty. And she has a white cotton jacket with a zip up the front and yellow tabs on the sides of the pockets and batwing sleeves. (I didn't see the yellow tabs but I knew they were there.) I'd only seen her ponytail, scraped high from her neck like that, bouncing, as she scrambled down the other side of the drove, following Dad, carrying his fishing umbrella for him and the fold-up green seat, just like I sometimes did when he let me. He bounces the keep-net in his other arm, loosening the catch. I watch as it springs free: miraculously lengthening, bouncing beside him, like a giant green snake.

He used to let me do that, release the net. He called it his slinky, like those metal cylindrical toys that tumble down stairs, slither in your hands, a handful of rings, gathering their own momentum. He'd let me lower the slinky into the water and I'd sit for hours, staring at whatever he caught, poking it with a stick, trying to feed the bigger fish with bait.

Look at the spines on this little bugger. It'd take your fingers off, he'd say, holding a perch in front of me, carefully opening the spines on its back into a fan. He'd lift it up to the sunlight to show me its tiger stripes, or point its face at me and make me look right into the white of its mouth, gaping at me like an open sock.

Now he has Dawn Staples to carry his tackle. He probably throws maggots down *her* bra, calls her the Titless Wonder, I think, tears welling up. (Titless Wonder is one of his pet names for me.)

They're a long way off now. But I can see that Dawn is leaning against my father, like she is the luckiest girl alive.

Two

I can see the best man's speech threatening now like a rain cloud: I have to get out of here. The best man is a friend of Andrew's from work, from the Probation Service. He perches on a wobbly white plastic chair, plucking at his tie in that gesture that men have, necks stretching like tortoises. He taps his spoon against his champagne glass, no doubt ready to eulogise Andrew's professional warmth, his miraculous way with wayward lost boys, but as we're in the garden, all the children switched to full volume, no one can hear him.

Pray silence for the best man! Andrew shouts, cupping a hand to his mouth. I see Billy glance over to him, and I wonder it too. Why didn't Andrew ask Billy to be the best man? The answer, I think, glancing round for my coat and bag, spying the covered bower with the wedding car behind it, white ribbons shining between the honeysuckle bushes, is the answer to all the questions in our family. We can just about cope, do the ritual things if a certain distance is observed. These kind of events orbit a forcefield. This is the closest we've been in years.

So I slip out for a moment. I duck under the ribbon-laced bower, taking a breath, and then I'm out in the street outside and it's after all only a normal Saturday afternoon in an English market town and we're a normal family unhappy in our own particular way, just as Tolstoy said, but that's all, surely I'm wrong, completely wrong-headed, oversensitive, as mad as they always thought me, to think otherwise. I walk quickly across a small green, the cathedral *looming*, the word they favour in guide books, Ely cathedral always *dominating* the skyline, but I never thought of it that way, to me the cathedral didn't so much loom as erupt, as if it had burst through the marshy Fen soil one night, something organic, something belonging here. The only solid thing in a landscape made of mist and water, smoke and mirrors. There was a description that we were read in school once, from the letters of Daniel Defoe, of the cathedral lit up, the only thing to be seen in fog, a yellow beacon, like a light-house, while Defoe rode his horse across the misty sea of the Fens to the Isle of Ely.

Today the doors are open and a sign is propped outside, advertising the stained-glass museum and the refurbished Lady Chapel, but I hurry on past, heading for the market square. Maybe it's Poppy. I'm missing Poppy — that must be the source of this feeling, this pressure in my ears; the pinching in my lungs. I refuse to regret my decision to come on my own: I suppose I always had it in mind that the weekend could be explosive, but nobody but me made me do it, and that's what I have to remember. Like jumping out of a plane with a parachute on your back, or dropping backwards from the boat with all your scuba gear attached, weighing you down. There's a second before you leap (or fall) when you think: oh God, I can't do this. But at the same time as paralysing terror, there's exhilaration, the joy of submission. Here, you think, if I just push myself that tiny little bit, if I summon all my courage for the leap. Once I'm tipped overboard, there's nothing to do but fall deeper, and remember to breathe.

It's the same now. I don't think I'm sick, although the pressure in my ear is becoming excruciating, a knife twisting in there. I stretch my jaw and hold my nose and blow out, then take deep breath after deep breath. None of it works, and it's not just my ear either, now my stomach is playing up, a horrible melting feeling, as if my stomach lining is being burnt off with paint-stripper. I reach in my bag and take two of my tablets, buying a bottle of water from a hot-dog stall. It's late afternoon and most places are closing up. Stall-holders are dismantling the market, a great smash of metal as the framework is pulled apart and loaded onto a truck.

Who might be watching me? Who might I know here? Everyone and no one is familiar. That could be a girl I was in school with. Ingleby, wasn't that her last name (her first one won't come), and she's smiling at me, too, but she's fatter, and her cheeks kind of jowly, she has three children with her, she's bought them all hot-dogs from the stall, and thankfully she's preoccupied with policing the amount of ketchup they're drowning them in. The smell of sweet hot fat from Ajays Freshly Cooked Rose Garland Doughnuts causes me another lurching sadness, knowing how much Poppy would like one. A car alarm whines, sudden and in panic; as if someone stood on a dog's paw. A trout-faced woman with puffy eyes — Mandy Baker's mother! Surely that's Sandy, Mandy Baker's mother! — is packing away the bookstall and the collectable beanies. I daren't catch her eye, I might be wrong, and yet I know, with delirious certainty, that I'm not. She hasn't seen me. She's packing a great stack of *Woman's Own* magazines into a Tesco's box, then putting a wilted copy of *Tales of Old Cambridgeshire* on top. I find myself resting my hand on a piece of Burwell ochre pottery. I've rolled to a standstill in front of her, after all these years, like a marble.

Can I help you? she says.

I snatch my hand away from the pottery, muttering: No, I — sorry, I was just looking —

I slide away and she carries on, pausing to straighten up and sip tea from a paper cup balanced on the edge of her nearly empty stall.

I glance back over my shoulder at her, but her head is bent. I can see the light spot in the centre of her dyed red hair, a scalp-pink circle, big as a coin. This tells me everything. This after all is Mandy Baker's mother, Sandy, who worked in Zara's Hair for years. Impossible to imagine then that she would become this puffy, shrivelled figure, who doesn't even care if strangers spy a vulnerable, forgotten spot on the back of her badly dyed head.

I have to say something. Ask Andrew, no matter how mad he thinks I am. I have to try and talk about it.

114

God, I don't know, maybe this is even the reason I came, and Andrew has given me my lead, a way in. I have to ask him what he meant.

I guess it's true I've bobbed through my life, floating rather than swimming. Dean accused me of this once and although he took it back later, seeing how much it upset me, it was the true part, the part I recognised, that hurt. He was talking specifics, about my relationships, the men I've been with, but as a general criticism he had a point. He was incredulous at my statement that until Ryan, the guy just before him, I'd never really fancied any of them, I was just responding to their interest in me.

You slept with boys you didn't even find attractive?

It's easy, I said. You've no idea, how powerful it is in girls, wanting to be sexy, desirable. It's confusing, it's an absolute turn-on. And don't forget, above all else, we're brought up not to hurt anyone's feelings.

Even to me, this last sounds lame.

But not just early relationships when you were a girl? I mean later, too? And for so long, and so many boyfriends, for years in fact . . .?

OK, OK, I shrieked, don't rub it in!

He changed the subject then. Made a weak joke, got out of bed, made us coffee. Standing in his white cotton shorts, his desire for me so easy and obvious in the sunlight of our exposed kitchen. He didn't even bother to pull the blind down: students passed by our floor to ceiling windows, chatting, carrying their tennis racquets, carrying, it seemed to me, their own easy straightforward desires.

Mandy had straightforward desires. Let's play The Bum Game, she'd say. She was insistent, bossy. This is what The Bum Game consisted of: one or the other of us would lie on our fronts, face down, eyes closed, pants pulled down. The other child (and more often than not it was Mandy: she was the game, I was the bum) would brush the prone one's bare skin with a series of objects whilst said child had to guess what they were. A hairbrush! A flower! Your hair! Mandy's long hair, she would swish close to my buttocks and I'd feel her breath, too, her mouth close to my skin. Was it innocent? Here we are upstairs in my bedroom, nose pressed into the nylon smell of the green squares of carpet. If we hear a noise, I leap up, pull up my knickers, snatch my dress down. So I'd say, no, not that innocent. But thrilling. To lie with eyes shut, still as a corpse, while Mandy tenderised the skin of my buttocks, made my bottom rise and fall to her touch, like a magician working with a snake.

You didn't know nine-year-old girls played these kind of games? I say. You thought we were all sweetness and light?

Dean doesn't remember any such childhood games. Or none that he feels compelled to share with me. But surely the Bum Game *is* sweetness and light? What could be sweeter than breathing life into every pore of skin, lighter than to experience every last inch of ourselves as tingling, as desirous, as alive? They are such scraps now — the things I can remember about

116

Mandy. I have to work hard at it, scrape up what little there is. And it's the odd ones, the prickly ones, or the ones with smoke around them, charred edges, that come most readily.

This for instance. It's Mandy by a swimming pool: it's a birthday party. Actually it's Mandy's birthday party, she's ten; here's her mother Sandy, smiling, trotting on heels, carrying the cake. Mandy's mother has a client at Zara's Hair, a woman from Thetford, posher than the rest of us, a woman who has loaned to us eight girls her small square of swimming pool, flat like a glinting turquoise tile in this otherwise dark and rambling garden. We are in our bikinis, the smell of Ambre Solaire rises from us in a hot cloud and there are colours, the colours that girls always bring, the colours of possibility, the red and the blue, the sharp turquoise blue. How is it that we dare to laugh like that, splashing, screaming. Mandy the loudest: she always was. Mandy standing up and jumping in, emerging with a great sputter and splash, whipping her blonde-dark hair like a dog, scattering droplets of water, beads falling on our skin. The smell of burning meat from the barbecue. The soft white baps, floury on our lips.

Mandy stays in the water, shivering, while bowls are brought to the water's edge by her mother and some of the other girls, the ones who want to curry favour. Me, for example. Cheese puffs. A hedgehog made from an orange and stuck with cocktail sticks spearing cubes of cheese and tinned pineapple.

117

Jenny — a rival for Mandy's attention, her body sour and long in her green swimsuit like a pickled gherkin, with hair as short as a boy — pushes me towards the water and I scream but don't fall, the scream that only a nine-year-old girl can give: it rends the air, splits ears, it encloses us, it's only ours, we scream with laughter. Mandy is scathing: your rotten hat, she says, pulling at my hat, and now it's floating on the water. That stupid hat, turquoise plastic, yellow flowers. I threw it away the other day but as it went in the black plastic bin liner, as the smell of old wine swallowed it up, I wanted to claw it back, wished Poppy hadn't given a bored, curt *no* to my offer to pass it on to her. I wanted to pull it out of the bin and back down thirty years and look more closely at it, look again. Was it really mine? How did it end up in my things, last through my college years, accompany me to America? Wasn't that Mandy's hat, or was I muddled, why did looking at those splashes of yellow daisies make me think of her? Maybe one day she borrowed it. She certainly borrowed it from Lolita, but no more than any of us: we all wanted to try it out, who wouldn't? How we pulled the hat down low over our eyes, examined our mouths in our pocket mirrors, practised our pouty smiles, noted the way our eyelashes brushed the underside of our eyebrows, wondered if a boy would ever admire that gesture as much as we did, ever kiss our closed eyelids.

Mandy's bikini top is striped pink and yellow. How flat they were, those bikini tops, against our blunt chests, often barely even serving their assumed role of covering up our nipples. Mine is turquoise towelling and ill-fitting — Mum made it. The pants were flat and straight across, the legs what they call now boy-legs (as if only boys have functional pants, ours always for some other purpose). It had a white rope tie under the chest and white plastic rings at the hips: they made circles on my skin when I took it off.

Mandy is splashing, then dragging herself out by her arms, shuffling on her bottom along the sun-heated concrete lining the pool and reaching for the Tupperware bowl of warm strawberries, strawberries that taste of plastic; dipping them in the bowl of stiff cream. Her flat fringe, wet against her forehead. Her foot, fine bones at the arch, the colour of a perfectly baked birthday cake, golden, rising, her toes like ten bright birthday candles, dipping small circles, little yellow light flames, in the water. Her stubborn bottom lip, what my Mum called her *pet lip*, peachier, fatter than mine.

Clever Mandy Baker, with her clever tongue, licking the cream from her very last summer.

The re-enactment of Mandy's "last known movements" has to take place on a Sunday, at the same time. Just like that Sunday, people doing their everyday things, the Inspector says. Jog their memories when they pop out to get some mint sauce to have with the lamb for their Sunday dinner. Two weeks have passed. There have been interviews, door to door enquiries, a couple of false leads, but not one sighting of Mandy. Now orange cones line the High Street in a path towards the river. Police cars top and tail at either end: between them cars with men leaning on them, fiddling with cameras. It's nothing like that Sunday. That Sunday two weeks ago our village barely saw a police car from one day to the next. Front page news was Dog Dirt Menace in High Street.

I'm wearing the purple and lilac dress and the shoes and the necklace. My teeth are chattering. Mum smooths my hair for the hundredth time, rapping my head sharply with the comb when I protest and try to duck away. Dad is chatting to the young policewoman beside him; she laughs once at something he says, turning her face towards him. Mum raps my head again, harder this time.

I glance anxiously around me but there is no sign of Mandy's mother.

OK, now, when you're ready then, Tina, says the policeman Crisp.

And so I set off on Mandy's bike, wobbling along the route they've marked out for me, and a dozen men lift their cameras, pointing their dark blank eyes at me.

It's the oddest feeling. To me, I am nothing like Mandy. I can't understand how anyone could be fooled, how anything could be helped. They think all ten-year-old girls look the same, that's why. It's like Dad said that once about coloured people, about how you couldn't tell them apart and Mum told him off, she said he was Prejudice, she said he was as bad as that bloke in *Love Thy Neighbour* who carries on about darkies all the time.

I feel as if I'm playing a horrible game of dressing up, playing a trick on her. I expect Mandy herself to step

120

out from behind that curve in the river bank, or to begin a slow walk from under the bridge, up to the High Street, a walk towards me, weaving between the cones, her yellow hair dripping, a furious look in her eyes, a mocking look. What do you think you are doing with my beads? With my lovely purple leather shoes? What are you doing with my bike?

My knees are like sherbert, my legs too weak to cycle and several times I have to stop. Small clumps of boys are watching. The lilac-headed customers from Zara's Hair huddle in a dangerous storm, like bees. The young WPC with the enormous chest, straining the buttons on her uniform, calls out her encouragement: that's fine, Tina, you're doing great, love!

Over one shoulder I see Dad moving towards her, his mouth towards her ear.

Grimly, I press down with my feet, nose the bike towards the river. Tears sting my eyes, blurring my view down the slight hill towards the bridge. I can't see the water yet, only the misty grey walls lining the bridge, or the dark smudge at the corner of my eye: a line of camera-laden men running beside me. I am playing at being a missing girl and when Mandy steps out from under that bridge, steps forward from wherever she has been, she is going to be furious with me. She definitely won't be my friend: she will find some way to punish me. The Bum Game will be over for ever.

And then the weirdest thing happens, in the middle of pedalling. I'm looking down at the pedal (I'm not doing it well, they didn't adjust the saddle for me and I'm smaller than Mandy) and at the white basket in front and the *I Love Donny* sticker and the white plastic handlebars and at the road in front of me and I have this feeling, such a strong feeling, that I've done this before. I've felt all these things before in exactly this combination: my lilac shoe on the plastic pedal, the slight trembling in my calf, my tongue slipping out to wet my dry lips. It's so strange: I know exactly what's coming next. I know that dog is going to bark just now (and it does) and I know that red car is going to pull out, in front of the blue one, with a man in sunglasses leaning his elbow out of the window and staring. And that's just what happens. It's all slow-motion, it's weird and kind of like I'm dreaming it but I know I'm not and it just keeps unravelling in front of me, doing all the things I know it's going to do. So now I'm scared, thinking: I've seen all this before so that means this must be what Mandy saw, this is what's happening to me — I've turned into her and I'm having her exact same *feelings*, seeing all the things she saw, last Sunday, one after the other, and so, if something awful happened, if something really terrible has happened to her, surely I can't stop it, now that it's started up, like a record playing, the needle getting closer and closer: surely that's going to happen to me now too? And thinking all this makes me wobble and it makes the grey tunnelling feeling start up in my head and the burning smell floods under my nose again and the voices and then before I can help it, the bike is slipping to the side and people are running at me and catching me, and the policeman Crisp says: give her some room

122

now, that's enough — move out now, please, some room for the girl!

Get her a drink of water, someone else shouts. Here's Mum, I can see her now, at the other end of the long tunnel, tiny but coming bigger, and someone comes out of a house and puts a glass of water to my mouth and Mum is sitting beside me, on the pavement, saying: it's all too much for her, it's her best friend, you know, and the tunnel disappears again and the world comes back, and I've no idea what's going to happen next; it's just a sunny day in our village with loads of policemen and newspaper men around, and bollards in a line down the High Street; but apart from that, everything is perfectly normal.

That's reconstruction, isn't that what they call it? As in: re-building, re-making, to be as close to the original as possible. I've reconstructed it again here, to the best of my ability, including the strange sensation of déjà vu, and my fear that I was experiencing things through another person's eyes, through Mandy's eyes in fact, which I never had before. But now that I think about it, didn't I say that the first time I had the weird fainting feeling was in church with my brothers, and now that I've dragged up the reconstruction, surely *that* must have been the first time? It strikes me that he's wrong, that professor, another memory scientist; I've been to lectures of his. Dean finds him really fascinating: Douwe Draaisma, the Dutch one, the one who looks a bit like Benny Hill. He says that we always remember forwards rather than backwards, so that if we're thinking of an event, an incident, rather than remember more recent events and play it backwards, we go back to the beginning and replay it, in a typical narrative line. But what keeps happening to me is that I remember something and it feels like that was the beginning, and then I remember again, and discover I was wrong, I can go further back. It's a trick I think that memory plays on us to make us feel this is the most we know, the most we can remember, and then surprises us. Like fishing in a murky pool you think is empty and then just as you are about to go home there's a tug. Something bites.

Here's another one: Russell. My first boyfriend. Russell William Sly. It's another ouija night round at Jenny's. Russell is a friend of Stephen's. Stephen is home this time, and they can't resist baiting us. We can't get the letters out in front of them to play, so we skitter upstairs to Jenny's room, balancing a *Blue Peter Annual* on the bed and carefully arranging the letters on the faces of Lesley Judd and John Noakes. (It's a weird cover, the Tenth Annual, with all four of the Blue Peter presenters holding a picture of themselves and then in that picture there they are again doing the same thing and then on and on until it gets too tiny to see — it drives me a bit insane, trying to imagine how small it really gets, or sometimes trying to draw it. It's Infinity, that's why it makes my head ache.) The boys are taking up all the space in the living room with their hamster smell.

Cherry fancies the dark-haired boy with the moustache; the one with his socked feet on Jenny's mum's smoked glass coffee table. His name is Russell. His trainers are in the hall, melting like sweaty cheese. Cherry keeps dreaming up excuses for us to go downstairs (Can we have some more jammie dodgers from the packet?) just so we can pass him.

Cherry isn't bossy like Jenny. It's Jenny who says: go downstairs, Tina. I dare you! I dare you to go down to the haunted cellar.

Jenny is laying out the letters.

We forgot the tumbler. You can get that while you're down there, she says.

She doesn't look up from the letters. I know she's actually telling me to get the tumbler, she's not interested at all in the boys downstairs, they're her brother's mates, that's all.

That Martin, though. He's all right, isn't he? Cherry says, her face scarlet suddenly. She collapses onto the bed behind Jenny, rolling about and squealing as if she's being tickled. She opens her mouth so wide that I can see that little dangly thing at the back, but then claps her hand over it with a smack.

She's just trying to throw you off the scent, Jenny says, her eyes still fixed on her task. So you'll fancy him and not Russell. Russell's got a full moustache, not just bum fluff. Go on though. The haunted cellar. Even my dad won't look down there. I'll give you that new nail-varnish I just bought if you open the door and take two steps. Count to ten.

She nods to a bottle of plum-coloured Miners polish on the dressing-table behind her.

OK, OK, I say. I don't know what it is about Jenny, why Cherry and I always do what she says.

The difficult bit is to walk past the living room, with the door open and the TV on and Jenny's brother and his friends in their great cloud of cigarette smoke. Only one of them looks up as I pass him and it's Martin: the fairer-haired one, the one with the big ears and the flat forehead as wide as a plate, his head too big for his lanky body, the one Cherry pretended to fancy, when I know the real beauty is Russell, the dark one. Russell has a brown moustache planted just like a perfect little hedge on his top lip, with his mouth beneath it wide and easy like a nice big lake and his teeth white and crisp and even. Russell doesn't look up, but he must sense I'm passing the doorway behind him by the expression on Plate Face's face. He says something I don't catch and the others laugh, then without even turning his head to look at me, Russell lifts his brown muscled arm in the light blue aertex shirt in the gesture the boys always make: fist clenched, one hand feeling up their own muscles. It's a compliment, I think. That is, I blush. They're always doing this, but no one has yet made this gesture to me. I know it's rude and I know what it means he'd like to do to me but the difficulty is: how am I supposed to react? There are two bad things for girls to be and they don't leave much room in the middle. One is tight and the other is a scrubber.

So I pretend not to have seen it and carry on into the kitchen but then Russell has rolled off the sofa like a puppy dog and bounded into the kitchen behind me. He stands very close, close enough to feel the heat from

126

my face. I breathe in the beer on his breath and the smell of his aftershave, which I know is really sophisticated, Aramis, I think it is, not that disgusting Great Smell of Brut. His eyes are dark, liquid. (These are the ways boys' eyes are described in the magazines I read. Melting. Soulful.) He looks like he just woke up. He runs a hand through his fringe and it falls back in perfect blow-dried style. I'm surprised to feel a kick, an odd little kick, low down inside me.

Hi, Cherry . . .

It's Tina. I'm Tina, I squeak.

Hey, Tina. Whatcha all doing up there?

Nothing . . . I just came down . . . to get some jammie dodgers . . .

Huh? Why don't you gi'ss a kiss then. Give us a kiss, will ya? Are you tight or what?

He moves towards me but I don't want to accidentally look like I think he means it so I aim for a neutral expression and keep my eyes wide, trying to make my eyelashes touch the top of my eyebrows. He bursts out laughing. His mates are suddenly in the kitchen, opening the fridge, swatting at each other like flies, farting and saying: jeeezzz, light that one!

Where's the fucking beer, Russ? What you doing in here?

He says nothing. He turns his back to me and pops open a can.

Later that night, I go downstairs again, passing the swampy living room den and Russ calls out: hey, Tina, come and look at this.

127

They have a magazine on the coffee table in front of them. I'm on my way to the haunted cellar. (I never got there the first time.) They're engulfed in smoke. The blue of the TV screen crackles away, like it's the only thing alive.

I step into their lair and politely stand on a marshy piece of carpet, sticky with something spilled, while they flick through the magazine on the low table in front of me, their eyes on my hot face. I stare at the pages: red glossy finger nails spreading dark pink folds, like showing you the inside of a walnut shell. I stand there for an age, the cork soles of my wedge-sandals nearly slipping into the bog, before saying politely: I have to go upstairs now.

And as I leave, they crack open with laughter, the room exploding.

Did you go to the haunted cellar? Did you look down the haunted cellar? Cherry screams at me, back in Jenny's room. A giant, sunny David Cassidy smiles down at us, clean and friendly, fingers cocked in the pockets of his jeans, as we set the tumbler to the centre of the board and try to compose ourselves, close our eyes.

No. It was scary enough with Jenny's brother and his mates. I think you owe me that nail-varnish. That living room is a Fetid Swamp! I practically drowned on the carpet in there!

You stink of smoke. Five minutes with them and you're probably hooked now. You'll be marked by their Evil Stench for life . . . Jenny says.

He's OK, though, Russell. He asked me to meet him. He whispered it: come and meet me down by the river. Thursday night, after school.

They fall about laughing.

Are you going?

Cherry is jealous and Jenny thinks I'm mad. What would I want with one of her brother's smelly friends? Big grown men too, aren't they a bit old for us?

It'll be a laugh, I say. Come on, at least wander down there with me. What happens on a Thursday? Sweet Fanny Adams.

What, to meet my own brother? Jenny says. No thanks!

I know, Cherry giggles. Let's ask the ouija board if Russ fancies you.

She hands me the tumbler and, without hesitating, I breathe the question into the glass. We press our fingers on the upturned tumbler. It immediately shoots from one letter to the next. PUPPY LOVE, the board spells. And swiftly, too.

Puppy love! Cherry shrieks. She was the one pushing, that time.

What, who's a puppy? Tina? Or Russ? asks Jenny.

And they called it Puppy Luhhurve . . . Cherry sings.

Later, I think about the magazine they showed me, wishing I could have picked it up, taken it home with me. I've seen them before in Jenny's house. Her brother has a half-built shed with punched out windows, reeking of damp and wood and I once hid in it to play a trick on Jenny and there was a whole crinkly stack. *Fiesta. Club International.* My mouth watered, gingerly turning the pages. All that clean bare flesh, shiny and

129

new. No one sagging or wrinkly, only chubby and fresh and bursting out of things, out of fabric, for instance. There were some pictures where I quickly turned the page: those frightened me. But everything was plump and compact and round and I understood at once the appeal. I read over and over words like pert and tight and felt I was really getting somewhere, really understanding at last. I could see that it was better when things burst against fabric, when flesh pressed against lace or black straps. I saw that they liked the restraint, but also the idea of spilling over, of things spilling out of control. Things? Girls. Us.

Up until then I'd thought that when I grew up I'd be a lady. That was the word. The one I was growing towards, the future. Go and ask *the lady* if they have it in your size, Mum would say in a shoe-shop. Mind that *lady*, if you brushed too close to one in the supermarket. What was a lady? She was nondescript, someone frumpy. Not nicely dressed in a white crimplene skirt with ric-rac round the hem or bell sleeves, those were still called girls. Ladies were shapeless, with bulky coats and headscarves. They had children. Ladies did boring jobs: shop-assistant, dinner-lady, lollipop-lady. Or they did unusual jobs, like lady-doctor or lady-dentist. Or lady-scientist. That was going to be me.

Years back, absently rubbing at an itch at the nether side of my thigh, I'd accidentally reached the hot hollow of my groin and discovered what a textbook I read in the library called a full *crisis of pleasure*: one that rocked my body, rattling through me like a gale

130

through a draughty house. The library book, which was called *Love Together*, didn't say that girls as young as nine (which I was at the time) could feel this: only happily married women. Of course I thought I was going to die. Or at the very least, go straight to hell. But when the gale subsided and I discovered that I was still alive and lying sweatily on my bedroom floor, I rolled on my back and stared at the ceiling and put my hands up to my face, which was flaming. Fab, as Mandy would say. I knew I was a freak: better not mention it to anyone.

Flicking through the pages of Stephen's magazines, I realised I wasn't a freak at all but probably just a sex kitten, or maybe a nympho. I was hiding for a good long while since Jenny had no idea that I'd ventured outside the house, so I had time to really study them, read all the letters and the little paragraphs about Naughty Nancy or Saucy Sam under the pictures. Girls always want sex, I realised at once. Even when we said we didn't, we did, after a while. If we didn't feel like it, we could be persuaded unless we were Frigid (I wasn't sure if this was a medical condition or something you were born with, like brown hair, but it sounded really terrible, like acne or warts; something to be absolutely dreaded). Especially girls in uniforms (nurse, teacher, waitress, hotel maid), they were the most likely to be nymphos, quite filthy in what they were hoping for. I crouched down in the corner of the dusty shed, opening each of the magazines, one after the other, After a while I realised what I was looking for.

There was so much about girls. Girls girls girls. It made me think of the end of the *Benny Hill Show* when this stupid bald man is chased all around by these girls in bikinis and they all want to slap his head. Girls — heaps and heaps of them: pouting, open mouths, so that as I turn each page they seemed to pile up, body after body, pink and brown and creamy; blonde and dark and red-headed. I felt dizzy looking at them all. It was as if a hundred gaping mouths of baby birds were shouting: feed me, feed me!

But what I was looking for, I didn't find. It was when Jenny called and I slapped the magazines shut and jumped up that I puzzled over it. I could see easily enough what boys saw in us, why we were exciting. But what was there about boys to get hot over? I'd seen my brothers in the bath. Nothing very thrilling there, but that's brothers, I suppose, that's different. In the whole stack of magazines, I flicked and flicked, page after page, searching, looking for Readers' Husbands, or something more specific. I thought one would surely leap in front of me, frozen; dazzled and upright like a hare in headlights, but it never did.

So after the re-enactment, after dressing up as Mandy, I don't know what I expected. I suppose I thought she would turn up. Or someone else would turn up, say that they'd found Mandy, that she'd run away somewhere. Or the police would be round our house, to tell us that they had found her.

We watch it on TV, with some excitement, with a kind of thrill, as if I was a model, as if I'd done something really exceptional.

Graham! Billy! Andrew! Our Tina's on the TV!

Mum yelling, standing in the doorway, her navy pinafore dress, the corduroy one with the patterned blue flowers on the hem; her hands rubber-gloved, and the smell of bleach wafting from the kitchen, along with the fainter one of toad-in-the-hole. The boys thunder down the stairs, swing themselves from the balcony at the last step, Billy falls over (he always does), starts yelling, over which Mum shouts again: come on, you'll miss her!

And there I am, on my bike, pretending to be Mandy.

Budge up, Doreen, Dad says to Mum, squashing beside us, feeling in his pockets for the sugar cubes he nicks from work to drop in his tea. (He's always forgetting about them, so that when Mum washes his clothes they're always dissolving, leaving bits of blue and white paper sticking to everything.)

Police today asked members of the public to search their memories for any sightings of missing girl, Mandy Baker, aged ten, in the village of . . .

Dad stirs his tea so noisily that Billy shouts *sssh sssh!* and Dad says, talking over the television, that if Billy tells him to ssh one more time he'll clout him. Andrew and Billy hunker down on the sofa. Billy throws the orange velour cushions on the floor, narrowly avoiding knocking over a glass of half-drunk lemon barley water on the low coffee table.

You're rubbish on that bike, Andrew says.

She looks like she's going to cry. Look at her eyes! Billy says.

We listen to the policeman talking about "fresh witnesses" and "tragedy and heartbreak" but I'm not really listening to that, I'm staring at myself, at that little tiny version of myself that I can see must indeed be me, must be what I look like to other people: that is, a girl, a thinnish, quite pretty girl, maybe cute and small, who knows, with a pointy face and pointy elbows, sharp corners everywhere, the fringe that goes up at the end, the fringe that Mum cut with the kitchen scissors, cut badly; big grey eyes, a sort of owl-like, watching kind of face, very serious, perhaps a bit frightened: and then the news item is finished and my wobbling figure in the lilac dress is gone, replaced by the same school photo of Mandy staring too directly at us from out of the television, her turned-up mouth in the shape that everyone thinks is a half-smile. Only I know what it really means. She is sarcastic, is Mandy. She will be laughing at them, how rotten they are; they got her half-smile so wrong.

Mum squeezes out from the sofa, goes back to the kitchen. Pulls off one of the rubber gloves, making a snapping noise, so loud that I hear it through the serving-hatch. Like a doctor trying to scare you. Angry.

She puts her face to the square hatch, leans right through.

And don't you go down by that river, you hear me? Don't you dare go there on your own, she says. She says it to me, not Andrew and Billy. She points one nasty gloved finger towards me.

What, they can, and I can't? And I'm older than them — that's not fair!

134

None of you, she says, flustered. None of you are to go down there unless me or your dad is with you.

The boys have already left. Tumbling out of the room and up the stairs again, Andrew punching Billy in the ribs, Billy shouting: stinker! Big bum!

Dad has said nothing throughout my moments of stardom. Now he is whistling. "Green Laurels" at first, then one of his tunes, his old-fashioned jazz tunes. I recognise it. I think it's "Summer Time and the Living is Easy".

Fish are jumping, I think. And the cotton is high.

And that's the beginning of our summer holidays, holidays all spoiled by Mandy. We aren't allowed to play near the river or the droves or the sailing club or any of the ditches, basically, anywhere near water. That just about rules out everywhere. And still no one "comes forward". No one tells us anything. When will they find Mandy? I ask, discovering the police again, in the kitchen with Mum, at home now, getting up to pull the yellow sun-flowered blinds themselves, without asking her permission; drinking from the familiar mugs, calling Mum Doreen and accepting the McVities she nestles next to their cups, the chocolate melting on their hands in the hot day. One time I hear them talking about Mandy's dad and mum saying: yes, Alf, he is a bit of a loner. I mean, I never blamed Sandy for leaving him, I don't think he said two words to her this last year . . . and another time she's saying: well, I don't have an address for him. Janice Richardson might know. All I heard is he's a brickie, from Chatteris, and Sandy had been seeing him for quite a while . . .

I don't ask: what happened to Mandy? That's the question I know they won't answer. (They'll lie: they'll say they have no idea.) I'm supposed to understand entirely and also not know at all. That's the underbelly, the up-you-go-to-bed-now-my-girl moment, the deep forests, the half-eaten, blood-spattered heels. It's the reason too you have to keep your bikini top on, even though the boys are allowed to run around with their chests plain, uncovered. That's the reason they fall silent when you're doing handstands like that, cart-wheels in front of your Uncle Jimmy, and suddenly tell you to run into the kitchen and get yourself some home-made lollies from the freezer, the plastic kind, so weak and pallid, lemon they're called but tasting only of yellow-coloured plastic, like sucking on barley-coloured sandals.

I know they think I know nothing, they are so keen to believe that I know nothing, and it's true, I'm puzzled, I don't have all the answers but I know *something*. Children are supposed to be innocent: it's our job. We're the ones with the souls, the little cherubs in the paintings, we're the angels. I have a picture book with all these curly haired golden children, which look a bit fat to be airborne to me, but nonetheless, there they are, floating above a tablet (like the kind of tablets Moses had, not a Disprin) with this prayer on it: *As here I lay me down to sleep/I pray the Lord my soul to keep.*

I have to say it every night, every single night, kneeling by my candlewick bedspread. And then, after Mandy, somehow she stopped insisting. I stumble over it one night, stalling at the lines: *And if I die before I wake/I pray the Lord my soul to take*. I can't get the "if I die" part out. It is too horrible. Girls don't die. Little girls my age don't die. I've already begun hideous nightmares, ones where Mum and Dad are replaced by aliens, robots so well constructed that they'd fool somebody else, they'd fool the police or the teachers, but only at night, on my own with them, do their eyes glow red as the centre of coals, and they get important stuff wrong, they don't know when my birthday is, or that I don't like carrots, and that's how I know that they're not my mum and dad at all, they're monsters, alien replacements.

There's no need to be paranoid, darling, the mother in *The Partridge Family* says. Bad things happen but there are still plenty of good people in the world. She's not talking about murder but about someone stealing a lunch-box. I wish my mum would say this. I wish she'd use those sweet, calming tones, instead of her own combination of horse's snorts and sudden blasts, rants that can last four to eight minutes. (I timed her once; that's how I know. I had a stop-watch as a Christmas present and since I don't like running, I didn't know what else to time.)

Mum's view is bleaker than that. Once, when I'm straddling my bike, this man calls out from a passing van: let's sniff your saddle then, love! I can't really think why he would want to say such a thing, much less do it, so I just ignore him, but he probably hadn't realised that Mum was with me, a few yards behind me on the pavement, whilst I cycled on the road. She stops dead, glaring around her, but the van is already far up ahead.

Disgusting! she screams, waving her fist at him.

Then to me she says: men, they're all the bloody same. Disgusting. They're animals! Ruled by their stupid — ruled by *that*.

This confuses me. If Stephen's magazines are to be believed, it's girls who can't stop thinking about sex, who are like animals. But of course, I can't tell Mum that I've read them, so I say nothing.

There are some terrible, wicked people in this world, Tina.

She's watching a TV programme when she says this, about this blonde woman who has murdered children and taped them screaming and won't tell the police where their bodies are buried on the moors. She turns the dial, changes the channel when I come in the room. Her voice is low and crackly, like a phone line that's gone all wrong and her face is blotchy, where she's been crying.

Why are there?

Why? What do you mean, why? I don't know. It's — it's not our place to question the Lord's Plan! Anyway, it's not His fault! It's the Devil —

Is the Devil to blame for Mandy?

Billy says: not the Devil, stupid. She just fell in the river.

He's been playing behind the sofa. Mum didn't even know he was there. Billy has rigged up camouflage and netting, he's playing with Action Man, making the hard-boiled doll crawl beneath it, hand-grenade in hand. I fetch my Sindy and use her to attack his man, batting him with her thin cupped claw, pecking him with her breasts.

How do you know she just fell in?

Well, she just did. She got off her bike, she slipped in the river and she drownded and floated away.

It's cramped behind the sofa and it smells of boys' socks and dirty hair. Mum has gone out of the room. I raise my head to watch her go out before I say anything.

You know nothing, I say, in a vinegary grown-up voice.

I write guiltily in her diary, the diary I bought for her birthday, filling in the days, Mandy's blank, un-written in days.

Bought some fruit gums. Read Anne's House of Dreams. Went to Cambridge to be measured for our new school uniforms with Susan Babcook and now she is being horrible to me and telling Jenny not to talk to me. Had a Milky Way. Guess what's number one? Horrible Suzie Quatro!!! Who will I sit next to at the new school if Mandy isn't back? A nice purple skirt came in a Freemans Parcel.

One time I am watching telly and the photo of Mandy flares on the screen. Seeing it, a bolt shooting right from my neck to my toes, I realise that despite all their best efforts, their attempts to protect me, despite Mandy's sarcastic half-smile, I'm scared. I'm suddenly back with Mandy in Debenham's, with her mum, and I remember we were choosing a bra for Mandy, giggling at the way Sandy ran her hands over the satin material first; a white teen bra, a bra with a name, a bra called Dolores, size 28 AA cup, with the tiny pink bows.

I have a sudden clear picture of that little bra, white and pink. Trampled in some mud somewhere. For the first time the thought forms that Mandy might not come back.

The newsreader on Anglia News speaks of a "woman coming forward" with "information".

Information! They must have found Mandy?

But when I ask her, Mum just sniffs and says it'll be a "false lead".

No, they said there was a *sighting*! In London or something, I heard it. Maybe they've found her? A girl "answering the description of Mandy Baker", that's what they said!

Mum goes into one of her angry splutters.

Sick, they are.

My excitement flickers as I wait, doubtfully, opening the glass doors to the kitchen to see what she's going to say next. She's scrubbing at the hobs, taking all the little rings apart to clean right under them, and she seems to have forgotten I'm there.

Who? I prompt.

Oh, just people. Really sick.

What do you mean?

Oh, making up stories. Some sick people. Do it for kicks.

Making up stories. Sick people do this. But the man on the telly said . . .

For a moment, the picture of Mandy being alive somewhere, down in London, feeding the pigeons at

140

Trafalgar Square, glows in front of me, vivid, strong. But Mum's words are stronger. The picture flickers and goes out. Mum gives a big noisy sigh and I think she is going to tell me. What sick people do, why. But she puts the rings back on the hob, ties up her apron and picks up the Jif bottle, starts scrubbing the kitchen counter-top. She scrubs hard, her elbows sticking out behind her, like the folded legs of grasshoppers. She scrubs a lot these days. I wander out again.

I try deliberately rolling out my favourite story, the one I use to cheer myself up. I'm in school, in the prefab, we're doing a lesson, and the day is sticky like candle wax, with wasps buzzing in through the open windows and stupid girls (not me) attracting them; flailing their hands about, fussing and screaming, and Mr Hellis saying: now come on, don't be silly, girls, they won't hurt you if you just stay calm. It's my best lesson: Fish and their Natural Habitat. I'm cutting out a fish shape from some pale pink paper, that thick paper that I don't like the smell of, or the colour either, a colour dull and sludgy not quite right for a nice fat carp; and the door to the prefab opens and there is Mandy. She says nothing, she slides to my desk as if she is on casters and stands beside me. I can smell her, the Cola smell, the lip gloss smell. She's wearing a sailor outfit: white collar, red cotton dress, ribbons flapping at the front. Susan is sitting in that place now, Mandy's cross, she feels jealous. Mandy flicks her hair away from her eyes, that movement she has, using both hands at once, flicking hair away from her face, tossing her head back. Move over, Mandy says. Susan moves over. Mandy is back.

A week later I read in Dad's newspaper that the sighting of Mandy is a "false lead." The police go down to London and ask questions but can't find anyone else to "corroborate" the story of the lady who saw her. She was on a number 38 bus and saw the child, fitting Mandy's description, outside a chip shop. A fair girl without shoes.

I think about this. I can imagine Mandy eating chips from a bag and wandering by herself: she wouldn't be scared at all. But why would she leave her bike behind? Why would she leave her shoes? I want Mum to be wrong about people making up stories and I often have such a powerful picture of Mandy beside me, doing something ordinary like picking a scab from her knee, or sticking a Donny sticker on her Rough Work book, that it's impossible to believe she's not somewhere in the world, like on holiday or just off school for a while.

Each day, I expect to turn up at school and for her to be there. She surely won't miss the Going up to Big School party? I know she had a new outfit for it. A pinafore dress, cream with coffee-coloured ric-rac trim on the pockets. But there are only a few weeks left. One morning Miss Hazlehurst helps us to empty out our drawers, giving us a big paper folder with all our drawings in. I notice that Mandy's drawer has been emptied already, the felt-tip label of her name removed. But when Miss Hazlehurst's taking down the drawings in the art room she peels one off and sees Mandy's name on the back and she notices me looking at her and says in a stiff way, would you like this one, Tina, this picture? I shake my head. It's not a good picture. It's a drawing of a princess, for a story about Rumpelstiltskin. The head is out of proportion with the body. Mandy was always rotten at drawing shoes.

The police call around just one more time. They don't call me in to ask me anything, but I hang around outside the kitchen door and hear the sighing in Mum's voice and the words "no more leads" and "poor Alf, the man's a wreck" and then that's it. That seems to be the last time anyone is going to mention her. There is no further mention of the case on the news. No body has been found.

Sometimes we see Mandy's dad in the village, sitting atop his tractor, driving as slow as anyone could ever drive, scattering muck and sugar-beets in the road, a whole black trail of them. None of the cars ever tries to pass him. Dad curses, the driver of the school bus beeps his horn, but Mr Baker just sits there, sometimes dragging on his cigarette, hogging up the whole road, driving just as slowly and as badly as he likes, leaving a black zigzag of mess behind him.

One of the boy's in Andrew's class makes up a song: Mandy Baker, Mandy Baker, ran away with a pumpkin-maker. It's a rotten song and they get told off for it by one of the teachers.

It's not just Mandy who has gone, school has finished too. I'm not going back there. We won't ever sit together in that prefab, drinking soapy milk through a straw or cutting out fish from coloured paper. This summer is all about the secondary school, the huge, spanking new comprehensive with the gummy smell in the halls and the looming carpark with its white lines to show where coaches from Burnt Fen and the Surrounding Farms should park; and later, the swarms of children buzzing together, their newly bought navy jackets flapping over their shoulders like wings, bright red markings, logos, uppermost. And Logo is a new word and a bit tricky, along with Options and Personal Development and Free Period. That last phrase makes Billy and Andrew laugh. Not that they know why, but it's something to do with their big sister and embarrasses them. Jam rag! they shout, ambushing me from the stairs with their cap-guns, firing at my cheek. Mandy would have slaughtered them for that. My brothers never scared her. The long strip of paper, the cap-gun ammunition, the black smoking dots wind in front of me, a long ribbon reaching between us. A weird smell: hot, chemically. That smell is my childhood. Gun smoke.

That day, the Sunday Mandy goes missing, we're all at the beach. Well, not all of us; not Dad. But Dad was out all yesterday at the Electricity Cut at Peterborough where he said he'd been standing knee-deep in bloody slimy black water for hours on end just to catch some chub and roach to use as bait for his big adventure today. Now he had to go and pick them up from their hiding place before heading off to the Relief Channel at Ten Mile Bank. We know it's a big day for him: he's been excited, edgy, sort of jumpy for a couple of days.

144

Anyway we'd never expect him to come with us, on a church outing. The beet factory is closed at the moment, it's the season for growing, not harvesting, and he always gets depressed around that time, doing other dodgy work, bits of farm-work that he hates. He hates eating his docky in a field with men he can't boss around, that's what he tells me. And Mandy's not here either and she was meant to come with us and she didn't, because in my own spiteful little non-Christian, non-forgiving head I accused her of stealing the Sindy hairbrush.

It's my favourite beach with the wavy grasses and the sand dunes for jumping in and the sea a long long way out on the longest flattest beach in history. Mum is lying on her back with a copy of *Woman's Realm* over her face, her knitting in a flowered plastic bag beside her to keep the sand off it. Andrew and Billy are bailing sand over my legs, patting it into a large hump dividing into fins at the bottom, a mermaid shape. My legs beneath the weight of sand feel cool and heavy.

You've got no legs. You're disabled like Melanie McMahan, Andrew says.

A shark ate your legs, agrees Billy.

My arms are folded: I'm ignoring them and their stupid boy remarks and I'm staring out at the sea. I'm thinking: one day I'm going to swim far, far away from here, to another country. I'm going to do something really important. I'm going to invent something, discover something. Work in a zoo, an aquarium. Find something really special, understand something really difficult, something true that no one knows already, no one else can see. I'm deciding. If I don't do this, I will always feel . . . unfinished.

I feel guilty about not inviting Mandy and so I'm seeing her everywhere: isn't that her in the yellow and pink bikini with the kite, or bending over that sandcastle with the red sun hat on, the sea licking her toes? When we grow up Mandy is going to be a model or a pop star and I'm going to be a really famous scientist and we are both going to have two children, probably twins. One boy and one girl, each. I close my eyes and picture this.

Picture the scrapbooks we made last summer on that nasty grey sugar paper. Our names on the inside flap, pink felt-tip pens, a heart instead of a dot for the *i* in Tina, a curly spiral *y* in Mandy. (She tried spelling her name Mandi, just to have the heart over the *i* thing, but scribbled it out, saying it looked rotten.) My favourite food, my favourite colour. My measurements (four feet one inch, weight six stone two pounds). My favourite boys, my favourite pop group. Me, me, me. Little things about my body, my territory. I know the story of Narcissus — we are told it in church and I know that staring into a pool of water to see your own reflection all the time will only make you twisted, and wicked, but on the other hand, dressing up and thinking about myself is really all there is. We make these comics for each other, Mandy and I. *Lovetime.*

On the back page of every issue she writes an end letter from a pop star she doesn't like, say, Dave Hill. *Hi there, well I hope you like my modern gear, my hat, the sort of helmet. I think it's great. I've been putting more glitter on my face and I look more horrible still. As you know, Slade's Number one, so are we glad. Bye, love Dave Hill.* And in the problem page: *My friend has turned into a goody-goody. Oh we're sure she's not. You just think that because you're not as good as her.*

The comics I write aren't called *Lovetime*, but *Girls World*. It's because I have a doll called that: Girls World, a life-sized, hollow plastic head. The hair is shiny, fair and nylon and there is makeup and hair accessories and it sits on your dressing-table to hold your things, your hair-clips, and it's fantastic, you can do anything you want with it, change the styles, paint the face, add lipstick, tiny plaits.

Andrew annoys me because he keeps getting it wrong and calling it Girl's Head and when I patiently explain to him its real name he says: what's the difference? Or: it is a head, though, isn't it? I put it on a high shelf, out of his reach, and hide the pink clips for her hair, which he's always chewing. Still he persists. I find her one day, under a net of Action Man camouflage, tiny grey hand-grenades attached to her hair with hair grips and sellotape.

How can it be Girls World when it's just a head? Girl's Head! Girl's Head! Andrew squeals, breathlessly. I'm holding him down on the bed, his arm bent behind him, and sitting on it. He says I'm breaking his arm, but I'm not giving in.

Her name is Girls World! She's the Doll with Endless Possibilities! Say it! I'm screaming, spit flying from my mouth.

He always calls my dolls the wrong things. He does it to annoy me. He calls them stupid things that don't make sense: he calls Sindy Bendy and Barbie Busty and Teeny Tiny Tears Weenie Whiney Weers and he does it because it makes me angry, he likes it when I turn into Mad Troll (his name for it) and jump on him and he only laughs and shrieks and enjoys it even more if I fight him because it's girls' fighting and useless.

Now Andrew is silent or occasionally humming a little tune. The back of Billy's neck is red and burnt and he is digging a trench around my mermaid's tail. Andrew is patting the sand down with the palms of his hands. Each time he does this, some sand on another part of me crumbles away like a bad pastry case and he has to start over. Neither of them is annoying me or teasing me, and if Mum were looking our way right now (which she isn't — she's pulling out a stripey fold-out chair, sharing her flask with another woman from the church, who is pulling out iced buns from a crocheted silver lace bag with holes in it), she'd be very pleased that we're all playing *nicely* for once.

Girls World. The beauty head. I got it last Christmas. And I showed Mandy, but I remember now that she laughed. She looks weird, she said. She's like those ladies under the fryer in my mum's shop, frazzling up their hair. She's ugly! Mandy said.

Who wants a head without a body? she scoffed, turning it in one hand, as if it was spooky and dreadful, instead of beautiful, miraculous; as if it was a Halloween pumpkin.

148

And I don't like thinking of this, staring out at the sea as it begins to creep in over the mud flats, my body buried from the waist down in the great mound of sand, so that I can't really feel it, my feet lost. How would it be to be just a head, not a body? In church they say that we are to be wary of the temptations of the flesh. So if we were just heads, one good thing is, this wouldn't happen. Most people, well, that is, my teacher, Mr Harris, he tells me it's wrong to think we only live in our heads anyway. When I asked him where is my mind, where am "I", am I in my brain and in that case, is it my brain making my thumb work or does my thumb have a sort of mind of its own (since I know my thumb can feel things which it tells my brain about)? Mr Harris told me this was a very interesting question and yes, aye, I'd hit on the real nub of many discussions about consciousness. Is there a ghost in the machine, he says, a mind telling us what to do, a soul, a self, or is it just a typical split in Western thinking that divides up mind and matter, or separates the head from the body. He told me I was a very interesting little girl and I would go far, but he didn't tell me the answer.

And then later, an hour or so later, that's when we meet the seahorse man. He's a foreign man, wearing a long white shirt and trousers, when everyone else is wearing shorts. He has grandchildren with him and he's at the table next to ours in the beach café, showing them something in a king-sized matchbox. I'm looking over at his table. Mum and the church lady are squeezing vinegar from a bottle onto all the various children's chips and I am the only one trying to hear what the man is saying. He says he picked it up on his travels. He winks at Mum and Mrs Jones and says something like: you know what they use them for in Asia. But Mum and Mrs Jones look away and are busy suddenly with mopping up spills on the table and if they do know, they don't say.

Whatever it is lies in his box with white tissue paper crinkling around it. What I want to know is how can he keep it in that dry box, surely it must need water, surely it should be swimming somewhere?

Having drifted from our table to stand next to theirs, now I am too shy to push forward to look. The man gently tugs at one of the grandchildren and she moves to let me closer.

There at last, nestling in the box, a dark curved twig, is the perfect shape of a tiny dried seahorse.

Is it real? I say.

Of course it is, he says.

It's dead, I say.

It looks so ancient, so stiff; a dark brown and grey colour, like a perfectly curled twig. He shows me its coronet and fin, the little spines visible as tiny white dots, the ridges covering the belly like a miniature paper lantern. He points out the chin spines and the eye spines and lets me run my thumb along them and I close my eyes and there it is again, my thumb telling me that they feel good and nicely scratching, with each spine just the perfect size to scratch inside the lines of my thumb. Then the man says how this one is a female because she has ridges all the way down her body, with no visible pouch, and that seahorse daddies carry the babies.

The daddies carry the babies, I repeat, softly.

He puts it in my palm and it's light as a leaf. I hold my palm stiffly, terrified I might crush it.

Ach, he says, don't worry, it's stronger than you think.

I hand it back to him reluctantly and he tucks it up in his box. It's the first dead thing I've ever touched. I suppose you could say it was the beginning of a life-long obsession.

If I close my eyes now, I can feel it as the man dropped it into my palm: how light, how fragile, how it looked like the shed skin of a seahorse, the empty shell of a seahorse, as if the real thing had just stepped out, leaving this ghost form behind it; curled like the outer rim of an ear, without the ear itself. If I held it up to the window light would shine through the tiny skin of its miniscule eye, making it gold again and vivid. Once dead, they are not as fragile as they seem, he was right about that. We had a Customs seizure only last week: a whole box of seahorses from Florida for identification, sloppily enfolded with bubble-wrap, but I know now that they're unlikely to crumble to dust, or for their long pointed noses to snap off, although they always look so brittle, so exquisitely tiny.

God, what if Yelena forgets my instructions, forgets to check the water, or to feed them enough, or to check the video tape? Or worse, allows some sophomores into the lab to see them? My mind boggles, picturing beer bottles floating in the tanks and dead seahorses rising to the top like a dark scum on the water. Always, when I'm away, it's this order of anxiety. Poppy first, although Dean is better with her than me and has seen her through enough of my absences (conferences, dives, spells in hospital for tests) for this to be a well-established fact. The seahorses next, despite all precautions and assurances from colleagues (after all, Yelena is not let loose in the labs on her own, there are others to supervise her) that they'll be fine. Dean last of all. I see this as a good thing, a sign of my lack of dependence on him, a sign of confidence and trust between us, maturity. Dean is not so sure. He sees this as absence too, my preferred method, he says, of dealing with everything.

Well, I've been away long enough. I walk back from the market and there are posters in every window of the two missing girls, badly photocopied, hastily produced. I stop for a moment, stare at one of the posters in Burrow's newsagents. Two girls, smiling, arms linked, a family snapshot, in a kitchen. Neither of them look the slightest bit like Mandy Baker. They're two girls I don't know, from a village near here. But they're staring straight at me.

So. We're at Andrew and Wendy's house. The wedding reception is over and we've driven there, those of us still sober enough funnelling the other ones into cars; cars packed with colliding perfumes, peach jackets, abandoned hats, bridesmaids' flowers. I'm one of the designated drivers and I overshoot: no one tells me until it's too late and I'm already halfway along the straight black road towards the village that Billy used to call Benny Hill. No one would get the reference any more, so I don't try it. It's only in the States that we're now showing old re-runs of the programme.

These roads are lined with ditches, filled with water. Last year, Charlene says, a girl from my school was driving and she overturned her car here and the car was stuck under the water and all three of her friends drowned. She doesn't need to remind me, driving here always holds this possibility for me and the camber of the road doesn't help. Once you hit sixty miles per hour, you can feel it. The road actually does want to tip you in. I reckon it's the water, trying to shake you off, creep its way back. It's a constant battle, keeping the Fens drained. The Fens are a thin black skin but the water holds all the power.

The house is an old farmhouse, The Beeches, Wendy's house, and the lights are on in every room and the whisky comes out, it's only about 10p.m. and downstairs they're continuing to party. Now I long to lie down, to collapse, I take one big swig of whisky and regret it, I tell Wendy I'm beat suddenly, it must be the jet-lag. I don't know if she believes me but she smiles in a friendly, easy way and says: let's go upstairs and sort out your bed. She finds me some bedding and shows me into the spare room, the tiniest room I've ever seen; just space for a fold-out bed where the top and tail touch each wall.

I don't know what this room used to be, Wendy says, apologetically, maybe a pantry or something. We use it

153

for a study. I hope it's not too small for you? She has bits of coloured confetti hanging from her hair, a lipstick mark where someone kissed her on one cheek. I murmur: it'll be fine, and she goes out, asking if I want her to switch off the light. Yes, thank you. I'm already lying down; too tired even to take my jacket off.

The room goes dark as if it were full of smoke. The damp smell of unaired sheets floats up from the pillow.

You weren't home, Mandy says, accusingly.

She's sitting on the edge of the bed. I feel the dent of her, the weight, at my feet. It takes me a moment to make her out, in the murk. I prop myself up on one elbow and stare at the grey shape: she doesn't look like Mandy, she only has half a face. One half is peachy, the upturned nose, the fringe, the high plump cheekbones, smattered with freckles. The other half is turned slightly away from me but I know it is empty, a smashed in cavern. A skull with streaks of green and yellow. Streaks, ribbons. I feel curiously calm. I'm thinking of how I feel inside a hot, damp cupboard, and wonder if it is the smell of my own sweat. I wonder how is it that I can make out some petals, confetti, scattering the floor, if the room is so dark.

What do you mean? I mumble. Did you come to my house?

I came to call for you. On my bike. You weren't there. Where were you? You should have been there.

Her voice is soft, but ordinary. The accent faintly rural, the timbre musical. I didn't know how well I remembered it. There is a smell around her, too, faintly salty, sour. Poppy calls this smell belly-button smell, or girl smell. Like the inside of trainers, like unwashed feet.

Mandy. I sit up. The bedroom is immediately dark, with just a split of yellow light under the door. The room is tipping like the inside of a ship, nausea swilling inside me. I stare at the end of the bed, where she was. Downstairs I can hear noises: the thump of music, or maybe even dancing. Overlayering that, just outside the door, are the softest sounds, rustling: the trail of a dressing gown cord, or pyjama bottoms, dusting the floor. I feel as if my heart is sputtering, unable to get back to a normal rhythm, like a car engine that won't turn over. I can't seem to make myself wake up, or rather, I am awake but the smell and the girl have gone.

A giggle outside the door. Maybe one of the girls, Chloe perhaps (the right age) might have come in my room? Tiptoed in, sat down, tiptoed out again. I run my hand over the bottom of the bed, over the hairy rough blanket, but there is no indentation where a child's weight would have been. There is no green streaky half-face when I close my eyes.

Right. Lying down and closing my eyes makes it worse, then. I'll have to get up again, go downstairs and join the party. I turn the light on and the room retreats, the biscuit-coloured blanket defiantly ordinary. My ear aches, pressure spreading to my jaw.

Sleeping girls are draped on every chair, heaped up like abandoned coats. Someone has put a CD on and it's Frank Sinatra, another of Dad's favourites. It looks

155

like only family members are left: Mum, Billy and Gaynor, Andrew, Wendy, this weird guy, Geoff, who seems to be someone Mum has brought along, a distant uncle. I spot a space on the sofa and sit down on it; Gaynor's outsized bottom, squeezed into the white trousers, is suddenly level with my face, wedged between me and Andrew, as she brings around a tray with more glasses and the half-bottle of Scotch on it. From behind this snowy mountain it's hard to get Andrew's attention but I manage to pat the space beside me and get him to sink down onto it, just as Gaynor spills some whisky on her sparkly flip-flops and leaves the room, shrieking.

My heart feels like my ears: as if some enormous pressure — as if two big hands — were squeezing it.

Andrew, I say. That comment. About Dad. What did you mean?

Huh?

The field-day one. Dad would have had a field-day.

Oh, you know. Girls, you know. Dad — and girls. Women. Christ, Tina, you know what I mean.

Girls or women?

Huh? Girls — I don't know, it's the same thing, isn't it?

I don't know. Is it? What age of girls are we talking about — thirteen? Fourteen? Younger? The same age as Charlene, or Chloe? Or are we talking Rose's age?

Rose, Tina? What are you on about — Rose is five, for God's sake. Our dad didn't leave Mum for a bloody five-year-old!

He's holding his whisky in front of him like a shield or a weapon, like he might involuntarily shake it suddenly, a spasm in his arm forcing him to jerk the lot all over me. But he has to hiss, too, he doesn't want the others to hear and it's the hiss somehow that allows me to carry on.

Andrew, I say quietly. Could we go upstairs? I want to ask you something, talk to you properly . . .

He nods, his expression inscrutable, and leads the way.

What is it now that's shaping itself in front of me? Staring into cracks, into crevices, or into the deep blank blue, while a balletic shape drifts up through the water: a turtle, legs gently paddling, drawn by invisible thread. The silver metallic bubbles rising from the other divers' gas tanks, the sound of my own breathing, trawling along beside me, like someone on a respirator, like a heavy breather, an old man, someone dying. And I saw Mandy Baker in the sea with me, Mandy Baker, yellow and turquoise and stippled, and I said it was the first time in thirty years, but I knew it was only partly true. There have been other times, partial glimpses. Each time I would surface, decide it was only currents and disguises, refraction or distortion — nothing I had words for, or that even took a proper shape. That's the difference. That's what's happening now.

So here's another. It's a day in summer when all of us, Billy, Andrew, me, are very small. I don't think I was even in school. We have lollies, I can remember the taste of them, lemon and scented, like eating perfume. We have t-shirts in a soft towelling material and there is another child with us, a girl, a neighbour, with two brown pigtails that I accidentally call piglets — "I like your piglets", trying to be especially nice and friendly, and everybody laughs at me. It's a day out. It's the seaside. We have buckets too and sand in our socks and the creases of our skin, of our hot and sticky legs but that must be later, that must be coming back. The piglets girl comes with us, her name is Caroline. She has round pink plastic sunglasses with glitter in the plastic and she screams when the sea touches her toes. There is that seaweed that turns hard and black when it's dry and you can pop it, Dad shows me how to pop it with his big nail, and make a satisfying sound, a lovely sound, and there are crabs, little tiny ones that mass in the sand like spilled beads and Dad can pick those up, he's not afraid of them. He's in a good mood, he's singing, his t-shirt is brown soft material that smells of him when he hoists me up onto his shoulders and he drives us there, he has a new van, I think he even has a new job, but I'm not sure about that bit.

Then suddenly there's a jagged, red-streaked blur. I'm returning to the van. I don't know where my brothers are. I'm not even five, I shouldn't be outside the van, here by the dunes by myself. I think perhaps my father is supposed to be watching me. And the piglets girl. Caroline. He's in the van with the back door open and Caroline is sitting on his knee.

She looks startled.

I wander towards them. I'm eating something. Maybe an ice-cream. I want my yellow spade, which is in the van. I didn't expect my father to be in there, sitting on that special fold out chair, with Caroline. Mum, my brothers, are on the beach. I thought Dad was fetching something, the picnic basket, the drinks. Look at that really big road they've built, down as far as the sea. Look, Dad! We've made a big road.

Caroline's face. Startled. Staring straight forward.

He closes the door to the van. His eyes, always bluer than sky, bluer than the bluest crayon, have huge black holes in them. He smiles at me, he ties the belt of his shorts. There are long tickling grasses in front of me, higher than my head. I'm carrying a bucket full of shells and stones and bits of seaweed: my "hoard". They say: why do you want that bloody great hoard in the car with you? Dad and Caroline and me are walking back down to the beach. The sand is gritty and it's not yellow either. Mum says: this is England, what do you expect? But it's hot. Hot enough to need my hat, my sun cream, a drink of lemon squash in a red beaker with a white lid with a special round hole in it and a little cap that peeks up so you can drink from it.

I need my hat on. I should be wearing my hat. My skin will burn. Mum says I have delicate skin. You can't just forget about her skin, Graham. I'm blonde and sensitive. Come on, Dad, you have to take me back, I need to have my hat on, my hat is by the sea and the sea might come and lick it, wash it away. You mustn't be here, with me, or with the piglets girl. We have to be with Mum, with the others.

I ask the ouija board whether it's true what Jenny says, that everyone in our village has seen Dad with Dawn

Staples, that he's a cradle-snatcher, that he's running round with her.

I don't like the answer.

One afternoon, after school, Mum comes home unusually early. I can see at once from her hot reddened cheeks, from the energy that crackles round her, that something is wrong. You're coming with me, she says. Get your coats. You can see for yourselves what your father gets up to of a Thursday evening while I'm slogging my guts out in that bloody shop.

My brothers are watching *Wacky Races* and it's come to a good bit with Dick Dastardly up to his old tricks again and Penelope Pitstop about to run over a whole load of giant tacks on the road and so they groan when Mum makes them get their shoes and pushes their arms into the sleeves of their coats, all the time muttering, through her teeth, a girl young enough to be his own daughter! And then just outside our door she bursts into tears and squashes the boys against her legs and looks over their heads at me, saying: no, I can't do it, I can't shame you all like that.

We traipse back indoors and put the telly on again. Penelope Pitstop whizzes to first prize. Mutley does his stupid laugh.

That night at Jenny's, when I go to the kitchen to get the Tizer and crisps, Russell is there, peeling away from the others to stand admiring me as I open the fridge. When his friends are out of earshot he puts his mouth close to my hair and whispers: why didn't you come? I waited for you, by the river . . .

160

Did he really, or is he teasing? I don't want to look like an idiot by taking him seriously, and I can't admit that I dithered over it, I wanted to, but in the end lost my nerve. So I stand there dumb as a dim-bat and he suddenly says: you're a cracker, you know that? Anyone ever tell you that? You're a real beauty.

No one has told me. But — and I wouldn't, of course, tell him this, or anyone in fact — I have wondered. I've wondered if all girls get men staring at them like this, if men are always shouting rude things to other girls. Perhaps it's just ordinary, happens to every girl, men hollering when you walk past the sugar-beet factory in the early autumn or you're on your bike in your t-shirt and shorts. Or perhaps I am unusually gorgeous. How will I know? Who on earth could I ask?

They come in the kitchen then, Stephen and Martin, so Russell leans forward, pretends to be lighting his cigarette on the gas cooker.

I can't get enough of looking at you, he says, when the others go out again. He brushes my bare arm with his sleeve, the Ben Sherman checks brushing against my fair hairs. They stand on end as if pulled by string, one after the other.

Look at you, he whispers.

He makes a noise that I can't make sense of but it sounds like Billy when he sees a plate of chips. I smile and move away from him, balancing the packet of cheese footballs under my chin, a bottle of Tizer in each hand.

But he plants himself in front of the stairway, starts whispering again. That's so cute — the way your hair curls. Just there.

He touches my cheekbone. He puts his face close.

You have gorgeous little tits, he says. His chest is against mine. Something inside my ribcage leaps towards him, as if I had a hamster in there. I shriek and duck away. Anyone might see us. Jenny might come to the top of the stairs, or her brother or his mates come out of the living room. Inside I'm singing with triumph. A grown up boy like Russell, a man, telling me I'm gorgeous! But to him I say: I have to go upstairs now.

Give us a kiss, he says.

I turn my back on him, run upstairs two at a time. I can feel him still standing there, watching me. I'm aware of my hips, my backside: that's the word Dad would use. Fair backside on her, he says, watching Miss World. Or: Backside like a bloody cart-horse, Miss Denmark. Nul points if you ask me. Russell's words are like magnets. The bits of me he talks about perk up immediately and rush towards him. I picture them clustering, like iron filings, to his mouth.

Russell says if I don't want to give men blue balls, I shouldn't wear my jeans so tight and move like that.

Later I push a chair under the handle of my bedroom door to lock it, and practise the walk. I squeeze my breasts together in my v-neck t-shirt and I think of the magazines and the girls he likes looking at and I feel a fizz running up and down my body as if I was an Alka-Seltzer dropped in a glass of water. Andrew makes me jump by banging on the bedroom door, shouting: Mum says come and set the table! She's been calling you for ages!

162

Mum's sister Auntie Janice is staying. This is something to do with Dad; they talk in whispers, stopping every time I come in the room, but the snatches I pick up are obvious enough: good riddance to bad rubbish. Better off without him. There's a bottle of Advocaat on the table in front of them and a jar with glacé cherries in it.

Make your mum another snowball, there's a good girl, Auntie Janice says. I fetch lemonade from the fridge, rinse Mum's glass, push the mixed yellow drink towards her on the table, open the jar to add another cherry. Mum's cheeks are red and blotchy and she hasn't changed out of her Lipton's green overall. What about the boys? she wails, suddenly, for no reason at all, then folds up on the table as if someone kicked her in her stomach.

I realise I'm staring. Sssh, sssh, Doreen, Tina's here, we'll manage, don't worry, Janice says, looking over Mum's blonde head at me, wiggling her eyebrows meaningfully towards the stove. A pan of baked beans is bubbling dry, so I switch it off. I hesitate for a second before turning to face the two of them. Then when no one says anything, when the kitchen is filled only with the regular shuddery breaths that Mum is making, I open the oven door, get the dish of faggots out, spoon one onto each plate next to the beans, get two cups down, fill them with lemon and barley water, fetch the ketchup and my brother's favourite plates — Thunderbirds for Billy, Bleep and Booster for Andrew — and carefully set out their tea.

Then I go back upstairs to my room without speaking to any of them.

He's left, I suppose. His fishing rod is still in the hall, his green wellies and umbrella propped against the shed, the smell of the muddy river all around them. When I opened the fridge to get the butter there was still a reassuring blue Tupperware tub alive with his fishing bait, wriggling maggots. The light on the fridge door tickled them into life.

Then worms will come and eat thee up, I think. It's another of Dad's favourite songs. Downstairs I can hear Billy shouting. A chair scraping, a childish voice screaming: I hate you, I hate you, your Brains Faggots in Gravy, your stupid cooking!! No wonder my dad left!

I think of her face and I hate her too. She's old, she can't keep him, is what I think. She has lines fanning out from around her eyes and her hair has this grey line at the parting, as if someone spilled some flour on her head, just there in the centre. I stand at the mirror on my dressing-table, examining my *cute as a button* upturned nose, standing sideways to see the shape of my bosoms, poking through my skinny-rib jumper.

Russell thinks I'm gorgeous. His words make me feel like a sock turned inside out, showing my underbelly, my matrix, my unknown heart. The wrong way out: not quite right. Last week I wrote to a magazine.

Dear Cathy and Clare, I have been looking at pictures of women in magazines, especially ones with big bosoms (I've tried to find the same sort of pictures of boys but I can't find any). I think I'm turning into a lesbian. Help!

Every morning I've been setting my alarm early to rush to the post before anyone else can. I bought the magazine but they didn't print my letter. Later I write another one, asking if anything bad will happen if you keep rubbing yourself. But I've been reading Mum's *Cosmopolitan* magazine, so I know the answer. In fact, I should probably be doing it more, if I want to be really healthy.

We all run riot without Dad. That's what Mum says. It's true the atmosphere changes. Billy and Andrew are noisy and wild, Mum turns Radio Caroline on high and sings along to songs that Dad used to call bloody bollocks, like her favourite singer, Shirley Bassey. I've never heard Mum sing before. There are piles of washing by the washing machine and cups and plates stacked up next to the sink, and Action Man's things and Meccano and Lego all over the living room carpet so that if you go in there with bare feet you are likely to end up with a tiny brick embedded in your heel; and conkers pickling in jars lining the bathroom windowsill and my collections, my shells and stones and all the years of beach pickings, Mum finally allows me to display them, in the bathroom. The house fills up. Bedtimes slip, morning drift. We miss Dad, we wonder why we aren't allowed to visit him, why she says "over my dead body" when Billy asks if we can go and see him in this house with his new girlfriend. But it's also as if some great lid has been lifted. Without him the four of us explode, we sprout overnight like mustard and cress.

* * *

Gorgeous, you are, Russell says to me, over and over, in a voice with a sort of husk in it, a voice that starts to slide. I am sitting on his knee in the kitchen; dangerous territory as his mates are only next-door, my friends upstairs. The door is shut, but from the way he is breathing I know that he feels the danger too. He is talking fast, lagging behind his own breath, then catching up with it, whispering how much he *wants* me, he's always using that word, and then he is on about some nonsense, the stars or cars possibly, bars even . . . and he has one arm around me, his fingers sneaking down the front of my bra. (Oh God, please don't let him find the pieces of material wodged there!) I shift position, my legs twitching a little, and he slips a hand under my denim skirt and starts stroking one leg, whilst I try to rest my foot nonchalantly on a pile of magazines near the cooker. A sound outside the door makes me start, thinking someone is about to come in, but when I move he says hoarsely: *stay!* And so I readjust my weight and sit myself back down in his lap and he carries on with his strokings. His face is pressed into my neck and I feel his warm breath there like a liquid running down my cheek, and smell its powerful smell, which isn't unpleasant, just new and kind of salty. But his words become more and more breathy and strange and his breath hotter and I become more and more conscious of him shifting his weight beneath me and a certain quiet intensity in his breath and then a sort of holding of his breath for the longest time, almost as if he has slipped away and vanished to somewhere else, and I think I know where he is, it's the

166

first time I have encountered it in someone else but I do at least know where it might be, how it might be a pleasure to be lost, suspended on the brink like that for the longest time. And then suddenly the phone goes, a great tearing sound and Russell sits up so hastily that he more or less tips me to the ground.

You shouldn't do that if you don't mean it, he hisses. The phone continues to shrill. Then it stops and we hear Stephen, in the next room, say "yeah?" into it.

What, what did I do? I whisper back, blinking, my cheeks hot, my hair full of bristling electricity.

You've no idea, have you?

He glares at me, and now he's angry, adjusting himself in his jeans, pulling his baggy shirt out and letting it fall loosely.

Of course he's wrong. I might be only thirteen but I can *read*. I found a copy of *The Joy of Sex* in Jenny's mum and dad's bathroom, under a pile of papers. There's a nasty-looking man with a beard, and weird stuff about desserts and starters in it, but plenty of other stuff too. And there's the papers. Dad used to get *News of the World* on Sundays. Mostly it's a lot of boring stuff like Fox Hunting Anne Rides into a New Row, but there's also tons of stuff about I was a Sex Slave or Share-a-Bed Wife Says Let's Stay Wed. Last week I read that in the year 2000 AD family life as we know it will die out. Instead husbands and wives will invite friends and neighbours over for naked orgies.

Sounds a bit exaggerated, but you never know. If they're right, I don't want to be left out.

★ ★ ★

Andrew heads for the furthermost bedroom where we won't be overheard: the girls' room. They're both asleep downstairs on the sofa, propped against various adults like giant soft toys. I follow him in, nursing my whisky. He switches on a lamp beside one of the beds and the room flushes pink. He sits on one bed, fastidiously moving several plastic ponies, lining them up on the window-ledge, all facing one direction, their shiny lilac tails aligned. He spends a moment on this, adjusting their positions so that each horse just nudges the tail of the one in front. (This is the brother who poked out the eyes on my favourite baby doll. Who tried to punch in the breasts on my Sindy.)

Neither of us speaks for a long time. Then abruptly Andrew puts his hands over his face, trawls through his hair, leans forward, resting his chin in his palms, his elbows on his knees. The white carnation, which has been sagging its head for a few hours, falls from his lapel, and lands in the middle of the girls' rug; a fluffy pink affair shaped like a heart. I stare at the flower, with its pin sticking up, just ready for a tender foot to step on. Neither of us moves to pick it up.

You want to bring all this up again, on my wedding day? I haven't seen you for years and years and this is all you want to talk about?

I don't know what to say to him. My eyes rake the room, taking in the rose chiffon curtains over Rose's bed, the trailing flower wall lights, the fluffy heart-shaped cushions, the beanie toys, the Bratz dolls, the Hello Kitty purses, the Princess jewellery box.

168

Andrew follows my gaze. We both stare at The Beach Bratz Party Pool, still in its box with its two little dolls, all doe eyes and pouting mouths. Ages four and up. Rotating dance floor, four awesome areas. Scorchin Hot Style. Baby Girls with a Passion for Fashion.

After you left, he says, I talked to Jenny. I mean, we were breaking up by then; it wasn't easy to talk to her. I told her what you said, about him, you know about how you'd seen him looking at other girls and you found it weird and wondered why no one else noticed. And Jenny said: yes, well we all found him creepy. And then she told me something I had no idea about. She told me that when she was really young, maybe about eight or nine, Dad — Dad molested her.

What?

Oh God, Tina, do you want details? She said it was in his shed. She came round to play with you and he invited her into the shed and then — I don't know, he showed her his dick or something and tried to touch her and she got scared and ran off. I didn't ask her to repeat it.

Jenny said this?

My ears explode. A whoosh as the pressure inside my head bursts like a balloon.

Yes.

He stares at me: are you OK?

Yes, yes, it's just my ears — the flight — you shouldn't fly after a dive and I went scuba-diving for the first time in years, just before leaving . . .

Andrew narrows his eyes at me, then stands up, moves to the window. On the window-ledge is a

169

jewellery box with a lilac furred lid; with one hand he opens this and a tiny mini ballerina pops up, rotates slowly to a few tinny notes. He seems not to know he has opened it and I don't know how to stop him. The tune — Brahms' lullaby — plays for three rounds before he snaps it shut.

I take long deep breaths, while Andrew says again: Are you OK?

When did Jenny tell you this? I ask.

Oh, years ago. I don't know. Around the time he — you know, probably after he died. I mean, not straight away. She's not that bloody heartless.

So that's — oh, fifteen years ago. And you've only just decided to tell me. All this time. All of you acting like I was a monster not to come to the funeral. Like he was Mr Innocent and my — whatever they were — my *reservations* about him, about the way he treated Mum and — all of us — were so unreasonable, unfair, isn't that what you all implied, I was being totally unfair to him?

Yes. I'm sorry.

The simplicity of his answer disarms me. Keep breathing, I tell myself. Breathe out, through your mouth. You still could be wrong. I'm sitting on the bed opposite him, holding a beanie cat, grey with soft floppy paws; turning it over and over in my hand. We had beanbags like this in school. Square green bags, with a weird sandy smell, made of rough canvas material. For games, I think, or maybe throwing. Safe throwing. Girls' throwing, as Billy would say.

170

I ask Andrew: I wonder if Jenny saying that means there were others? Did she mention any others? I've got a hazy memory of other girls, this little girl — a really tiny one. Remember a trip to the beach? How we often had other children with us, and there was this one girl, really young, with brown pigtails.

He shakes his head. I don't know, he says. You know, I was so shocked. And I kept saying to Jenny, why didn't you tell me years ago, why didn't you tell your mum or someone else and she just said: it was embarrassing. I knew immediately you'd been right then. What you said years before and we'd all jumped on you. Then I worried, I thought you weren't telling us the whole story when you said it was just a feeling, just a — what's that American word — just a *vibe*. I wondered if Dad had done that to you too, or worse, and —

I shake my head, the air thick with embarrassment between us, but he keeps on, his head in his hands again, chin dropped, voice quieter and quieter:

There was this one time when I heard you were in Mum's bedroom really crying and Mum was out and Dad was trying to get you to stay in the room and go to sleep. I could hear him in there, and Billy and me we were supposed to be asleep already but you were crying, you wanted Mum and I heard you crying and then Dad shouting and then he locked the door, he was inside with you and I was really scared. So I crept downstairs and I got this knife from the kitchen and I remember I was shaking, really shaking, I thought I was going to wet myself I was so scared, and I tried to shove the knife under the door for you and I put my ear to the

171

door and the voice Dad was using, I knew it was wrong, it was horrible and I could hear you doing that thing where you really can't breathe, you're catching your breath and really gulping but I just stood outside the door, waiting and waiting, and I thought, if she screams, if I hear her really scream, next time, this time, I'm going to kick the door down, barge right in and stab him. But I didn't, I just stood there outside the door, shaking and shaking, and I wrapped the knife up, I put some toilet paper round it so that he wouldn't see it and I hid it, in the pedal bin, in the bathroom, I thought I could still get it, if I needed it . . .

But I don't remember this at all, I really don't. I search my mind, my store of memories, *I rack my brain*. I even picture myself doing this, ransacking the years like so many socks and jumpers, rummaging through people and books and photographs, but even when there's an almighty mess, when it looks like someone went in and burgled me: nothing. Nothing about being locked in a bedroom with Dad. Nothing about a knife, or Andrew crying outside.

I can see the kind of pyjamas my brothers used to wear: faded, once khaki in colour, now a sort of sludge-brown. I can remember our bathroom: the orange and green lino in the pattern of autumn leaves, the fluffy yellow rug shaped like a crescent moon, tucked neatly round the stalk of the toilet. (I know it's not called a stalk but in my mind the toilet is a toadstool, a stalk with a cap on top). I can remember Mum tutting and making that horse-snorting noise and telling them both they'd better learn to *aim* better because she was sick of forever washing the crescent moon rug; and my astonishment at why they didn't just sit down like me.

I suddenly picture another occasion entirely: the time when Andrew smashed his Mickey Mouse watch — we're in the farmyard at Mandy's and there's a huge pile of sugar-beets behind us, sugar-beets that have gone off, stinking to high heaven, as Mandy says, only good for animal feed. And Andrew is on Mandy's bike, trying it out and he's about seven or eight years old and he's too small for it and can't really reach the pedals properly so he skids on the stony old drive with this sickening skittish crunch and drops the bike, crying, and Mandy and I run over to him but we stop dead when he takes his hand away from his mouth, because the bottom half of his chin is covered in blood. Andrew has two front teeth all red and one of them is like a shutter, flapping, so Mandy does this little scream and runs indoors to get her mum and her mum comes out with Dettol and cotton wool and Andrew screams, he really screams when she dabs it to his chin, and his hand flies up to bat her away and then I see that his watch, his beloved birthday watch with the Mickey Mouse face is crushed to smithereens.

I don't remember, I tell him.

You were really sobbing. I put it back. The knife. A day or two later.

I sit chewing on my lip, and wishing I could say something that would make Andrew feel better. It's extraordinary that he should drag up this memory, this scene that means so much to him, that he obviously

173

thinks will help me, or confirm something, and then to find that his offering means nothing to me.

Really, Andrew. I don't remember, I say again.

He thinks Dad molested me. This is the worst thing he could imagine. But could he be right? Is it really possible that I can have been molested and suddenly "discover" it, realise it, years later, in one great moment of truth? No, this doesn't fit at all. I run it past myself, and no bell goes off. What I'm trying to think about, *talk* about is more nebulous, but cumulative. It's not specifics, but feelings. All my memories of Dad have a weird feeling around them, a weird colour, or smell. They pop up — Dad and Dawn Staples, Dad and the piglets girl — and it's not that they're different, not that they surprise me, but that they're familiar. The disquiet is the same. It was always there, like the voice that told me not to walk down the lane near Jenny's house. I just didn't listen.

Andrew rests his chin in his hands, stroking his chin and staring away from me, out towards the window.

I didn't want kids myself, he says. Not for the longest time. I didn't think I'd be much of a dad. It's — a sort of late bonus, this. The girls. Wendy's girls.

He makes a gesture around the room, a sweep of his hand. These girls are so *tidy*. My eyes fall on another box. One of them, Rose perhaps, seems to prefer to keep her toys in their packaging, rather than actually play with them. Sylvanian Family Sister's Bedroom Set. Every Little Girl's Dream. Includes over 30 accessories, including a dressing-table with a three-way mirror.

He was scary, wasn't he, Dad. When he was mad.

174

It's a huge admission, the most Andrew's ever said. I should be pleased.

He stands up, as if the conversation is over. He bends to pick up his carnation, fixes it back on his lapel. There is a beat, an instant when I hear echoes in my head of my mother's voice saying *haven't you caused enough trouble for one day, my girl?* Isn't this enough, this acknowledgment that my harsh judgment of Dad all those years ago, my criticism of his shoddy behaviour towards Mum and us, and his "thing about girls" was truer than I knew? Nevertheless I press on. What Andrew said about Jenny made the final tug. Now it's unspooling right in front of me and it's too late to rewind.

Andrew. The thing I wanted to talk about. Do you remember a girl in our school, our primary school, I mean? The one who went missing. Do you remember Mandy Baker?

Our favourite game on the school playing field, I mean second favourite after The Bum Game, is Levitation. It's another invention of Mandy's. This requires several girls, at least four. One for all your four corners, Mandy says. One girl kneels at each socked foot, one at each hand. The soles of your socks are stained green, grass dots your checked skirt, your hair. You lie on your back and the girls, Mandy, Jenny, Vicky, Judy — anything really as long as it ends in "y" — stroke your hands and feet, short repetitive movements, in a rhythm. They chant, quietly: *Blood-sucker, blood-sucker, sucking all your blood, sucker.* You picture the insect they call a blood-sucker, a small, orangey-coloured sugar-beetle, smaller than an earwig, harmless, you think. They chant and stroke and you lie with your eyes closed, watching the clouds slide red and pink on the back of your eyelids. And then the girls sit back on their heels and shout: levitate! And with the cessation of the stroking and the chanting, your body feels deprived, suddenly, cut off from the oxygen of touch and rhythm and there it is: you do. Float right up to the sky. You can feel the air, the light, blowing beneath your back, the backs of your legs: it feels like a child's warm breath. You can feel the clouds closer to your pink, petal-fine eyelids. You keep your eyes closed. No one ever sees this. You're far enough away from the teachers, or the other children, on a part of the playing field that's out of bounds, near the hedges, near the border.

Mandy puts her face close to yours and whispers: six inches that time! You rose six inches, right off the ground!

The other girls shriek manically.

They're impressed. You open your eyes and the ground races up to meet you: solid, hard, green, ticklish. You put your hand beneath your knees to check, but your eyes are open now so you've no way of knowing. The grass smells of cats' pee and neighbours' gardens and the mudpie games of your brothers. You bump back down to earth.

Best so far, Mandy says.

She's your friend today, for the rest of the day, you're her favourite. You're a star, she says: you can black out at the drop of a hat. You've learned this, how to blank,

176

disappear, absent yourself. You can rise six inches in the air, hover there above everyone. Air is your medium, for now. You love to be lost. You love this best of all, this feeling. To be weary, exhausted, for it all to be over. Your favourite word is *spent*.

Andrew stops in the doorway. A dangling fluffy spider bounces against the door, leopard-print legs softly knocking against the wood. The carnation droops from its pin.

Yeah, I remember her. That little Baker girl. Of course I remember her. She was your age, wasn't she? In your class. We used to play with her sometimes, didn't she live on a farm? But she had a flighty mother or something. The mother left.

I nod. Sandy, I say. You remember, she worked in a hairdresser's shop.

Why? Why do you ask about Mandy? Have you heard something?

No. I wondered if you had.

What do you mean, you mean lately? he asks. What, is this something to do with these girls going missing? The ones in the news right now? I thought — I seem to remember they mentioned Mandy on the news once as possibly one of the Ripper's early victims. You know, he started in the seventies didn't he, the Yorkshire Ripper, wasn't he a long-distance lorry driver? He travelled the country . . .

Yes, I remember hearing that —

Yeah, the Ripper, that was a big thing when you were at Leeds, wasn't it? I remember coming up to stay with you once and that voice on the tannoy in the Arndale Centre, that Geordie accent: I'm going to strike again . . .

Yes. I remember. Doesn't mean he did it though. They never proved a link. They never found — they never found a body.

And later, I'm sure her name came up in connection with someone else. Some other strangler or serial killer.

But there was never any proof, was there? It was just a theory, I mean, they probably explained away hundreds of missing girls that way —

Well, seems likely enough to me.

Does it? Does it really?

My voice is sharp, challenging. He gives me a dazed look.

Have they found her body or something?

I shake my head. *Andrew. Please — work it out. Don't make me be the one to say it.*

It's hideous, he says. Bloody journalists. It makes you sick. I don't remember this amount of stuff in the papers when we were kids, do you? I think they really go over the top with it these days. How can it help — you know, the families, any of it.

When I don't answer he answers his question himself: Oh well, I suppose it might help jog someone's memory but it's — too much. Giving the girls bloody nightmares. Chloe's obsessed. We have to switch the telly off — it's too much.

I'm still silent, and now I think he's prattling, deliberately postponing. He fiddles with his carnation,

178

trying to fix it. He opens the bedroom door. Music thumps up the staircase.

Wendy knew her mum, he says. The hairdresser. The one with the weird makeup, Sandy did you say her name was? Kind of Marc Bolan sparkles under her eyes and baby-doll bunches in her hair. This was after Mandy went missing. I mean years later. She went a bit batty . . .

I've been thinking a lot, I blurt out. Since I got here. About Dad, and Mandy. Whether, you know. Whether he — whether it could have been him.

Christ, Tina.

He gasps then, a winded noise. He sits down on the bed, his legs collapsing: the carnation drops on the rug. Neither of us moves to pick it up. I watch as his eyes change colour, the pupils dilating, filling the grey centres with deep black dots, widening until his eyes are two black pools, fixing on me. I hesitate, then press on:

It's possible, isn't it? Dad was home that day. We were all out, do you remember, we went to the beach? To Hunstanton, I think. The police never really questioned him, they kind of assumed it was Mandy's dad and then they couldn't find a body so there was never any proof.

You think Dad did it.

I say nothing.

You think Dad did something like that — did away with her, murdered her?

He tries again: you can think those kind of things, about Dad?

I want to cry. I feel hot and cold and sick and strange. I've said the strangest, sickest thing.

What, what — proof — do you have? What could make you think that about him?

My chest tightens, squeezing the air from my lungs. His eyes are black, stark. Despite what he's saying, I see the shapes shifting in front of his eyes, the readjustments. It's this that's frightening me, it's this, more than anything else, that's making what I said possible.

No, he says.

Then, lifting his head, more forcefully: God, no, are you mad? It's a small place, Tina, remember? Everyone knew everyone. Dad couldn't have got away with a thing like that without someone knowing. How could he? What proof have you got, I mean, why do you even think it?

I tuck my hands under my thighs, trying to control the violent trembling in my body.

I don't know, I don't know!

It's true, I don't know why I think it, but now that it's out, now that it's out here, in the room with us —

I've been getting these — hunches, I say. Flashes. I can't explain.

Flashes?

I don't know!

Flashes? Tell me? Like your funny turns, you mean, the ones you used to have?

Yes, yes, I suppose so. Well, sort of pictures. It started when I — I first saw this weird hallucination of Mandy,

180

on holiday. I'd been smoking, so I just thought it was that. But since then, since coming here —

Did Dad ever tell you anything? Is that why you're saying it? You know, I accept he was — I accept what you said about him having a — a *thing* for girls. But murder? He was our dad. Surely you can't think he was capable of that?

Everything I've said is in here with us. There's barely room to breathe, so choking is the squall I've just unleashed. I know he can feel it too, that despite what he's saying, he wants to run out screaming, like I do, gulping up the clean air.

I don't know! I say, my voice wild, a squeal. I barely recognise it.

Andrew's body is limp, his face expressionless. After minutes, long pregnant minutes, he says: flashes. You based all this on — pictures? Then suddenly: Tina, you're not going to tell Mum?

Mum! Oh my God . . .

Is that why you came? To talk to her?

No, I — God, I didn't even think —

Why then? Why are you saying this?

His voice is saturated in wine. The alcohol — no doubt coursing through him since midday — has reached his brain finally, kicking in to dampen the blow, to sedate him. His question doesn't seem to relate to what I've just told him at all. He repeats it, unaware that he's already asked me. Why. Why are you saying this. In fact he seems to be talking to someone else, someone just behind me. His eyes are staring at a spot on the pink painted walls and he shakes his head: a tiny shake.

Andrew! Are you up there? It's Wendy, calling up the stairs. She needs some help, carrying the girls up to their beds. Chloe is a lump, she says.

Andrew's face changes. He straightens up, gives another shake of his head. This time he's successful: whatever it was, it's gone. Moving to the bedroom door, opening it wider, he turns back to the room to stare at me and then at the girls' beds. He tugs at the chiffon curtain that surrounds Chloe's bed, tying it to one side with a silky lilac ribbon. I can see that he knows the drill, has done this many times before. He turns down Rose's Tinkerbell duvet cover. *Twinkle twinkle, I'm so pretty.* Then he picks up his carnation from the floor for the second time and fixes it securely to his lapel.

Leaning in to whisper, his voice trembles: Tina. You really are stark raving bonkers. Now, if you don't mind. I just got married today. My new wife is calling me. I'm needed here.

And he turns his back on the parted pink chiffon curtain, turns his back on me. I'm shuddering now and I'm deeply, horribly cold, my bones chilled right at the centre, at the marrow-bone jelly, that's what we used to call it and that's what I picture now, at the heart of me: a transparent jelly, a nothing.

The look on Andrew's face. It was like watching a face dissolving in a fire. I'd taken all his props away. I saw him resist, try not to believe me, scroll through our childhood, but then I saw him stop, bump up against something, something that disbelief or denial couldn't carry him past. And I wonder if my own face, as the words finally strung themselves together, beads on a necklace, shoving up, budging closer, did the same weird melting thing? Like we were both looking into the same shadowy corner and watching something move inside it. Then the shadow shifts again, becomes something else: a curtain, a table. Becomes the maddest stupidest ugliest thought I've ever had. It's already reshaping, crouching back in a dark corner somewhere, retreating. Unimaginable.

On the plane, I had a nightmare. I was dozing, and when I woke up the plane had ruptured at one end, and was filling with blue sky. We were all plunging to our deaths. There was something horrible beside me on the seat, something I couldn't see and knew I mustn't look at. *Just make it not be true*, I said to myself, over and over. *Stop thinking like this and everything will be fine. Wake yourself up.*

Andrew's black irises return to grey. He's needed, he says. He's a big man, my brother, six foot two in his socks, and at thirty-nine he still cycles and runs, prides himself on his athletic build. His new wife needs him to help lift his new step-daughters upstairs to their princess bedroom, the one he helped decorate, the room he painted when he first fell in love; the one that seemed girly and silly, even ridiculous to him at the time, but now seems to represent everything he wants from his new life. It's deeply familiar, like stories he was read as a boy; ones about girls locked up in towers, or lost in forests, their entire worlds cast into darkness by an evil spell. Girls who always need lifting somewhere, or waking up; or rescuing. The difference is that his task right now is not to waken the girls but to move silently, lift them gently; to make sure they stay asleep.

OK, here are the reasons why what I've just said is totally incredible, impossible. Mad, utterly mad.

I've no evidence, no proof, nothing to go on, not one shred of anything at all that could link Dad and Mandy. No one else has ever suggested it. Mum has never ever said anything at all with even a hint of any connection between Dad and Mandy's disappearance. No one ever questioned Dad, no one else suspected him. Thirty years have gone by and no one in this world has even considered it. Yes, Dad could be scary and he had a temper and a thing for girls. None of that is evidence. None of that makes him a murderer.

I'm jet-lagged, I'm distressed, I'm back in England for the first time in fifteen years, I've been drinking, I'm being attacked by the weirdest memories and I'm taking some heavy medication.

Saying it doesn't make it true. Sure, I've said it to Andrew, I've opened the box, the can of worms, whatever, but I can still put the lid back on. I can stop thinking about it, apologise, say it must have been another of my funny turns; I can concentrate; erase the sight of Andrew's melting face. I can make it not be true.

Words fail me, Mum used to say. What about pictures? Pictures don't fail me, that's the trouble. Pictures keep right on coming.

This is me in school, in the sick bay, at the end of term, having one of my funny turns.

Here's Andrew, nine years old, his red and blue striped tie all skew-whiff, holding me a paper cup of water and staring into my face.

She's done it before, he says.

You've done it before, your brother says. Here's Matron, looking at her watch. She smells of chamomile lotion and green scratchy paper towels. She hasn't much time for hysterical girls.

Well, you're right as rain now. Though you did look a bit green around the gills, that's true. We've rung home and your mum's there right now. She says it's fine for your brother to walk you down the hill to your house and then Andrew can pop back here in time for school dinner, all right?

Murky, watery voices hover around me. Staring at Matron's broad cheeks, the flattened out nose and the slightly bulging eyes doesn't quite dispel my sense of being inside a nightmare; one that started like the others, like the time in church and the time of the reconstruction with a burning smell and a headache, a blinding headache and then voices and pictures again. The pictures themselves aren't frightening: they're just ordinary things — a person's face that I don't know, a haystack, a little girl holding out a gold ring, but it's how thick and fast they come, how unfamiliar they all are but how I keep feeling that I know them all, that I've seen them before. It feels like someone cracked open my brain like a walnut shell and poured the

185

wrong person's *stuff* in there and now I can't get rid of it.

Andrew's embarrassment at having the weird sister shifts at once to excitement. We get to skive off. He puffs up his chest and tucks his shirt into his trousers and takes the note that Matron hands him.

We've never walked out of the school gates on our own on a school day, when the others are still at their desks. My class is in a music lesson in the hall with the radio on: Singing Together. The voices singing *Wee willy wackety whoo John Dougal alain go rushety roo roo rooo* fade behind us and the minute we're the other side of the gate we burst into screeches of laughter, as if daring one of the teachers to come out and stop us.

I can read your mind, I tell Andrew.

He starts running.

You're thinking: oh no, I'll miss pink pudding with pink custard for afters . . .

He's down the road already, past the steps of the Baptist church, his skinny arms pumping. But then he stops. Hey, look at that!

A dark ball of dust, the size of a small car, is rolling up the road towards us, just exactly like something out of the Wild West. Out of *The Virginian*, Andrew's favourite television programme. The air around us is suddenly dark, as if we walked into a deep grey cloud. We stop dead, putting our hands over our eyes where the grey dust is pelting our faces, stinging our eyes.

Yippeee! Andrew screams.

Peeping through our fingers we see the same dustballs gathering all over the horizon towards where the sugarbeet factory and the cathedral should be, but instead there is just more grey, deep and hanging, as if the world is smothered in smoke. The black top soil from two empty fields right in front of us lifts in billows of soft dust, swirling up and joining the clouds. The two cars on the road have their lights on but it's like fog, we can barely see them.

Yippeee! Andrew screams again. It's a long time since we've been in a Fen Blow this good. We can hardly walk, the wind is so fierce. We have to walk backwards, but it's such a warm day that we don't have coats or jumpers to cover our faces, so we tug up our shirts, stuffing them into our mouths to stop the dust getting in.

Everywhere we can taste the soil: black, peaty, gritty. Grass and wheat and the mudpies we used to make when we were littler, with daisies encrusted on them. It tastes of worms and sometimes an iron taste like blood and it dissolves on your tongue, in a black soft way, leaving tiny gritty stones behind. It's special: it's the blackest soil in the whole world, Dad says, but he won't like the blow, not the way we do, because it means lost money for the farmers: all the seeds will fly away before they've hardly started.

By the time we get home our shirts are streaked with grey, damp from being in our mouths, and our faces are patchy with black eyes too, where we've balled up our hands to make binoculars, and our hair is gritted with the stuff and we both look, Mum says, like the golliwogs on the jam jars. It's not right, she keeps saying, it's not the season for blows — they usually

187

happen in the spring when the soil is black and bare, it's a freak, a freak of nature, that's what it is, she says, it's a terrible sign on top of everything else that's gone to pot in this village! (As she says this she's tugging our filthy shirts over our heads and our vests too and stuffing them into her washing basket.) And I tell you what, it's bloody Alf's fault — I know I shouldn't speak ill — but that man's stupid, leaving his fields so bare, hacking down that row of trees, now there's nothing left to hold back the gale . . . Andrew sniggers, wiggling his fingers above his ears like horns whilst she has her back to him, kneeling at the door of the washing machine and she sees him with the eyes in the back of her head; wheels around:

And there'll be no going back to school for you my boy, you'll have to wait here till the blow settles itself down —

Yippeeee!

Andrew whoops a war dance round the kitchen, snatching up a warm scone from the table.

This is the best day, he says. Tina, I wish you'd get more of your funny turns.

I can still read your mind, Andrew, I'm like Uri Geller. Never mind bending spoons, just stand a little closer. Let me tell you something terrible and see if you believe me. Leave that curtain, turn around. I need to see your eyes.

This is a letter I wrote to Mandy's magazine, *Lovetime*.

Dear Lovetime. I feel so guilty because I don't like my dad. Sometimes I really hate him and wish I had a different one. Do other girls feel this way?

188

And Mandy's reply: Well maybe there is a good reason for this. Don't worry about whether other girls feel the same way. They don't. Your dad is a bit funny. Just be yourself. Try hard to be nice to him and don't disgust it with anyone else.

Andrew said I was bonkers, but he didn't say it wasn't possible.

I'm awake, I'm the only one. The house is flattened, slumped, the guests felled like trees. Light seeps in through the dusty yellow-spotted curtains. I guess it must be about six-thirty or seven.

This old farmhouse is on a tilt too, like the road; one side of it sinking into the earth, a ship going down. Andrew says they will never manage to sell it, though they might get a pay-out from the insurance company. I pull on jeans and a white camisole, pad barefoot out of my room and downstairs, to find my shoes, picking my way between glasses and cigarette-laden saucers (no ashtrays, Wendy doesn't want to *sanction* smoking, she says). Still swilling in alcohol, the slant of the kitchen undoes me, makes me stumble and want to roll like a ball down to one end. Ridiculously, I forgot to bring my trainers, I've only these pointy peach shoes to wear. Tapping noisily on the tiles, I fill the kettle with water and after a few attempts manage to light the creaky gas stove. PG Tips. I've missed English tea. The familiar box almost cheers me up: it's always Liptons, in Amherst, tea that Mum would describe as weak as weasel water.

This medication is failing me; that's all. I should probably ring Dean; see if he can't recommend something else, refer me to a pharmacist, change the dose.

Just because Dad had a thing for girls, I mean, just because Andrew told me about Jenny doesn't make him a murderer. What else do I have to go on? Only my intuition and . . . Mandy. Mandy's *visits*.

I glance around, checking, glancing into corners, quickly. The room is a post-party shipwreck: paper streamers littering the carpet, draping the back of the sofa, clinging to the paintings. Seaweed. Nothing moves, or creeps, or flickers.

One time I did a Google search. Profile of a Pedophile. (The spelling in the States, the lack of an "a" making it seem modern, not something ancient and Greek, but new and progressive, perhaps related to feet, or pedals; like that sports shop they call, without any embarrassment, The Athlete's Foot.) The web is full of these profiles. The old image of the dirty rain-coated weirdo is out of fashion and in its place is the friend of the family, clever and often charming, wooing and "grooming" his victims. (The gift of the gab. Dad certainly had that.) In some descriptions it's likely they have weird hobbies or childlike qualities of their own. In others they're family men with a certain ordinary acceptability. The more sympathetic sites mention that pedophiles are usually victims of sexual abuse themselves. The cycle of abuse theory is practically an article of faith but if the reason for becoming a sex offender is the fact of being abused in childhood, why

190

do so few abused women become offenders? Surely it's not the abuse that makes someone into a pedophile, but more how they make sense of it, what shapes it makes within them. The only consistent fact seems to be that they are 97 per cent of the time men.

Well, that includes Dad then. But it doesn't bring me any closer. Maybe it's the kind of thing Andrew knows about? It's his work, after all. Troubled boys. Naughty boys. Thing is, I get the impression, from the way he talks of it, they're fairly innocuous, the kind of things he deals with. Reprimands, Community Service cases. Cannabis. Nicking cars and burglary. Boys who can still be turned around; boys like Billy. I've never heard Andrew mention any kind of sex offences, let alone murder.

These are rational thoughts, this is me talking to myself. I'm doing things, making tea, going back into the kitchen, I'm chatting away to myself in this matter of fact way: was Dad a child-molester, was Dad a murderer and then in amongst it, underneath it, somewhere all around it, this other stuff is going on. Fragments. Dad sitting on a sofa. That's all I keep getting. Dad on a sofa, and the curtains drawn, and a sunny day. And I feel sorry and guilty and sadder than sad for even thinking it, because I never can ask him and it's wrong to speak ill of the dead but they won't stop coming, these images, now I've let them in; they're like ants, an army, they're crawling all over me.

She must have known. They always say that. No one ever believes, when the Ripper or Fred West or whoever is arrested (but surely Dad's not like Fred West, how can I think of Dad in the same sentence as Fred West), that the wife or the girlfriend or the women in his life didn't know. As if knowing is easy. As if they themselves would know readily and squarely, face it without squirming: that the person whose underpants they had washed this morning could rape and strangle a child.

There was this girl at university, a girl I vaguely knew, whose boyfriend stabbed her to death. We were all shocked, but I remember one girl saying: oh well, he hit her, you know. But if you asked her, she'd deny it. How can you deny something like that? How stupid can you be? I remember thinking the opposite. That surely it would be easier to deny it. How much harder to believe it, imagine it. That the boyfriend with the shocking temper who gave you the giant Valentine Card with the teddy bear on the front is really capable of something he hasn't yet done, something even he can't believe he's going to do.

I asked Mum once, I don't know how old I was but I must have been small, maybe it was not long after Billy was born: was Dad pleased when you had me? Did he hold me when I was a little baby? Did he come to the hospital?

What a funny question! Of course he came to the hospital! You're his daughter . . .

Did he buy you flowers though? Did he pick me up?

She made her usual noises and protestations. I can't remember what else she said, but what I do remember is, when I pressed her, she couldn't say what kind of flowers he brought. Were they freesias? Were they roses? Were they yellow tulips, daffs? What does it matter,

Tina, she finally snapped, he brought me flowers, I'm sure of it! He was bloody pleased when you were born!

And then when Poppy was born, and Dean and I brought her home from the hospital, I had such a strange reaction. We wanted to bathe her outside in the sunshine. So I got a bowl of water and put it on the grass outside the apartment, and I watched as Dean took Poppy's little sleepsuit off, tugging gently at the yellow-daisied cotton, peeling it over her naked arms and legs, then dabbing the tag on her umbilical cord with cotton wool in disinfectant, just as we'd been shown in the hospital. And then I watched him bathe her, cradling her head with one hand and soaping her legs with the other; and she's splashing and gazing up at him with her goggly new eyes, making her mouth into a triangle shape, doing this funny thing she used to do with her chin, tucking it deep into her neck; and I'm suddenly furious, I'm shouting at Dean for no reason at all, he's not doing anything wrong and I don't understand why it's causing me such pain to see him so tender with our tiny new daughter and he's saying: what, what have I done? and putting Poppy on the outspread white towel and snuggling her up and carrying her inside where I'm sitting on the sofa, sobbing. I am inconsolable and this is a first, an absolute first for me. Dean has never seen me sob like that, before or since: it's just not me. We think later — Dean being a doctor suggests it — that my reaction was probably some form of post-partum blues, natural enough in a new mother in a foreign country, without the support of her parents. I know dimly that it's something else. Something savage and directed at my daughter. Something like: what did she do to deserve such love, such a good, loving father? Why her, and not me?

If I could run them past me, every memory I have of Dad, from nought to twenty-five, the age I was when he died, every last detail of my childhood, the story of my life, if I could reel it out and unravel it, one long piece of ticker-tape, would I know then, would that give me the answer?

But there are so few. It's not ticker-tape at all. What would be the first, *my very first memory* they call it, don't they, as if it arrives discrete, a beginning, like it's all one neat line, instead of millions of tiny wavery threads. This is the story of my father. This is the story of Mandy Baker going missing. This is the story of my funny turns. This is the story of my brother's wedding . . .

I remember a study I read by Blonsky about first memories. And how often a first memory involves injury, accidents, bruises, burns, bites. Exactly the kinds of things Freud was suggesting we'd repress. So maybe, Blonsky claims, Freud was utterly, gloriously wrong and the very things we *remember* not repress are always the traumatic, the significant.

Every time I try to fish up my first memory, it changes. I've caught one here but it's not fully formed. It's Dad throwing me up in the air. Rough and tumble, he used to say, when he was in a good mood: Come here, you, let's have a lickle bit of old rough and tumble! And then he'd lift me high, and throw me, and catch me, or lie on the floor and let me crawl all over him, pummel him with my fists. He smelled of soap and tobacco and wool and some of the time the sugary burnt-cabbage smell of the sugar-beet factory. Smell is easy. I can see his face with his blue eyes and his hooked nose, and his rough skin. He seemed shaggy, like a bear. Maybe the bear was because of the brown sweater he wore, made of some heavy, knobbly wool, or because of his hair (I now see, looking at photographs, that he had dark thick sideburns) or the fact that the hairs on his chest were so prominent that they snaked at the neck of his shirt, giving me the impression that his entire body was probably covered in dark fur; or some association with the phrase bear hug which I might once have heard. Or perhaps his tickling, how he would roll me and then sometimes grab me by the feet and drag me towards him on the sofa, then bury my neck in a storm of kisses. *They tugged his hair with their hands, put their feet upon his back and rolled him about, or they took a hazel-switch and beat him, and when he growled they laughed.*

Rose Red and Snow White again. *Oh Snowy-white and Rosey-Red, will you beat your lover dead?* My father behaved like the bear in that story, and I behaved like the little girls in it, tugging at the fur on the bear, squealing with delight and jumping and bouncing on him. My mother scolded him. She disliked these games. She'd hover, a flowered blur in her apron at the corner of my eye, sometimes saying: Now, Graham, in a warning way, if my shrieks rose to a scalding pitch.

195

I remember my mother telling him I am not a *boy*, meaning: it's fine to play those games with my brothers but I'm too delicate, or the whole game is indelicate: my bare legs kicking, my skirt flying up, my bum in the air.

He has a signet ring, too small for him, on his little finger, left hand. The flesh bulges out either side: that ring is stuck for ever. I'm frightened when he tells me this. His first girlfriend gave it to him, when he was ten; it was *her* father's and she'd nicked it out of a biscuit tin and Dad — or Graham, as he was called then — had to hide it for the first few years until his finger grew big enough at fourteen for him to wear it, and by then the girl had moved away, but the other man's ring, he's been wearing it every day since.

And now I wonder, was he wearing that ring when he died? My brothers never mentioned it. There were belongings, but not many and none of them found their way to me. I said I didn't want to know. I didn't say it bitterly; it was just a fact. Dad didn't have much, by then. He was living in a bedsit in Littleport. His girlfriend had left him, his sons, whom he had left years ago, weren't much interested. His only daughter had told the whole family she found him repulsive — repulsive, yes, that was the word, that was the actual word I used — and did he know this, did it get back to him somehow, did he find out by osmosis, ESP when I muttered the word? Within two weeks I'd had the rescue letter from Amherst, the scholarship offer. That's it, I thought. I don't have to look at this again.

And so, I guess it was a Thursday in September, while the kids in the village were buying their

196

back-to-school shoes or collecting conkers from the horse chestnuts lining the river, that Dad unthreaded his dressing gown cord from the belt loops of his gown and nailed it instead to the beam in his shed. Then he moved his fishing wellies out of the way, unfolded his green fold-up chair, the one he had sat on for many a long hour by the River Great Ouse and, using a schoolboy knot, learned on the farm at the age of eight, he climbed onto it; kicked the chair away. He leapt into it, that clear space he made for himself.

Of course, neither of my brothers told me these details. I supplied them myself. They told me he left no note and that neither of them had spoken to him for months. Billy said he had even passed him at the garage in Ely and Dad had cut him dead, pretended not to see him.

Cut him dead. It was Billy who cut him down, Billy who found him, Billy, the one who loved him best and therefore felt the most slighted, the most wounded, was the one who had to kick the door down (cleverly locked from inside), holding his t-shirt over his mouth to try to blot out the smell, use the garden shears, still dark and smeary with grass, to cut the rough striped brown and blue Marks and Spencer's dressing gown cord, a present, wasn't that dressing gown a present, years ago, from one of us, from Mum perhaps, who was over in Cambridge by now, who couldn't care less, she said, if he wanted to run around with every fifteen-year-old girl in Ely but who didn't know when she said it quite what she was not caring less about, how tall the order. He was, after all was said and done, still the father of her three children, the only father you've got, she sniffed down the phone. The only father we *had*, I adjusted, but not out loud. I had already told her my studies were too pressing and I wouldn't be coming to the funeral.

Well, I'll send some flowers on your behalf, she said, some irises. You know he loved those.

Already I could feel the re-writing of him, how innocuous he would become; a man who loved irises, who sang "Green Grows the Laurel" beautifully, who wore a signet ring he'd had since his first childhood love, at ten. And then I thought of another thing, a confusing thing: how the goalposts kept changing, maybe leaving us for a fifteen-year-old girl (this latest girl had her sixteenth birthday quickly afterwards, so no one troubled the police) hadn't seemed so strange to Dad, since he'd met Mum at not much older, and his own mother had been that age when she had him.

I figured that out once. Grandma was only thirty when she died, and Dad was fifteen, it was just before he met Mum. So that means Grandma must have had Dad at fifteen. But Grandad was always old. I remember him with a big nose and a snowy beard like Santa, or God, only much more fierce and ugly. He had blue eyes too, like Dad's, only Grandad's eyes seemed even more strange, being in that pale pink and white face, like two chips of blue, like the pieces of stone in pebble-dash walls.

He had webbed feet, Dad said. This meant he was a fisherman too, but of course, for the longest time, I didn't understand it.

198

Dad's first memory — the one he told me — is of the floods of '47. He's two years old. He remembers the smell of the water and mud everywhere and it smelled like wet newspaper to him, he says he'll never forget that smell. And the men in their foreign uniforms, German prisoners of war he says they must have been, lining up along the river bank, working with the other men. Grandad lifting him up onto a horse, and the two of them staring over at the fields near Queen Adelaide, one flat grey sea, with the cathedral rising above it, like a ship, just like in the old days, before the land was drained.

His other first memory is something to do with some new slippers. I remember him telling me this, but also, it feels real, like a memory of my own, with all the details, the colour. Sometimes I wonder about that. If memories can be inherited genetically, by our brains, if we even need to be told them. Because in this one, though I wasn't born, I can even see the slippers, which are tartan and big (Dad always had big feet) and soft inside with a pale blue felt material.

He says the slippers were a Christmas present from Grandad. It was snowy, he was living at Burnt Fen by then at the pig farm and it was his job, little as he was, to go out and feed the pigs. But not in his new slippers! He didn't want to take them off, so he went out in the snow in them. And the next thing he knew, there's Grandad coming out of the house, really running towards him and shouting, and he knows it's the slippers, he knows he's in big, big trouble, so get this (he tells me), he takes them off and flings them way over towards the pig-sties.

I thought I'd be in less trouble that way, he chuckles softly. I'm on his knee when he tells me this and I feel the chuckle inside his chest, rattling.

Did you get in trouble? I ask.

O'course. Your grandad beat me so hard it made his own hand bleed. He only stopped when Mother screamed at him that he was ruining her clean walls with the blood, splattering everywhere.

How can you make your hand bleed by beating someone?

Well, he already had a cut there. It opened the wound. What a mess. Mother was furious with him since she had to wash all my clothes as well. She couldn't send me into school looking like I'd been in a blood-bath.

How old were you?

Six, I suppose.

He didn't have many memories of Grandad after that. Just the farm and the pigs. And then the boy who came to work with them, Danny, his best friend. The one he rode the pigs with. Danny came the year his mother died. When he tells me about that, about Grandma's dying young, there's something not right, something false in how he describes it, how pure she was, how perfect. I always have the oddest feeling whenever Dad talks about anything emotional, anything that really matters: of the falseness, the wrongness of the words. As if he has the phrases but not the feeling. I don't know where the feelings are, the ones he's reaching for. I know he must have loved his mother, no boy in the world doesn't feel sad when his mother dies,

200

and here he is talking of how *pure* she was, how *lovely*, and telling me how I have great big eyes, just like her; so why, when he talks of her, do I want to climb off his knee, move away from him, why don't I feel sadder, more sorry for him?

Was that something to do with it, the loss of his mother (but so many boys lose mothers — without becoming child molesters, murderers!)? What could I find out about him, now, what on earth could explain it, or tell me if I'm right? Even if he were here right now, if I could ask him, I doubt I'd be able to figure it out. Instead, what I long to do, what I'm afraid to do, is try it out on the others. And by the way, you guys, did it ever occur to you that Dad might be not just a crap father and a sexual obsessive but a murderer too, he might have done away with Mandy Baker?

The house is stirring. I hear footsteps, the slide of slippers on the floor above. I sip my tea. I open the folded newspaper beside me, yesterday's *Cambridge Evening News* with its depressing headline: Search Extends for Missing Girls: Man and Girlfriend Questioned and beneath that: Natasha Bids for Fame as England's Sexiest Teacher. I can't help reading on: a PE teacher from Cambourne has made the grade for the finals of the television programme for Britain's sexiest teachers. Natasha Gray, who recently completed a BEd in Physical Education at Bedford's De Montfort University, is one of five finalists for the ITV show after impressing producers during an interview and screen test.

Andrew said that Chloe — nine, ten is she? — is becoming obsessed. I think of her watching the television, seeing them again, their photograph; hoping for news — the way that I kept hoping, kept believing, that Mandy was out there somewhere, on the top of a double-decker, or eating Spangles, wandering over Tower Bridge — and in the meantime, Chloe glances beside her and reads that Natasha's looking forward to the thrill of meeting her TV idol, Michael Greco from *EastEnders*. You could study for three years to be a teacher. You could go to the moon. You could even discover the gene for autism or a new seahorse species that no one in the world has seen before; but for God's sake, if you're a girl you'd better make sure you're sexy.

My heart slumps. I pick up the phone and dial my home number. I don't try to calculate the hour, or what Dean might be doing. I need to talk to him. It's either that or catch the next plane back.

It's Integrated Science and the topic is Personal Development and the teacher, Mr Davies, says we can ask him any question we like, anything at all, and what's more to save embarrassment he'll let us write it down, anonymously. He promises to answer every one.

Jenny writes down, why do men lick girls' private parts? She hands this in with the other notes. (She tells me afterwards that this question was hers.) Mr Davies reads it out, quietly, in his serious voice, and his answer is brief. Some men like it, he says. A cough. Some women like it. Next.

202

It's a test. A test for Mr Davies. Will he let us down? My questions are different. I've asked two. First I ask: what is an orgy? I got the word from *News of the World* again. I know the answer. But I want to hear Mr Davies's version. I want to know if he's been to one, a real one, could he describe it in detail please. Someone writes down: Sir — how many times have you had sex?

We expect a number. Twelve, twenty, a hundred times maybe. We are shocked by the answer. Mr Davies says it's like asking how many times you'd had a bath. After a while, you lose count.

We are stunned then. Mrs Davies, his wife, is a young English teacher in our school. She has swinging black hair and big round glasses, with black plastic frames. The boys watch her walk down the corridor in her close-fitting, tan-coloured slacks, and giggle. They write things about her on the wall between the boys' and girls' toilets.

So I ask the ouija board. I ask it the question Russell keeps asking me. Shall I meet him down by the river, go the Whole Way?

Mr Davies, I write on a torn-out sheet from my rough book, what is a pederast?

I'd read it in a book on the ancient Greeks. What is a pervert, a fetishist, a sodomite? I fold them up. We are only allowed two questions each and I've had mine. So it's back to *Fiesta* and *Cosmopolitan* and *Forum* magazine. All the reproductive stuff, I've got that covered. Tadpoles, eggs, fallopian tubes like sheep's horns. Yeah, yeah. I could do an O level in those, no trouble. But perversions. Tastes, desires. Wants. Decisions. When, who, why.

Only the ouija board to help me with that.

I whisper my question. I mist up the glass with my breath and then put it back down on the table. We all put our little fingers on the glass and wait. Cherry giggles. The glass waits and then moves jerkily from letter to letter. It spells out YES.

Dean — is that you?

The phone is hot, pressed against my ear. I'm still on the sofa with the newspaper beside me, the TV screen flickering; the volume turned down. I can barely hear Dean's voice for a fuzz of static. I try to picture him. Where will he be, the kitchen, the walkabout phone? Popping a beer from the fridge, opening it with the purple Amherst College bottle opener, slamming the door shut with a movement of his hip. No, no, I'm completely wrong, it's late, he's still up, he's been waiting for my call.

Tina? Honey? How's things? How was the wedding?

Yeah. Fine. It was fine. I — Dean, I've been talking to my brother and —

This is a bad line —

It's about my dad! I mentioned to Andrew about this girl who went missing, you remember me telling you about Mandy Baker —

Dean says, interrupting, warningly: Poppy's here. She can't sleep. She wants to talk to you.

He's on the speaker-phone, then. I don't know if he knew what I was about to say, but he is good at reading me, he seems to think whatever it is isn't maybe the best thing for Poppy to hear right now. She's missing me. Poppy comes on the line sounding sleepy and muffled and it's all chit-chat about her friend Karizma who is having a slumber party tomorrow night and what are my nieces like and then when Dean goes in the other room she says can she go to Hampshire Mall on her own at the weekend, because Dad says she can't and he's just *so* old-fashioned . . .

Tricky. Of course, being away from her, I want to be the good guy, the one she doesn't complain about. But Dean and I have agreed that when it comes to Poppy's safety, I'm not the best judge. My decisions are crap, in fact. I'm inconsistent: either insisting she stays in when it's perfectly reasonable for her to want to be outdoors, or else forgetting to care at all. This realisation came when Dean came in from work when Poppy was about seven to find I was deeply involved in an article on Pair Bonding and Parental Investment in *Hippocampus zosterae* and had no idea where she was. After some frantic phone calling we found her at a friend's. But Dean's assessment, which I've come to accept, is that my waywardness from about the age of twelve, the fact that I spent all day and every day and most of the evenings, too, away from home, was not so much a sign of my early maturity (as I vaguely suggested) or my independent spirit (my second, more defensive suggestion). No. It was a sign of abject neglect on the part of my parents. Dad was never there, and Mum's only concern was where he was. Poppy, it's understood, will have a different kind of upbringing. We don't talk

205

about class but the reality is, she will have the upbringing of a protected middle-class child, because that's what she is. The daughter of a primary care doctor and a marine biologist, living on the campus of one of the most prestigious liberal arts colleges in America.

Hampshire Mall? I repeat, playing for time. You know what, I fly Monday night. Couldn't it wait until then?

Poppy simply makes a breathing noise, an intake of breath, but I recognise it for what it is: deep frustration. I know exactly what she'll be doing: sitting on the sofa with the phone sandwiched between ear and shoulder, her head on one side, her stubby dark braids spidery over the handset, wearing her pyjamas with the Old Navy sparkly flag on them.

My eyes fall to the newspaper beside me again, to the two smiling girls. But these were loved girls, I'm thinking. These girls, from everything I've read, the family party they attended the day they went missing, the stricken families: there's no question. They were properly looked after. I mean, how vigilant do you have to be? Wasn't Mandy cherished too?

Maybe there was, in Mandy's case, a hiatus. I mean, Sandy had left. A second or two when her parents glanced away and a chasm opened up, and Mandy fell into it. But what parent in the world isn't capable of making those kinds of errors, those occasions of imperfect attention?

You're a very lucky girl! I want to shout, but that would be ridiculous. Why should Poppy be grateful? Because she didn't have a dad like mine? Because she's

206

alive and safe when other girls, girls she doesn't even know, aren't?

A flood of weariness washes over me as I wait for Poppy to speak.

OK, honey, we'll talk about it when I get back, I tell her. Love you. You be good now, for Daddy.

I'll see you Monday, she says. Love you too, Mom.

My first proper dive, I'm with Dean. Dean and I haven't been together long, I'm twenty-five. We're in the Caribbean, Turks and Caicos, our first holiday together and we're forty feet down, with the sound of my excited breathing filling up my head. Calm down, calm down, he tells me, with his hands, the same gesture a conductor would make, meaning: softly now. Or King Canute, suppressing the waves. I'm grinning and grinning and staring into his mask, at his grave brown eyes, so fixed on me, making sure, making sure I'm safe, while he fiddles with my scuba gear, adjusts my buoyancy compensator, to allow me to fall deeper.

I'm falling all right: my body bubbles with almost hysterical pleasure. I hear my own breathing, rasping in the regulator like an obscene phone call. It's so dangerous, sexy, to be so far under the sea, so utterly reliant on this new boyfriend, this practical, trustworthy Dean. The fact that he's my doctor, he knows my medical history, my tendency to funny turns, but gave me the OK to dive, that he chose to vouch for me to the divemaster, that he told me to tick the insurance form "No" when it asked about blackouts (technically,

207

he said, you've never had a full blackout), all this makes me delirious with love for him.

Could I swim to the surface if my air fails me now? I love it when Dean reaches for my belt, drags me towards him. Don't look up! he writes on his diver's pad. I shake my head . . . and look up. Above me, an ethereal blue stillness. A solitary turtle is scooped through it, weightlessly. I watch its slow paddling legs wafting away from us. My buoyant body tries to follow: I'm bubbles in a champagne flute, rising to the top.

Dean points out butterfly fish, the colour of lapis lazuli, and white feather-duster worms. He points out furry purple sea cucumbers, and a yellow trumpet fish hiding behind the coral; a puffer fish so close it almost kisses me, and sea-fans that look as if they're made of nylon nets, with tiny laced spider crabs at the centres. But it's the blue that thrills me. The other-worldliness, the lost in space feeling, bobbing like a lost cork, somehow neither living nor dead, looking into the heart of light, the stillness.

So finally, in the sea-grasses, we see one. My first. That is, my first live seahorse, in the wild. *Hippocampus reidi*. And that's when it happens. I'm bobbing and bobbing and smiling at Dean and watching the bubbles purl from him in a silver froth and that's when something from long ago slides back into me and I feel myself doing it again: hooking my tail around whatever I can find, bobbing. I'm still and watchful and paused. I know I've survived this way, many times, it has served me perfectly well. Dean is smiling encouragingly at me, making the OK sign with his fingers and thumb, and then gives a hitchhiker's jerk towards the surface, meaning shall we go up?

It's then, forty feet under, I decide: I'm safe now. Why go back to England, spend my life in a lab, or at conferences, darkened offices, grey English life, filling out grant application forms, never doing any fieldwork? I'm going to stay here in America. I'm going to ascend slowly and carefully, the way I've been taught by Dean. And when I get to the surface, I'll do the vanishing trick again. I'll change colour, grow long green fronds, barnacles, whatever. And I'm never going to think about England, or Dad, or any of it, ever again.

Well, that was the plan. But here I am and Mandy, she's spoiled everything, she just keeps on knocking at the door. I came to your house, she says again, when I open it — the phrase disembodied, the grin of the Cheshire Cat, no child in sight — but did she, is she telling me the truth?

Mandy was days away from her eleventh birthday. She knew I had bought her a present. Maybe she came round my house to call for me and to see if she could squeeze some hints out of me, get an idea what the present was. It's Sunday, 2p.m. She's had her Sunday dinner. Her stomach is full of pork crackling, roast potatoes, cabbage (not much of that, she hates cabbage), mashed potatoes, carrots and swede mashed together, an orange and yellow mess, she hates that too. She's a fussy eater, Mandy.

Or else she is coming with the Sindy hairbrush. That's it. She feels guilty, she wants to return it, wants to make up. I prefer this, the idea that she wanted to make friends with me again, that she felt remorseful, in the wrong. That little lilac brush, dropped in a pocket. Did she have a pocket? I know exactly what she was wearing: the lilac and purple print dress with the new beads. That dress didn't have pockets, at least the replica one — the one I wore — didn't. The Sindy hairbrush wasn't in the basket of her bike, either, unless it slipped through. That's possible. The basket had small holes in it. The hairbrush was tiny.

She cycles to our house. Her beads rap against her chest, she likes these beads (new), she looks forward to showing me them, even maybe letting me wear them for a moment, doing up the silver clasp at my neck, the kind with a tiny hook that has to be pulled back by your little finger, sometimes springing from you, fiddly; a task for us to master.

She knocks on our door. We have a brass knocker shaped like the head of a lion, a ring that you lift comes right out of its mouth, placed a little high for a child to easily reach. (Mum's deliberate choice; she doesn't want bloody kids knocking all hours of the night and day.) Mandy stands on tiptoe, lifts herself up in her (also) new shoes, the leather squeaking. Bought on the same trip to Debenham's. Birthday gifts, meant to be saved, but Sandy can never wait, likes Mandy to choose her own presents. A flake of doorpaint, a yellow flake floats to the ground as she releases our door knocker with one loud knock. Mandy chews the skin at the side of her nails, tasting blood. Pokes a finger up her nose, and waits.

210

Once, I found a friend of Poppy's Casey; a sullen, nosy girl with a face as blank as pudding, waiting on our step when I came home with groceries from Bread and Circus. Poppy's over at Karizma's, I said. But her dad's home. I wonder why he didn't let you in?

I put the paper bags down to find my keys but the door opened easily, I could hear Dean whistling, and the coffee machine bubbling.

I'm not allowed in, Casey said in her sulky way. If a man is home alone, don't go in the house. That's what my mom says.

A flicker of anger ran through me then, like electricity. Don't be ridiculous, this is my husband, Dean, this is Poppy's dad . . .

I didn't say it though. I might have thought it, but I can be proud of that at least, I didn't say it, I didn't fill that girl's head with the unhelpful advice that you could feel completely safe with some men just because they happened to be your best friend's father. *It's a sorry old world where everyone's so paranoid, where children know everything, there's no mystery any more.* The kind of remark Mum would make. Can it be true, though? And what about the fact that she told Mandy not to call round uninvited? I remember that vividly. I never understood it at the time, but she said it. What was it she didn't like about it? *They all know everything these days! In my day girls were innocent, we knew nothing.*

I wonder if she did, really, know nothing. I wonder if my father was home, that day, and if he answered the door.

★ ★ ★

He has been sleeping. He has one long red crease, a straight line, like the imprint of a pen, from his eyebrow, over his eye and down one cheek. He sees this girl, this ten-year-old blonde girl, the cheeky friend of his daughter on his doorstep. She's a mouthy one, that Mandy. He knows this. He looks at her and the roof of his mouth crackles. She flicks at her hair, that movement, that tarty movement. They all do it. Looking down like this, he is close enough to see flakes of dandruff in her scalp in the light crown. He is wearing an old t-shirt, nylon, green with mud-brown stripes. His loose black denim jeans, no belt. In one pocket his fingers curl around fishing twine.

Tina's not here, he says. It is a desperate sentence: it comes out in a blurt, like someone kicked him. He sees the bike beside her, upturned on the drive, saddle tilting up, abandoned. It's that saddle, white, plastic, shiny, slightly damp in the heat. He thinks. Slightly damp. His heart is pounding. But she's a mouthy girl. It won't work out. He glances over at the tall privet hedge, dark cabbage green, he trimmed it himself only last week, he knows how deep it is, how it obscures all possible views of our doorstep.

(Did he know what he is about to do? Has he admitted it to himself? I'm not sure about this bit. I'm not sure it is ever that deliberate, or could be, if he could admit it. More a case of *a bit of a one with the girls*. With the little girls. That's all. Maybe that's as far as his own thinking on the subject will go.)

Come in and wait if you like.

He should never have said it. That's surely the moment, isn't it? Is that the moment he could turn back, peel back time, unravel it, undo himself? But perhaps like me, like Mandy, like most of us, he too has no idea. Is he really the Enchanter: deliberate, wicked; or does he appear to himself as evil always must, in another form? What could he have done, what, what? Slide back to that position on the Dralon sofa. That dream he was having, before the red crease folded into his face, before he opened the door. Wasn't it a cliché indeed, a dream of the farm, himself as a boy, the smell of hay bales? That deep, old, innocent sleep.

When my father opens the door, Mandy doesn't hesitate. She leaves her bike upturned on the gravel path, she takes her finger out of her nose. She steps onto our hessian mat, oaten-brown, with WELCOME embedded in darker, chocolate brown letters. She wipes her shoes. She notes the lingering smell of mint sauce and other people's cooking that belongs to our house, scenting even the towels and the soap in the washbasin. Also the muddy smell, the water smell clinging to the boots and the jackets, hanging over the downstairs stair-rail. A smell that means that Tina's dad is home.

Now he's saying, come in here and wait if you like. There's telly on in here. I'm just watching the tennis.

That sound, the summer sound of a ball, a racquet, a surge from the crowd. Mandy steps in. Billy's fortress dominates the living room floor, the little soldiers facing outwards, poised. Tiny guns trained on her.

She sits on the sofa, the green Dralon sofa, with the rubbed clean Lucozade stain, the one she's seen a thousand times in Tina's house; at the end furthest from Tina's dad. The house is strange without Tina and her brothers, the sound of the Hoover droning. Tina's father is looking at her.

Tina won't be long, he says.

He looks towards the window, gets up, knees giving a sudden creak, a snap, a sound like a cap-gun firing. He draws the curtain.

Can't see a thing, he says, nodding to the telly. The light's right on the ball.

His voice isn't quite right. Mandy notices it, thinks: he needs to cough. He has a cough in there, or a strangle or a swallow. A swallow, that's what she means. Not a strangle. That's something else. The wrong word. Mandy doesn't often get words wrong. Mandy, remember, is clever.

Mandy is used to my dad ignoring her. He is good at ignoring. He ignores us really well. He can drive us somewhere, act like he's the only one in the car, opening windows, turning off the radio, never asking: is that OK for you, girls?

So what she isn't used to is him moving close to her. Him saying something ridiculous, something horrible and predictable, something sinister, like his compliment to me. You have a beautiful singing voice, was that it? The false note. This from a father whose favourite joke was Go and play in the River Nene! Now I know why I remember it. The weird sound of that sentence. Like striking a bell, and instead of a sweet peal, a great clang rings out, loud and true.

I don't know, something like: you have pretty hair.

Or one of his words I never understood. You're a rare bonnka, you know that?

Yes, that would be it.

And wanting to touch it, to touch her silky, newly washed, child's hair. Green Apple VO5 shampoo, we used, in those days. And our hair, it really did smell of them. It made your mouth water as it oozed out of the bottle: nuclear green and reeking of apples.

This is as far as I can get. It's — conjecture, isn't that the word? *Sheer* conjecture, they always say, as if it's gossamer thin, transparent, something you could hold up to the light; isn't that what they also say, the evidence was full of holes? Andrew's response when I mentioned Mandy was predictable enough, but it was too quick, too ready. I've barely taken in what he told me about Jenny. And his memory of Dad in my room, weirdly unremembered, drawing a blank from me. Interesting, though, that *he* remembered it, that it came out so readily, the moment I raised the subject. It's as though he and I have arrived in the exact same place, despite coming from different directions.

So here I am in Andrew's kitchen, the kitchen at The Beeches, after putting the phone down, saying love you to Poppy, falling so easily back into her way of talking; starting my sentences with You know what, calling her honey. I finish my cup of tea, wash a few glasses: a token. Empty some wine bottles, find a bin bag and quickly fill it with empty packets of confetti and bottles and the contents of makeshift ashtrays and the hard broken icing of wedding cake, paper napkins with silver bells on, paper plates. Andrew's carnation has found its way into a Rizla tin with cigarette ends in it, and after only a second's pause, I fling that in as well. Screwing the top on the near empty whisky bottle and scooping a ringlet of pink ribbons into the bin bag I spot my car keys and, grabbing my brother's jacket from the peg near the back door, I decide that a drive is what I need, a drive will clear my head.

Turning the key in the ignition with one hand, I'm saying to myself, not out loud, but persuasively nevertheless, that I have no idea where I'm going.

And it's a bright morning, blanched and clean, the colour of mist. Mum always hated this landscape. It's the openness. Exposed. Mum loves hills and valleys, crooked paths and dark built-up hedges, crumbling stone cottages: the Yorkshire of the James Herriot programme, a Yorkshire she'd never visited. To me Yorkshire is oppressively pretty and, well, just not flat enough. Not enough sky. Bleak, plain, uncluttered: that's what I've always loved. The way you can see the horizon from more or less anywhere. When I'd progressed from those drawings with a white space in the centre and learned to make the sky and land join up, I still drew it with sky filling most of the page and a tiny black bar of land at the bottom. Land of the Three Quarter Sky. That's what it used to be called, the Fens.

A sky you can touch, taste, with nothing in it but a fine thread of geese, like the tail of a child's kite. The

216

light is so bright that the straight lines of the ditches shine like strips of silver foil and the horizon is another straight line, this time of poplars. Stiff, uniform, shorn bristles on a chin. Fields and fields: artificial as squares of black and green carpet. A land entirely man-made. Constantly requiring effort, belief, imagination, just to make it exist.

Today there's the hum of a helicopter, a flashing tail-light. The sound is weary, anxious: the missing girls again. In the distance I see a whole row of cars, black beetles. Figures, vans, a police helicopter. Press. Maybe even the immediate arrival of sightseers, come to check out the *quiet English village beset by tragedy*. As if bad things only happen on council estates in Hackney.

When Poppy first started in second grade at Wild Woods elementary she had to do a project about Leaf Peepers. I honestly thought they were some kind of butterfly, or bugs or frogs perhaps. Dean laughed at my expression when he told me: it was the local name for the tourists who come to Amherst to see the Fall. To see the leaves turn from green to red on the Holyoke mountains. Leaf Peepers and now these other kind of peepers. Disaster Peepers, maybe. Murder Peepers.

Is that what I am? A Missing Girl Peeper? A Dead Father Peeper? Why can't I let it drop?

As I head the car towards the village, I'm thinking about Mandy's bike. They found her bike by the river, so how did it get there, if she came to our house? Could he have taken it there, later, in his van perhaps? Or am I wrong to think she came to the house, did it happen, in fact, at the river, or did she meet him there first, come to our house with him in the van, leave the bike behind? My foot on the accelerator is pressing hard. These straight, bumpy roads, pointing into the chalky, empty sky: so easy to fly off the ends of the earth. I don't think I ever drove a good car in the Fens before. I only rode pillion on the back of some boy's motorbike, clinging to his leather-jacketed waist; or bounced around in the cabin of some truck, one of Dad's workmates. It's one long road really, cleaving through the middle of a spatter of houses, fields either side of those, there's nothing much to stop me driving right through it. But I'm stopping.

There's the lane to Jenny's house. Walled with privet hedges. I get out of the car. I look down the opening to the lane, noticing how high the hedges are, how cleverly chosen this particular lane is, and wonder, did those boys — because surely they were only boys, really — plan what they were going to do? Did they wait for me, watch for me, or was it an entirely random choice, a surprise even to them?

I think that until this weekend I've probably chosen to believe that those two boys or someone just like them were what happened to Mandy. Someone whose motivations I could never figure out. Someone blurred, without detail, inexplicable.

Once, I said to Dean that every single woman I knew, every woman friend I've spoken to, has had at least one dodgy encounter growing up. That is, if you include everything, every small incident from the flasher on an empty train station to the masturbator on a Greyhound bus trip to the feeler-upper when you're

218

on the tube going to school, to the guy who tries to grab you when you're sunbathing on a deserted beach. Thing is, I said, they don't sound that serious, but when you're twelve or fifteen, how are you to know? If this is going to be something you giggle about with your mates later, or something that appears in a newspaper two days from now?

Dean said: God. Who knew. I can't imagine anyone I know waving their dick around, or feeling up kids on the subway, so who are these guys? If that's true, your statistic, who the fuck is doing this stuff?

Staring down the lane, I hear a dog barking. I know that if I turn my head suddenly, I'll be able to see myself, skinny and pale, with my dyed auburn hair; the light shining through it, like a dandelion flower. I'll be staring straight out at my future self, eyes wide, asking: I know I'm going to die one day, but is it now, is this it?

What about Mandy, then? At what moment did she think like this, did she ever see, understand, what was happening? This thought floods over me like a wave of nausea. When Mandy stared out into the future, what did she see, beyond the obliterating shape of my father? She didn't have a pale woman in peach-coloured shoes to save her. She didn't see me.

I don't turn my head. I climb back in the car, drive a little further. I park two blocks — a hundred yards — away from my old school, pulling on the brake, stepping out from the car. The sign is still there — a red triangle with the black shadows of children playing, but the school has gone and the sign now has the word PLAYGROUND above it. A playground has been built. Bright red roundabout, unscuffed turf. A bench for the mothers. Not a child in sight.

Our school has been converted into a house. Our old playground is now tennis courts. Washing hangs in the yard where we used to bounce a ball up to the wall and catch it, chanting: Plainzies, catchies, merry-go-round to backsides, high ball, low ball . . . The windowsill with its jars of tadpoles, its drying trays of mustard and cress, our primitive science experiments, now hosts a slim green vase, a huge spray of lilies. A few doors down, the Methodist church has been converted into a trendy new house, too, the words Primitive Methodist still over the porch.

Opposite is the Baptist church. A sign that reads: Jesus Christ: the same yesterday, and today, and for ever. Hebrews 13: 8. But nothing else is the same. The shop has gone. The pub and the British Legion club have gone. The pottery has gone. The post office has also been converted into a house, one with the old postbox still embedded in the front wall. Everywhere there are *Sold* signs and scaffolding and builders' vans parked up. The prices are astonishing. To an outsider it would look prosperous. But when our school closed in the late seventies, villagers predicted exactly this. The village will die without the school, they said. The village shop needs the mothers walking past, so does the post office. Seems it took longer than they predicted, but in many ways they were right. This is not the same place. The buildings might be recognisable but it's nothing like the place inside me: the imprint. Or it's the same but shifted: a pack of cards reshuffled. It seems empty, un-peopled, as if it's a replica of itself, not real at all, but *pretend*.

Pretend you're a pop star and I'm your best friend, Mandy says.

Here I am in the school playground, with Mandy. We're sitting on the grass with our scrapbooks and our magazines, cutting out pictures of Clodagh Rogers winning the Eurovision Song Contest. Here I am walking home with my brother in the middle of a Fen Blow. Here is a farmer, his hat pulled down low to his eyes, following the beet harvester, spiking the abandoned beets with a swift and practised movement, tossing them into the cart with his long scythe, without once lifting his eyes from the ground. Here's the beet factory in the distance, with its plumes of steam, pointing to the sky. And here's my father coming towards me, late, late at night, walking along the drove with a torch and a bottle of beer, he's drunk, he's left his kids, his family, he's left his job at the factory, he's given it all up, and he's heading right towards me. He's going to try to crawl into my head, and tell me, and only me, exactly what he has done.

Three

Dean doesn't think I'm mad, or schizophrenic, haunted, possessed, seeing ghosts, or psychic. He says I have "absence seizures": temporal lobe epilepsy. It's 1987, I'm in his surgery on campus, after three other visits to him complaining of a hodge-podge of symptoms: a) semi-fainting, not quite fainting, more a sliding away, preceded by a burning smell and then followed by a really clear scroll of pictures, like a waking dream or b) a horrible feeling of whirling down a long tunnel, sometimes hearing voices, as natural and loud as if someone was in the room with me or c) a pleasant sensation, also preceded by a burning smell but quite joyous this time, sometimes accompanied by pictures and voices but mostly just an overwhelming sensation that I'm happier than any human being ever was, that I'm God, in fact, and know the answer to everything. Two days ago, I found myself on the floor in the Amherst College lab, with an upturned jar of crustaceans beside me, which I'd been about to feed to Scott and Zelda, and all I could remember was that my father had been right beside me, slipping the belt of his dressing gown through its belt loops and telling me what he was about to do.

He had already done it, two months before, a week after I left England. My brothers told me that the girl he'd been living with had left him for a boy closer to her own age; but at this point, in 1987, no one had told me the exact details. I only knew it was suicide, not the dressing gown cord, not how. Dean, in his role as my doctor, the campus doctor, asks gently if any recent events have triggered these symptoms and I stare at him. I'm thinking about my seahorses. Right now they are in an intense mating phase. This morning Zelda was bending double, flexing like a snake, hanging upside down from the frond and nodding her head towards Scott, who, after a second or two's delay, assumed the same position, dangling there like a piece of bendy bacon rind, curling towards her. I've never seen her behave this way. Usually she plays so hard to get. Something has shifted. We're counselled not to anthropomorphise them of course and with seahorses, there is a natural check on this, they don't have strong personalities like some fish; they're self-contained, enigmatic. Even so, I find myself thinking about her in this way. She fancies another seahorse at last. She's woken up.

No, I tell Dean. No recent traumas.

And you couldn't be pregnant? (He doesn't look at me when he says this. Writes something down.)

No.

(Heat springs to my cheeks. I know I'm blushing: this very young, brown-eyed man is surely not going to give me a *physical*?)

Tell me a little more about these positive symptoms. The times when you experience — what did you call it — raptures?

So I tell him about the few occasions, mostly during teenage years, "funny turns" that began like the others, but then nose-dived into something else. In the midst of the sensation of slipping down a tunnel I'd get a feeling so fantastically *happy*, coupled with a sense that I knew everything in the whole world and also a feeling that I was getting bigger and bigger like a giant bladder, until it would be impossible for me to hold any more of all the feelings I had, so that I almost wanted to explode and die right there, in the midst of it. We were studying Tennyson, I say. I can still remember my favourite lines: *Behold, we know not anything . . . And all at once it seemed at last/ The living soul was flashed on mine.* They seemed to fit, I say. It's the most I've ever told anyone.

The results of the EEG tests are back. Dean is astonished that I could possibly get to the age of twenty-five without realising, or ever being diagnosed. I tell him that I've assumed I'm schizophrenic, suffering from paranoid delusions, and that seemed a fair enough explanation, at least for a while. Several visits to hospitals in England came to the same conclusion. I managed to avoid — stop taking — the prescribed medication, as there were long periods where no voices troubled me. Dean says that from what I describe, from

227

the rapturous bit, I may have a form of epilepsy known colloquially as Ecstatic Epilepsy. To cheer me up and because I mentioned Tennyson, he tells me that Dostoevsky shared my affliction and advises me to read *The Idiot*.

Epilepsy — isn't that people who fall on the floor and twitch? You have to stick a sock in their mouth to stop them biting their own tongue? I don't do that.

Well, that's a common but rather clichéd notion of what epilepsy is. Not every epileptic has grand mal seizures. The kind you describe. In your case, the simple partial seizures affect only a small part of the brain, meaning that you stay awake without consciousness being affected. From what you've said, you have only rarely experienced a loss of consciousness — where both hemispheres of the brain are affected. This is a secondary generalised seizure. I wonder if you're sure that nothing has happened recently, nothing that could have triggered the more severe seizure?

And so then I tell him about Dad. He listens and he says I'm sorry once, and he doesn't look at his watch. The sound of coughing and chairs scraping and voices outside in the reception of the surgery dies down; the square of sky beside his desk washes to a deep blue and I know that time is passing, that perhaps I've been here a very long time.

Then finally there's a knock on the door and Patty, the red-haired receptionist, cocks her head round it and says that she is leaving and shall she lock up and Dean (Doctor Yalom at this point) coughs and sits back a

228

little (he has been leaning towards me) and says, no problem, he'll take care of it.

A pause. I've been crying. I'm pressing at my eyes with a tissue. I stand up, taking the strap of my purse from behind the chair.

We could continue this discussion, Dean says. His voice is so quiet it's almost a floor-board creaking, a mumble. I have to crane my neck, dip my head towards him, to hear it. I notice that he mimics my gesture, in a subtle, barely perceptible way, he bends and dips his own head.

This may cost me my position, he says. But perhaps you would like to meet me for dinner?

Only it's not dinner but breakfast, the next day, in the Blacksheep Café, where he has asked me to meet him, Sunday being his only day off. I've arrived early, am thumbing through *The Advocate*, the words dancing meaninglessly around the page, instead my eyes somehow determined to fix on the green and black sheep painted on the café floor. I smile as I spot Dean in the line at the counter. He darts me a quick wave, trying not to wobble the tray he's carrying. He looks different outside of the surgery. Younger. Taller. Thinner? Bendier. Yes, that's it. He has a slight stoop, no doubt to compensate for his ridiculous height. I realise I've never seen him standing up before.

He brings me an Equal Exchange Fairly Traded gourmet coffee and a huge crumbly pecan scone with two wrapped squares of butter.

The band — a jazz combo — starts up as he reaches my table. Putting on the Ritz.

You don't take sugar? he says, sitting down opposite me. The tray tips slightly, spilling some coffee. He doesn't notice. He is staring at me, narrowing his eyes. I think for one awful, frozen moment that he's going to pay me a compliment, tell me I look gorgeous or something, but instead he says: it's one of only two reckless acts I've made in my life so far, asking you out. I hope you don't think I make a habit of it.

When I say nothing he says: the other — in case you're interested — was switching from Arts to Medicine.

So that's how Dean and I begin. Over coffee, he seems to regret his directness and reverts to being a physician, talking to me at great length about the areas of the brain affected by the kind of experiences I describe. Seizures happen when normal activity in the brain is disrupted by unusually intense electrical activity. Some generalised seizures can still be non-convulsive, and so subtle that a bystander wouldn't even know they were occurring. We don't really talk of grand mal and petit mal any longer — we talk of epileptic syndromes. It's common for epilepsy to begin in childhood and the kind you describe is more common amongst girls. We don't really know why. Actually, there's plenty we don't really know or understand about it.

I can hardly hear him for the jazz band, but I nod energetically, as if in agreement with every word.

230

The burning smell, the fear, the voices, the premonitions, he says, are all recognised symptoms of the kind of epilepsy he's talking about. Some people also report déjà vu. These things, the *aura* (a medical term, but I of course picture a New Age manifestation; colours around my head, violet, I decide, a cloud of violet), suggest that the area of damage is the amygdala and the hippocampus, the seat in the brain for emotions and memory . . .

The band stops. Coffee-drinkers slap down their cups, clap excitedly. Suddenly the café is quiet.

Hippocampus, I say. The seahorse.

Of course, he knows the Greek. He doesn't seem at all surprised — or intrigued — by the connection, even when I tell him what I'm doing here at Amherst College; when I tell him about my PhD.

It's shaped like a seahorse, that part of the brain, is that why it's called hippocampus? I ask him.

It's like this.

He picks up his paper napkin and draws a brain on it with an ink pen. He shows me with an arrow the almond of the amygdala and the frontal, parietal, occipital and temporal lobes. With another arrow he points out the curve of the hippocampus. He has fine, beautiful writing, the ink slightly blurring on the paper, as if he were trying to write under water.

Yes, he says casually. It is now assumed, there is some evidence, that it's the hippocampus, the seahorse if you like, that stores memory in the brain.

He sips his latte; a small moustache of foam appears on his upper lip.

Now he is carefully drawing the walnut-shaped cerebellum and shading the curves around the cerebral cortex. It was Wilder Penfield, the famous neurosurgeon working in Montreal, who thought that memory was located just here in the temporal lobes, he says. (He points with his pen, making a blue blob.) He was working with epileptics. He knew from Jackson's previous studies that odd sensations, dreamy states or déjà vu could be, you know, *provoked* by electrodes in patients with some forms of epilepsy but then this one patient suddenly relived everything. Everything he had ever lived as a moving picture. Mind-blowing. Like a drowning man: the mother of all flashbacks.

Do you think . . . I start. I take a sip of coffee and try again: is it possible that the things seen in an — what is it — absence seizure, I mean, does it mean automatically that they're not real?

Depends what you mean by real.

(This, I learn later, is a classic Dean response. Hedging his bets.)

Well some of my visions are — pretty specific. I don't recognise all of them. Some of them feel complete, sort of detailed. As if, well. The only way I can describe it, is it's like having the memories of someone else. Yes, that's exactly what it's like. Like, my brain got muddled up with somebody else's. I don't know whose. Their memories. Their dreams. Their experiences. It's freaky.

He butters his scone. His eyebrows draw together, he folds the napkin neatly, tucks it under his plate, white side up, hiding the drawing.

Sorry, Tina. This diagnosis must be a shock to you?

232

No. Not a shock. A relief. Unless you're going to tell me that — well, will it stop me doing anything? Driving, for instance?

The form you have is very mild — we can control it with drugs . . .

Well then. I prefer to be epileptic than schizophrenic. I'd rather be disabled than a nutcase, in the scheme of things. In the hierarchy of human stigmatisation. And — I hope you won't think this is rude — whatever you say, it's only one explanation. In ten years, there might be another one. I mean, I'll accept it for now and I'm not going to be difficult but — well, in my heart, I think I'm a sort of Joan of Arc, receiving messages. I just haven't figured out what they are yet. You're not going to tell me that even *she* had epilepsy?

He laughs at this. After a moment's consideration he says: they do say it about St Paul. That he was epileptic.

Dean's laugh is light, a sound like rice being shaken in a bottle. He asks me about my seahorses, is it campaigning, conservation, that sort of thing? I tell him I'm much too lazy for that; I'm just a researcher. But what I learn does lead to better protection. I tell him about the trade in seahorses, the figures. An 80 per cent reduction in their numbers in the last ten years. How much I love being in the lab, watching them. My work with the dwarf hippocampus species, their reproductive patterns; their survival techniques. Does he know, I ask him, that some seahorses are monogamous, they mate for life?

He doesn't know.

233

Last year Ted died. We tried to introduce a new mate for Sylvia but she's been rejecting him for nearly a year now.

He gives a slight shake of his head, as if this is too unlikely to be believed.

Most people know that seahorse fathers have the babies. That's the bit that interests them — the androgyny. But there's so much more to them than that — I mean I knew that when I was ten years old, after this book I read by Gerald Durrell, but what's really not commonly known are their amazing survival techniques, how they can grow appendages that look like fronds to disguise themselves, change colour. They almost turn into something else. Another creature. One time, years ago, I mean when I was still an undergraduate, I was working as a volunteer at London Zoo and feeding these *Hippocampus kuda* and they had dark red algae in the tank with them and it had grown on all the seahorses too, like little wigs: a dark red. If you looked for them from above, all you could see was red algae — they'd made themselves invisible. It was brilliant. A friend of mine did a study on a seahorse in Australia who managed to change itself into the same bright orange as the ticker tape she was using to map an area of the sea-grass bed.

Amazing, Dean says. How do they do that?

We don't know. That's what interests me. There's so much we don't know. We don't know way more than we do know. It can be frustrating at times, but mostly it's just incredibly exciting!

234

He kisses me then. He's been looking at me and I've been wanting him to and he leans across the table and puts one hand on the back of my head and pulls me to him. His mouth tastes of coffee; his stubble scratches my chin. When he pulls away the skin around my mouth feels hot, as if scalded.

The band starts up again, the double-bass vibrating through the small packed room. I lean against the wire, heart-shaped chairback and watch Dean's fingers tapping on the table as he turns to watch the band.

I could show you . . . I say . . . show you my seahorses.

He turns back and smiles at me. I love the way you talk about them, he says. I love the way you call them "my seahorses", he shouts, over the trumpet player.

Sorry, Dean said. Sorry about your father.

I nodded and I didn't want to say any more and I didn't want to tell him how. But then a picture floated up, such a powerful picture, from so long ago. Dad, after he'd left us. We didn't see him much. He didn't call round. The Campaign started and the lorries returned: every day a long convoy of filthy laden wagons.

So one day, I walked to the beet factory after school, a four-mile walk, along the drove with the river beside me and the road on the other side. It was winter, but not cold and I passed a heron, staring into the water; one I saw every day from the school bus, grey head hunching into its wings, like an old man in a raincoat, like the fishermen who sat along the river banks, in the exact same position. As I got closer the trucks were more frequent. The drivers hooted their horns at me and the heaps of beets they carried, looking like a stack of great brown potatoes, grew higher and higher and the smell as I got closer to the factory became more powerful: sweet, burnt.

The river glistened beside me, oily with possibility, simmering with mischief. I was not supposed to walk along the drove, by the high river, after school. Not since Mandy, not since ever. I dangled my denim satchel by my legs. I wore white socks and boys' shoes, shoes with laces and a flat heel: that was the style that year. Their warnings didn't trouble me. I felt already that Mum said these things because she had to, because the other mothers did, but her attention was fixed elsewhere.

A driver I recognised stopped at the factory entrance with a great trundling lorry loaded up with beets and as he went in I slipped under the barrier.

I glanced uneasily around the yard.

I'm looking for Mr Humber, I planned to say. The foreman. Humber, they called him.

But no one stopped me. It was late, the sun now beginning to slide. The great huge sky with the tiny trucks, the tiny heap of beets beneath it. The sun like a glittery pink sequin, then just a spot, then a line of pink. Two plumes of white smoke poured up into the sky. Two clouds pointing upwards, two foul, stinking fingers at the night sky, at the cathedral; at the magnificence, the dominance, like the guide books said, at the awe-inspiring. The beet factory was what dominated my landscape, its square long block of a building: the cathedral was a misty shadow behind it, the shape of a snail.

236

I'm looking for my father, the Breedling, the Fen Tiger. He's left us.

The Breedlings walked through the old Fen on stilts, like water creatures. They were the ones with the webbed feet, they were where all the myths came from: the isolation, the in-breeding. They were older even than the Tigers, who were descended from them. That's where they got their fighting spirit, I was told. To oppose the Adventurers, the ones who wanted to drain the land and ruin their living. When I saw their pictures in the textbooks, wading, an eel in each hand, all I could think of was Dad, fishing.

I saw his van. The white van with windows in the back, an old wreck he'd won from his father years and years ago in a snooker game. It was grimy and the windows were steamed up and leaning my face up close I don't know what I expected. I couldn't make out much. I thought I saw a sock, a flash of white, a football sock of Billy's. A bottle. Lots of beer bottles, on the floor and on the seats, green, catching the light. Silver bottle tops. Cigarette butts. And then I drew back, my eyes accustomed to the light.

Dad was lying across the back seat, his knees drawn up to his chest. In the light from the factory windows he was just murky, a grey-brown figure. He was not the foreman, or a Tiger, or a proud Breedling. He was drunk, or asleep, during a working day. Curled up, hiding in the back of his van, in the shape of a prawn, or a foetus. The shape of memory: a dark curled seahorse.

★ ★ ★

So I take Dean to the Life Sciences Building on campus that same day, and since I'm the one on feeding duty, I have a key. It's newly opened, the building; we used to be in something that hubbled and bubbled like the lab of Dr Frankenstein. Dean knows the Pratt Museum of course and he did some post-doctorate study in the Merrill Science Center, but this building is new to him. It gleams with newness: I proudly show him my bench, my tiny corner of the lab, with my lined-up tanks with their sea-grasses, and each with a pair of seahorses, twining and bending like strips of bacon rind, their dorsal fins fluttering in a blur of grey.

We have to feed them four times a day, I explain. They don't have a stomach, or teeth. They suck their food down.

I let him do it while I'm measuring the pH and noting it down; I lift off the lid of the tank so that he can scatter a handful of leaping shrimps from the white plastic tub. I tick off *feed: 6p.m., tank HP 185* from the whiteboard above the tank. Dean puts his face close to the glass and I show him with this pair how to identify Scott from Zelda, the female: she's the one with the short body, without the pouch beneath. He watches as she makes a deadly ambush on a floating shrimp. We hear the snaffle, like the snapping of fingers, in water. Then I tell him about my PhD: why I'm here. The tagging experiments — we're trying the Elastomer Visible Implant system, never before used on seahorses.

If it works, it would be brilliant to use on them in their natural habitat, to track them, I say, as I fish Scott out with a net.

238

They're so easy to catch, Dean marvels. They seem kind of slow, or stupid . . .

Scott lies very still in the bottom of the net. The only sign of agitation is the faint clicking noise he's making with his snout. I place some damp green tissue paper over his eyes and tail to calm him, and gently place him onto the bench, on another piece of wet paper. Under the green blindfold his gills softly expand and contract, like a paper lantern.

They're not stupid, I say. They just don't swim very fast. They don't really need to, since they have so few predators. Except for us, of course . . .

I have to act quickly. I show Dean how we inject the seahorses with the fluorescent dye, close to the pectoral fin, and how the liquid solidifies and shows up, bright and clear, in any situation. So much simpler than the usual necklace tagging, which might choke them as they grow, or get lost if it's loose enough to allow for growth. I'm holding Scott in my palm as I do this, his tail curling round my little finger.

Look how his tail does that, Dean says.

It looks like affection, but it's a mistake to see it that way. It's just a reflex. They have to hang on tight to whatever is available.

Maybe I say this sharply, I don't know. I'm aware of Dean's expression, of him studying me as I release Scott back into the water, where he drifts slowly to the bottom of the tank and then just as indolently hooks his tail around his favourite frond.

They're so tiny . . . Dean tries again.

I say nothing. I'm checking the water pH and making sure I've put everything back as it should be. I reach for the lab light as we leave.

Wait.

He kisses me again and this time I respond. I feel safe in here, with my seahorses, with the bubbling sound, the salty, antiseptic smell. Zelda floats to the edge of the tank, close to where our faces are, nodding her head rhythmically.

It's not curiosity, I say, when I can breathe again. She's just hanging there. That's her favourite spot. She's not nodding, not really. That's just how it appears to us.

Dean runs his hands down my back and my spine straightens, as if I were string being pulled. I take his face in my hands and tip it towards me, like a cup. He kisses me over and over. I press myself against him, one hand on the bench top beside me for support. The seahorses are poised. Paused. Their tails hook around the shared pale green frond. They are not watching us of course. They are not nodding and egging us on. It just looks that way.

The first time with Dean is in his surgery, after hours. He locks the door and shoves the table with all the swabs and hypodermics in front of it as a double measure. I'm shivering, my teeth actually chattering, so he has to get me a plastic cup and fill it with brandy (medicinal, he laughs, I keep it for medicinal occasions). The brandy makes my throat burn but instead of blurring my focus it only makes it sharper, fiercer. I keep my eyes open. There is something so new, so curious about this experience that I want to be alert, not dreamy the way I usually am; I want to see what happens. As Dean reaches forward to lift my t-shirt over my head, I feel nervous and giggly. I step out of my jeans and my underwear and make no attempt to be coquettish, or kiss him back. I just stand there staring at him, drinking him in, then put my hand out to unbutton his shirt, trace the dark lines of hair on his chest with one finger. I'm expecting an image of me, my own sexy nymphet self, to lodge between us like a mirror. That's what usually happens, that's how it is for me. I learned it, I think, growing up: to turn my desire inwards, to fetishise myself. But now at last it's someone else. Now it's him: dark and glorious, his mouth smelling of coffee, his skin of the nylon carpet and something like leaves of mint, and a doctory smell too, clean like soap or disinfectant. His body is slim, his skin pale and freckled. He is all long clean lines, his muscles finely tuned, like the strings on a guitar, the hair on his chest and his thighs a dark, soft fur. He draws the grey blinds, then pulls out a grey felt blanket and gets me to snuggle down right under the bed (we can't bring ourselves to lie on it: that would be too much like an examination). Above me is the underside of the bed: metal and tubular, silver and grey like a wide Fen sky, beneath me the thin, faintly itchy, felt blanket.

He has never heard anyone use the word shag, he says. It's so English! It makes him smile. He tries me out on a few expressions and we discover that I don't know the American meaning of the word chubby, but it's perfect, once he's explained it, it makes us snicker like children, how apt it is. I pretend to misunderstand, put my hand there, say, is this what you mean? and we giggle some more.

I picture myself back home in England suddenly, when he says again how much he loves my accent. The felty earth, turned over by the plough, mist wafting from it like smoke in the early hours of the morning, making it look as if the ground itself is moving. Is the earth moving? Is that what I'm thinking of, my literal imagination once again interfering, my Metaphor Disorder, refusing to leave me, even now, in the most intimate places, language accompanying me, still making its stupid commentary, its jokey remarks, right up to the edge. And then at last, my head empties and language swoops away and only this — the empty page between the sky and the earth — is left.

Before I leave England for good, I want to see Dad, and say goodbye. It doesn't take much effort to find him, although I never have, in all these years. I don't tell my brothers, or Mum, but one Saturday evening, I go to the Sugar Beet Social Club, and it's that easy. There he is, on a high stool at the bar, rolling a cigarette, as if he's been there all the time, which he probably has.

He's drunk. I've no idea if anything I say to him sinks in. I'm your daughter, remember? The one that you left.

It's not like me to come here, to do something like this and the courage soon seeps out of me. I hate you, I want to say. I tell him I'm going to the States on a fellowship.

The alchohol makes everything about him sloppy: his voice, his posture, the edges of his face. Staring at him, I feel as if he's melting. He's a giant pile of ice at the bar, slopping down to nothing.

He leans forward, burbles something about his girlfriend. I'm horrified, does he think I'm her? She should have tried harder, he says. If she'd been a good girl, she would have done. His eyes look frightened, suddenly, they widen so much that I actually turn around, look behind us, expecting to see the girlfriend here, in the pub with us.

Well, bye then, Dad, I say, trying to escape. He holds my hand.

Even his sweaty hand is melting. I've left it way too late.

Russell says: meet me by the river.
The book we all read in the school library is Desmond Morris, *The Naked Ape*. On the front, three figures: a man, a woman and a child, all naked, seen from behind. Three sets of buttocks: Daddy Bear, Mummy Bear, Baby Bear. "The male then begins a series of rhythmical pelvic thrusts. These can vary considerably in strength and speed, but in an uninhibited situation, they are usually rather rapid and deeply penetrating." Me, I've read those last two lines quite often. It's like running a metal detector over my body, waiting for the buzz. It always goes off, right at the same place.

I've seen my two brothers lying on their backs in the bath, with their penises folding to the side, like tiny dead fish, floating on the water. Russell says that if I don't let him do it, right now, his balls will explode.

He's agitated, rushing. I don't feel the same sense of hurry, except a fear of being seen, that someone might pass by. We're inside an abandoned mill on the other side of Russell's village, a short walk from the river. Inside the mill is very small, cramped in fact, without the room to lie down. It's an old wooden drainage pump, Russell says, to drain the land, not to mill anything; but I don't understand the difference, so I just nod my head and try not to look too closely at the wooden cog behind me, at the wooden beams, the scattering from a bird's nest above us, feathers on the painted floor. Someone is doing this mill up; painting it black. Is it a good place to hide, if there are such obvious signs of recent use?

Russell points to the empty beer cans, the cigarette packet in one corner.

It's fine, he says. I've been here before.

We have to scramble in through a square opening but once in, the mill is open, there isn't a door. From behind Russell I can see a huge sky, washed with streaks of white and the tall sedge, stretching towards it, strong and thick and green, the tall blades, the soft feathery heads, like trolls' heads of yellow hair. (I have a collection of plastic trolls of all sizes and hair colours, lined up on my windowsill at home. I'm too old for them now of course, but I won't let Mum throw them out.)

Russell has something in a foil package, a Durex, he calls it. It's the first time I've seen one. When the boys at school said Durex before, I was always confused, I thought it was the name at the bottom of the glasses we drank from in the school dining hall. I don't tell Russell this. It's bad enough that I'm in my school uniform: the unflattering white blouse, crimplene skirt, the striped navy tie.

He doesn't kiss me. He tells me to lie down as best I can and hitch up my skirt. I wish I could switch off this piercing white sunlight, I wish it didn't smell so powerfully of paint in here, of the strong, wet-looking black paint on the beams, which now I come to think of it, I realise is probably tar. I step out of my school knickers, the navy ones, really ashamed now that I didn't think to put some others on, something more enticing. I hear him sigh as I fold them neatly beside me, and do as he says, sit down, lie back, lean against the awkward beam.

He kneels down, puts his legs between mine. He is still in his jeans, which are pushed down to his thighs, along with his pants. I feel sorry for him for wearing his jeans like this, it's embarrassing, it makes him seem ridiculous. I wish he'd taken them right off, but then I suppose it would be more difficult to explain, if we get caught.

This might hurt a bit, he says.

I wonder whether he thinks I'm a virgin. I've tried looking at myself with a mirror and a torch, trying to figure out the mysteries of my own anatomy, but right now I'm closed like a fist, I'm hard and bone down there, like sandpaper, surely there's no opening at all, nothing at all to allow him in. I close my eyes and grit my teeth. He pushes. I scream and his hand shoots out, covers my mouth. I smell the rubber on his palm, the cigarette taste.

We both remain very still, stuck. So still that I can hear the sedge rustling, hear a bird moving in the highest point of the mill, above me. A grey feather floats past my ear, the ear painfully squashed against the wood. I think of the phrase: *he entered me*. I don't know where it's from. *The Exorcist* maybe, or a magazine. How easy they make it sound, how full-blown.

Oh baby, Russell says, and begins moving. Battering ram, I think. We've been studying the siege of Jerusalem lately. I picture the ramparts and then my school notebook, my pencil illustration. He is battering at me. I try to relax. Surely it will hurt less if I relax?

Still, I can't really tell if he is inside me or not. It feels as if he isn't. The pain is of two kinds: tiny, sharp and piercing, like the pain of skin, a paper cut. And deeper, higher up, a pain in my belly, the same pain I've been having a lot lately, and Mum says are period pains, although I don't yet have periods. I observe these two kinds of pain carefully, opening my eyes — I can see a pigeon in the top point of the roof — and then closing them quickly. The smell of rubber and the black tar paint smell is overwhelming, it's a good thing Russell still has his hand over my mouth, as I feel he is holding it in for me, holding in my desire to gag, or scream.

Tarred and feathered, I think, as Russell releases his hand, lets out one long stuttering moan, jerks hard one last time at me. It's been on the news lately. Tarring and feathering. The troubles in Northern Ireland. Mum

246

tends to turn that kind of news over, but the image remains: a wet black figure, stuck with feathers like a weird bird, caught in an oil slick; barely recognisable as human, except for the eyes staring out, white and petrified.

He tells me we'll try again. Don't worry, it will be better next time. He stands up and with a tissue over his hand takes off the condom, screwing up the soggy bundle and then chucking it in a corner of the mill. Then he zips up his jeans and tells me I'm gorgeous. And I'm not to tell a soul.

Dad has these bad dreams. This is when he is still living with us. My bed is pushed against the wall next to theirs and so I hear him sometimes. It wakes me, this great rumbling yell Dad makes behind the purple daisy wallpaper and I always wake up panting, as if I've been running upstairs, with the scary growling noise from Dad, twisting at the end into a yelp, almost a scream.

My bed is narrow and with a white painted headboard, transfers of two baby bunnies and a mother duck with two ducklings. The headboard is babyish, I hate it, but it used to be my cot, Dad converted the cot into this bed. The cover is candlewick, pale lilac with raised up bits, picked at and reduced to knobbles in no particular pattern. I mean, not flowers any more or leaves like they were supposed to be, but more weird, funny things: shells and crabs and twisters and whirls. It has fringes that tickle your face when you hide under it.

I can never get back to sleep when one of Dad's bad dreams has woken me. My heart won't stop pounding. I hear him go into the bathroom and then I hear the toilet flush and then his bedroom door open and their bed creak. And after a while I can usually hear him snoring, so I know he's fine again; whatever it was has been forgotten.

But if I close my eyes, his nightmares will sneak under.

Sometimes I'm in a field and a bull is chasing me. Sometimes a pig. Sometimes I'm riding on the pig and I keep falling off. It has a prize rosette round its neck and the place we are is Burnt Fen Farm or perhaps the farm Dad grew up on, and there's mud slapping everywhere and the pig is running fast and squealing.

Dad says pigs are clever, we're not to call each other stupid pig. But then another time he says: she always used to kill one or two of her little uns, the gilt, if we didn't move her. She'd lie down on them. We'd hear them, screaming and squawking, and the stupid old sow would be snoring away, and that was me and Danny's job: we had to get our foot under her, roll her off them. We put a bar there eventually, to stop it. Many's a time I'd find a piglet, squashed flat like a tyre.

That's what I think his dream is, when I hear him yelling. A poor little runt, a piglet, screaming, crushed to death by its own lazy, milk-laden mother. It wakes me, and then it's impossible, I can never get back to sleep. I'm stuck here with a weight pressing on my chest, flattening my mouth. A puff of a scream, with no sound escaping.

So. Here I am, standing by the river in my old village, having probably ruined my brother's wedding weekend, looking for signs. I stare at everything, like a newcomer, a journalist. A sign from the Fen Waterways Tourism Regeneration Board. *The Story of the Fens*. I stride on, march up towards the drove, hearing a sound so familiar that I catch my breath, hold it, until I hear it again. A reeling sound. Then one, two plops, like stones being flung into the water. I watch a fisherman nearest to me cast again, two lines at once. The ball of bright orange, the float, hits the water; a bird hovers over it. I'd forgotten that sound. That whip, that whistle, as the line swipes the wind.

How many hours did I sit beside him, biting my nails, eating my sherbert pips, listening to that sound, in between the crackle of Radio Caroline? I was the only one in the family who would go with him. I loved it, those afternoons, I didn't care that he didn't talk to me. I just liked to sit beside him, to feel included. I knew that men didn't like it that girls weren't interested in the racing results or the football or whether we should enter the common market, so they had nothing to talk to their daughters about. I thought I would try hard, and at least like fishing.

I need Tina to hold all me tackle, he'd say, winking at Mum. I never knew what he meant by this but I knew it made Mum cross, that he shouldn't be saying it. But I clutch at this phrase; it's relevant isn't it? Surely the kind of man who molests children, who possibly even kills one, is not the kind of man who can be open about himself; make warped, pointed jokes like that?

Unless Dad really did want somebody — me — to know what he was up to?

Once, I was in a café in Boston in the Back Bay area with Dean. Or, Charley's on Newbury, I guess it was, Dean loves the coffee there. Well, a kid threw a water bomb at an old guy behind us. It landed at his feet with a great smack. Water made a sudden dark blot on the pavement at his feet, the spattered guts of a blue balloon. The place kind of froze. People, moments before fanning themselves with menus, stopped. The thrower was behind a wall. And then we heard giggling, the voices of children, boys, and the waitress carrying a whole stack of plates, said: well, would you look at that! And we all started up, talking again, returning to our lattes and cappuccinos, and it was fine.

But we were scared, all of us, for a second. It was loud: we thought at first it was something worse. A gun perhaps. This was early October in 2001. We were still shell-shocked. We looked at one another: our gaze stunned, stripped. All the horror we'd been imagining, all the images, all the taped phone messages, things we'd been trying to take in, trying also to blot out. There were thirty seconds when we let them in again. Something slipped through. Something closed up again.

Maybe there were thirty seconds in his life when Dad glimpsed himself, really saw what he had done, but just before the chink closed up, he handed the glimpse to me.

On the way back to Andrew and Wendy's house, I put my hand in the deep pockets of his green Barbour jacket. I'm feeling for the car keys, which in fact I have stupidly left in the car's ignition, with the door unlocked. But I'm barely conscious of any of that. What

I'm noticing is what is in the pocket. My fingers curl around it and I bring it out to stare at it.

A Sindy hairbrush. It doesn't look new. My mind is wheeling with the possibilities. The silver S on the back: yes, I remember it perfectly, but what an interloper, an old relic, what an odd little item. Old coins, shards of broken pots, yes, but a plastic doll's hairbrush? I'm ten years old. I love this hairbrush. No wonder Mandy wanted to steal it from me.

But that's ridiculous. It must belong to one of the girls, to Rose perhaps. Rose would be the right age. I'm sure they still make them; girls still play with them. What other explanation can there be?

I drop it again into the pocket, where it nestles amongst its bed of crumbs and fluff. I switch on the engine, directing the car away from the river. In the rear-view mirror I glimpse a helicopter, hovering in the white sky, like a kestrel with its wings spread, poised, searching for a mouse, and as I'm pulling away I can't quite snatch my eyes from it. Vigilance. Searching. Not giving up yet. I know what they say, everyone does. If a child isn't found in the first twenty-four hours, the outlook is bad. But what parent can give up hope, when your heart keeps pumping it out, like adrenaline? I remember Mandy's mother, the only time I bumped into her later, when I was older. And not knowing what to say, and being with Mum, and Mum never one to hold back, Mum making all these sad noises, murmuring and commiserating and Sandy suddenly saying: I still make her a cup of tea every morning. Two sugars, just how she liked it. Just in case, you know. Make her feel welcome if she turns up.

Mum found this so *sad* and so *sweet*, and said so, all the way round Lipton's while I trailed behind her, lugging the basket as she threw in the Ski yoghurts and Dairylea triangles. I found it creepy. I couldn't shake the picture of a great line of cold tea, one for every day of the year, every year she was missing, lining up alongside Mandy's bed. And not even her real bed either, since she'd never lived at Sandy's house, the one with the fancy man in it; but a camp bed, dark green, with folded wire legs, like a long insect. A line of cups of undrunk cold tea, snaking its way down the stairs and out to the street. Did Mandy even like tea? In our house, children weren't allowed tea, only squash or juice, or pop. Tea and coffee steamed with a toxic, mysterious, grown-up smell, strong as tobacco and just as threatening. I couldn't remember ever seeing Mandy drink tea.

Sandy produced a shudder in me by then. It was the weird hairstyle, high bunches pulled so tight with cherry-red bobbles at the top of her head that her eyebrows were nearly stretched off her face. She'd become thin as a string bean, like an overgrown child herself, in lime green waterproof macs patterned with white circles, flapping bell sleeves, floppy-brimmed hats. I had no sympathy for her. It's only now it's occurring to me that Sandy wasn't the village weirdo: she was a mother whose child went missing. My heart leaps like a yoyo suddenly, thinking of Poppy.

252

Picturing her running up the beach, a year or so ago, crying after a swim in a freezing sea, ending in a stubbed toe; nine years old but at that moment younger; her legs almost bending with the effort of running to me, her chest heaving with sobs and how I ran towards her with the beach towel, the baby-blue one with the pictures of peach-coloured crabs and shells; how glad I was to be allowed to do this, surprised too, grateful: to hold it out to her, wrap it round her and sit with her in my arms; my face in her hair, her smell salty and seaweedy, her skin wet, crusted with sand.

Only we would understand, I think, and my heart is still leaping and falling on its wild string. Only Dean and I would know her, know Poppy fully and properly, know that ten is not on the way to somewhere, ten is not a half-life, a beginning, any more than forty is.

I drive slowly past the old bus stop, empty now of the teenagers who always massed there, heads together around their chips. Penguins huddling a bucket of fish. The glass is still kicked through. And then I reverse, cross the river again. As I do, I smell the water: soily and green. The smell of those green wellies Dad could never remove, without sitting on the bottom stair and asking one of us to yank at them. No need to pull me leg off, too! he'd say. I hated it, the slippery mud all over my hands, my lap, the way I always tumbled over when the boot finally yielded, and how he laughed at me.

Two cars are parked up by the bridge. That's not many fishermen for a Sunday. The water is low, I notice, as I drive over the bridge, the ruler, the same one that always told us how high the levels, the same one that warned of the great floods of '47, has snapped in half, but now, there's little need of it. Anyone can see that the river, thick and brown as coffee, is lower than it's been for years.

If Mandy's body is in that river, surely she would have surfaced by now?

I drive back towards The Beeches. I'm as tired as I've ever been, I've an overwhelming desire to put my head down and do what everyone else seems to be doing: sleep for a hundred years. I've resolved nothing. If Andrew wants to let it drop, I don't even know if I'll protest.

When I reach the house, driving over the scrunching gravel, Andrew's standing at the door, like a sentry, looking grey and hung-over or maybe something else. He's been waiting for me.

Tina. I've been thinking about what you said. I think you should go to the police. I really do. I'll take you if you like.

Hi there. How are you feeling this morning? Where's Mum? Where's the girls?

I mean it, Tina. I threw up. After you'd gone, I threw up, I felt so sick, thinking about it, about whether it could be true. You've got to — tell somebody else.

I climb out of the car. So I was right. What I saw travel over his face was some kind of recognition, some realigning of his memories with what I said. He looks washed out, his face bleached of emotion.

Where is everyone else? I ask again. What I mean is: did you tell Mum, or Wendy?

254

The National Trust. Wendy's taken them out for the day.

I follow him towards the kitchen, carrying the jacket I borrowed over one arm. A waft of fading roses and horse manure snakes up to me as I duck in through the brambles on the porch.

What are you doing with Dad's jacket? Andrew asks.

Dad's jacket? I thought it was yours.

All the questions I had about the Sindy hairbrush explode again.

In the kitchen he explains that the Barbour jacket is something Billy rescued from Dad's shed, along with a few other things, some decent boots, some jump-leads, a couple of keep-nets; asking Andrew if he wanted them. Over the years most of it has been thrown or given away, but the jacket, good quality and perfectly waterproof, has just ended up hanging from whichever peg in whichever house Andrew happens to be living in. It's almost the first thing he did, he says sheepishly, on arriving at Wendy's. Stake his territory, hang the old coat up, like a flag.

Don't you actually wear it? I ask. Did you ever put your hand in the pocket?

I dig mine deep, and show him the Sindy hairbrush. I explain that I think it was mine, that I think Mandy "borrowed" it from me and that I've always had a hunch that she might have tried to return it, on the day she went missing.

He doesn't leap up and scream and shout. He smoothes his hand over and over his forehead, trying to erase something. I think of windscreen wipers. I want to put my hand over his, make him stop.

You're sure it's not someone else's? Andrew asks. Could it be Chloe's or Rose's? Or even one of Billy's girls?

I shake my head. It looks like mine, I say.

I don't know, Andrew keeps saying, as if I asked him something.

His eyes are red, the lids beneath them swollen pouches. I think of the bellies of my seahorses: Scott and Henry. I wonder if Andrew's been crying.

Andrew offers to drive me to the police station. Not Ely, he says, that will be too swamped with this current case, with all the publicity. We'll go to Parkside instead. His mind is made up about this and I recognise his desire for action, to show faith; I'm grateful for it. Dean would say it's a male thing. You tell us about your feelings, men want to help by *doing* something. Where once this might have irritated me, now I only see how far my brother has come. Those fights over Girls World and the names of things, silly girl things, dolls and such. He's conceded at last.

Does this mean you believe me? I ask. That you think Dad did it?

He rubs his hands over his face again. I think at first he's not going to answer.

Then he says: you know when I told you about getting that knife when I heard you with Dad and crying and stuff and I thought I would try and save you? And you didn't remember?

I nod.

256

Well, I suppose we just remember different things. I don't want to believe Dad could be capable of something like — murder. I mean, who would want to think that about their own father, even if he was a shit. But. Oh, I don't know. When I think of myself, of us, growing up, I know there was something — weird. A heavy, horrible kind of cloud. Sex, I don't know. I never knew what it was. It's affected me my whole life, I mean, not just Dad topping himself but the whole thing. A weird flavour, that's all. And so what you say, it — it could be possible. It's not outside of the realms of possibility.

The flavour of our childhood. I had no idea that just him saying that, just my brother, one of only three witnesses who were there, part of the same family, could have this effect. Make me see the fields again, the fields at the back of our house. Flattened, chocolate-brown, the sugar-beets dotted amongst the furrows, each lying in the nest of their browning lopped leaves. A hundred scalped heads.

On the way, Andrew tells me he also talked to Billy. He's driving, but it's my car, the hire car. He's never driven a 5 Series, he says, stroking the dashboard and opening and closing the glove compartment. He chucks the disgusting air-freshener out of the window. He gives me a tired smile: pretty posh now, aren't we, Sis?

Settling into the passenger seat, I watch as familiar roads unravel into non-familiar buildings. The Fens abruptly stop as we approach the train station in Ely. A new superstore, new roundabout. On the outskirts, light-bricked, new houses. Cathedral View. They're like the homes of Poppy's Sylvanian Kittens — the Bear Family, Mr Webster the Milkman, every home with fridge and full accessories.

What did Billy say? I ask at last.

You've got to ease up on him, is all Andrew says. He didn't escape like you and me. He stayed right here. He knows everyone. He had to field all the questions, when Dad —

You think you escaped? I ask, surprised.

Billy hasn't told Mum. He went very quiet, Andrew says. And since it was on the phone, I couldn't really gauge his reaction. But somehow, Andrew adds, I didn't feel he was that — shocked. Not like me. He wasn't surprised enough, if you know what I mean. I get the feeling that there's nothing that would surprise Billy about Dad.

All these years of saying nothing, of knowing nothing. Years of being in a dark smoky fog, never thinking of Dad, of Mandy, with only shadows at the corners to trouble me; like being constantly underwater. Then suddenly, two people know. Andrew, Billy. I'm giddy, light-headed, coming up for air. But I know that in the next conversation I'll have to plunge back down again, like Hades; back to the underworld, the murk, the caves; back to wherever he carried her to.

We don't discuss what I'm going to say. Andrew will wait for me in the reception area. He's phoned in advance to make sure we'll be able to see someone: the woman on the phone was harassed and non-communicative — we're in the middle of a very

258

important investigation here, perhaps you've noticed? she asked sarcastically, at one point. We've got it completely wrong. The other case is being dealt with here too, it's dominating all the police stations for miles around. We're told we might have a long wait, but a DI Rickton would be available to see us.

Outside there is a BBC van with camera crews and equipment rigged up, and cars parked on every inch of road. Most have windows peeled and radios murmuring, and leaning beside them, journalists, smoking and drinking from Starbucks cups or speaking into mobile phones. All around the station is this hum, this noise. Like the whole place is flanked by insects.

Andrew plunks a kiss on my cheek.

You're sure you want to do this on your own? You don't want me to come in with you?

I'm sure.

DI Rickton eventually comes to reception to meet me and I notice only his pointed, blue-black leather shoes. They're a dapper little note that seems to want to tell me that out of uniform, in his other life, he's not an upholder of the law: he's hip. He ushers me into Custody, the only place, right now, he says, where we can grab a bit of peace.

What I find out is this: they have no further information on the case. Mandy Baker's body was never found, therefore she is still officially a Missing Person. Such cases are kept open for one hundred years, so there are plenty more years to go. As it was thirty years ago, and a paper file, it is not easy for him to lay his hands on the records. It may be that it has not yet been transcribed to the computer. As you can see, he says, it's an unusual time here. A very big case going on. We are — *extraordinarily* busy. (He has the faintest hint of an accent, when he says this word. Not from round here, I think. Essex, maybe, or somewhere further south. But then I wonder, is it just an association, a prejudice; something to do with his wide-boy appearance, filling in the details for me, falsely joining the dots?) He asks whether it's this fresh case of the Missing Girls prompting me to — remember — the case of Mandy Baker? I say no. It's coincidence.

If I could give him a day or two, he says, he will do his level best to locate her file, but he very much doubts there will be anything in it I don't already know.

Level best, he says. *Level*. Flat. I picture a field, again . . .

Then he leans back, folding one knee over the other, so that I can see his socks, black, silky looking, and asks me what makes me think *my father* is the one who killed her?

I stumble through the Sindy hairbrush story, even showing it to him at one point. He holds it between finger and thumb, as if pinching a fly by the wings, says: but you're not sure she actually took it from you, you don't know that this child *had* it, it might have just been *lost*, presumably . . .?

So then I go on about Dad's tastes in girls, and how there's a world of difference between girls of fifteen and girls of ten and so I'd never really considered a possible connection with Mandy before now. (Is this true? What

260

about other feelings, other times? Never considered, or never *dared* to consider, which is it?) I feel myself blushing. I wonder if he will ask me the inevitable question, did Dad abuse me? But he doesn't, so I stagger on. How this is now corroborated by what my brother's ex-wife says about Dad molesting her as a girl. At this he perks up, leans forward again, picks up his pen.

And your father lives where, a village the other side of Ely, you said? Is he on the Sex Offenders Register, do you know?

No, no, he's dead now, he died fifteen years ago.

He sits back again. The end of the pen slots into his mouth, where he taps it against his teeth. It's extremely warm in the tiny interview room. There are no windows, only three chairs and a metal table with a tape-recorder on it, three tapes in sealed plastic. He is not taping me, but only jotting down the odd word in a notepad. His eyes follow mine as I scan the room. I feel the damp patches under my armpits and the heat stinging in my cheeks.

I'm sorry we have to talk in here, he says. In Custody. There's not one single proper interview room free, I'm afraid. Full of nutters saying they know what happened to these girls. You wouldn't believe it, who crawls out of the woodwork during a case like this.

He is staring closely at me. I picture the people crawling out of the woodwork and wonder if in his mind, I'm one of them. He stops tapping and lays the pen beside his notebook on the table. His tone is softer. Cautious: you see, as your father is — dead, it would take a very great deal of new evidence to persuade the Crown Prosecution that it was worth exhuming the body, for DNA tests. And then, since this little girl is, as I said, still officially only *Missing* and there's no body been found, well, there's nothing new really to go on . . . just, you know, your *hunch*, so to speak.

And the Sindy hairbrush.

Yes. And the — child's toy. Which may or may not have been in the missing girl's possession.

A pause.

Not all child molesters are murderers, he says. Though in the public's mind the two are very often confused.

I know that, I reply.

Would you like a glass of water Mrs — Ms . . . Tina, wasn't it?

I would like a glass of water. He opens the door, asks another officer to bring it. Outside the door of the Custody room the hubbub is heard again. I read the signs, the paperwork stuck to the walls. Arrested Persons to Stand Within this Red Square. Property Room. *Arrested Persons: Your Rights*. The water is a long while arriving. DI Rickton is excited, wants to hurry me along. He has to make a statement to the press. He spits on a tissue, cleans his shoes. Something has happened. The bodies of two girls have been found.

After Russell and I do it in the windmill I notice that I smell different and wonder, does anyone else notice? My belly aches and all around me is a sort of tinny smell, rusty; especially powerful whenever I undress. I run myself deep bubble baths, full of my brothers' Matey bubbles, staying in so long that Mum raps on the door and tells me I'll wrinkle up. After three days I wake one morning to find a rusty-brown stain on the sheets, the shape of a leaf, right where I've been lying and for a moment I stare at it, wondering how on earth it got there, so beautifully formed, but then I notice there's blood on my nightdress too and I'm excited, in a calm sort of way, realising the magical thing has happened at last: I've *started*. This is the code we use, our secret, embarrassed question to one another: have you started yet? And I'm the last in my class, and it seems that Russell has had something to do with it. Has speeded me up perhaps, or given me a jog in the right direction. It's what he said, at the time, it's perfectly natural, it's natural it should hurt too. Becoming a Woman, that's how I think of it, that's something I've read somewhere. It doesn't mean periods but losing your virginity. Only it's not *losing* any more, either, they don't use that word in *Cosmopolitan* or *19*, only this weird book I've found in the library, *Married Love*, the sort of book Mum would have read. Mum would say I was losing something, she grew up in the fifties: she's old-fashioned.

You become a woman by letting a man inside you, as if you were half of something and now you are complete. I've no idea how you become a man: the magazines and books don't really talk about that. But then they don't talk about men as virgins either, as pure and innocent, although judging from my brothers, they must have been if not innocent, at least ignorant, once.

(Russell says he loves that about me. He always says it, when I don't know something, like what a sixty-nine is. You're so pure and innocent, he says, always both the words together, in that order: it makes him laugh.) I try not to have these thoughts, to dwell on any of this. I'm terrified they can tell, that Mum can tell, just by looking at me. Can she read my mind?

Mr Davies, the Science teacher, has lent me this book, *Kinflicks* by Lisa Alther. I think he's embarrassed about it, he sort of mutters something like: I think you'll enjoy this, Tina, someone with your questioning mind. But even the cover shocks me. It's a woman leaping, her knees bent, and she's wearing what look like military tassels, only on her nipples. I stare and stare at these but I can't really figure out how they're attached or what they're for.

I hide the book. Even the jacket would turn Mum into a raging stallion, huffing and snorting. *Teenage Sex Freaks, Serious Sophomores, Lesbian Hippies, Thwarted Suburban Mothers — America is full of them, but none quite like our heroine, who is all of these and more.*

I hide the fat paperback in my schoolbag and read it alone in my room when I'm supposed to be doing my homework, shoving it under my pillow if Andrew or Billy bursts in, screaming about some toy plane of Billy's or fighting over his precious collection of Brand New Decimal Coins which has somehow got not so brand new any more and has been dispersed in different corners all over the house, which as Billy keeps wailing, tearily . . . lowers their value!

264

At least, I've found out what blue balls are, and realise Russell wasn't lying. There's a whole chapter called "Blue Balls in Bibleland". There's even a bit that is remarkably like the first time I sat on Russell's lap at Jenny's house, when Ginny Babcock (the heroine) says: "The truth was, I feared sperm almost as much as I feared communists." And at last, there are plenty of descriptions of the male body, most of them recognisable, if not flattering. "I felt as though I was an animal trainer, trying to lead a recalcitrant baby elephant by the trunk."

I can't look at Mr Davies the next day at school. I've no idea why he's lent me this book. Mum doesn't read much. At home we have a medical dictionary and Dad's old fishing books and *Rude Rosa* (not what I thought, sadly, just Inspiring Stories for Girls) and *The Power of Positive Thinking* by Norman Vincent Peale, which I've read three times. Although it couldn't be more different from *Kinflicks*, he mentions communists too. "For example, when you are with a group of people at luncheon, do not comment that Communists will soon take over the country. In the first place, Communists are not going to take over the country and by so asserting you create a depressing reaction in the minds of others."

I think this book is what Mum reads to cheer herself up about Dad. The Power of Prayer to Solve Every Heartache. But she also has a copy of *The Exorcist*, which I know she doesn't want me to see, as it's hidden in the bathroom cabinet, behind a double-thick pack of Andrex. I have to read this in tiny chunks, while

265

running the bath, and somehow this makes the snatched paragraphs linger, like fragments of nightmares:

"Our Father, he began. Regan spat and hit Merrin in the face with a yellowish glob of mucus. It oozed slowly down the exorcist's cheek."

Jenny's brother has a copy too and she reads us long sections while we wait for our nail varnish to dry: "Then a thick and putrid greenish vomit began to pump from Regan's mouth in slow and regular spurts that oozed like lava over her lip and flowed like waves into Merrin's hand."

Ugghh!!! we all squeal. We throw ourselves on the bed, kicking our legs. Cherry is laughing so much she says, between chokes, that she's wet herself. Jenny makes gagging signs with her fingers down her throat.

We've abandoned the ouija board now but we have a new game called Telepathy and I'm brilliant at it. We've tried bending spoons, we've watched Uri Geller do it and read people's minds too and it doesn't look that hard.

It isn't. I'm easily the best. You must be cheating! Cherry shrieks, as once again I draw on my paper a shape resembling two people and a black dog and Cherry opens out her own paper (drawn in another room) to show me something similar. Her shapes are better drawn, the dog is clearly Jenny's dog, Prince, where mine could be any old creature, but still, the idea is the same. Two figures and a creature. I just closed my eyes, and that's what popped into my head. They want to know how I do it. They want their own turn, to see if they can do it to me.

266

We tear up pieces of paper. I go outside of Jenny's bedroom and stand on the landing, lean my back against the raised bumps of the wallpaper, try not to notice Jenny's nasty old carpet, torn to shreds in places by the dog, reduced to nothing more than crumbling grey underlay. I can hear the boys downstairs; the sound of the telly and the jingle of an advert: *Topic. A hazelnut in every bite — I remember!* I draw a girl's face, with long hair and big eyes, long eyelashes. I nearly always draw this, so that should be easy for them to guess. I fold it up into the smallest square I can.

The sitting room door opens with a burst of noise and Russell comes out into the hall, to go to the downstairs loo. He doesn't glance up at the landing; I'm just behind the white-painted banister. I watch the top of his dark head, his wrist with his identity bracelet, the large fingers, already going for his zip, preoccupied, self-contained. This is when I like him: when he is not paying any attention to me. If he saw me now, I know it would start. How gorgeous I am, when am I going to meet him again, how cute I look in this school skirt. We all hitch the skirts folding the waistband under a couple of times, but now suddenly I'm self-conscious; I've started to wear mine down at the proper, unfashionable length, down to my knees. He doesn't look up anyway.

Come on, we're ready! Jenny shouts.

I throw myself on the bed, put my hands to my temples and we all screw up our eyes and concentrate. Jenny's room stinks of sandalwood incense, mixed with the damp smell of dog-hairs and hairspray and Charlie Girl perfume. I start to cough. I squeeze the folded up

267

paper in my hand and concentrate as hard as I can on what I drew, and Jenny and Cherry stare at me seriously and then draw on their own paper.

Jenny draws a house. Cherry writes, Remember you're a Womble.

It's a face! I shriek. You're both useless! I open my paper and show them the face and they both look at their own paper. Cherry throws hers on the bed. Jenny tears hers up.

Jenny starts pouring Anne French cleansing lotion onto some cotton wool and goes over to her bedroom mirror to remove her kohl pencil. Can I borrow that? Cherry says. They're acting like they've lost interest, that they don't care that they're rotten at Telepathy.

I'm relieved, of course. I'm meeting Russell again, tomorrow night. Their powers of mind-reading are absolutely useless. It's I alone who have the gift.

I am in my bedroom: the room is dark and full of water. I'm nine, ten, who knows. I'm holding onto something with my tail, my magnificent, curly, strong, prehensile tail and what is it that I'm holding onto? Grass perhaps or maybe the leg of a chair, a piece of furniture. I'm bobbing, in this watery bed, and I'm nodding my head and behind me I feel something beating, fast, like wings, keeping me afloat, but something is coming towards me, something terrifying, with a cavernous mouth, weaving, zigzagging.

It wants to eat me. It wants to devour me or pierce me, puncture me. I think it's whispering to me. I know lots of things all at once that don't make sense: that I could die of this much knowledge, that you should never look at stuff too directly, like the sun, it'll burn your eyes. But then I also know that I'm not going to die, no, not at all. I know I have tricks up my sleeve, that even with this full weight on me, squashing all the breathing out of me, I won't snap in two like a twig, I'll do something else, change colour, grow extra arms or legs, maybe an extra head. The fluttering beats at my back, but I'm not an angel, either, though they might all want me to be, an angel or a rose, that's how they think of us: pure as air, pure enough to believe in, to lead themselves back, to wash themselves in. Yes, here it is right now, the beginning, the first time it happens. All around my ears, I feel it. My head bobbing up towards the surface, stretching away from the rest of me. I'm sprouting a neon-coloured head, waving limey fronds in the water.

When Andrew and I arrive back at The Beeches Wendy and Mum and the girls are glued to the television. I see through the open door to the living room a blue television screen flickering, with all four of them on the sofa, silent, while on the screen is a field, cordoned with blue and white police tape, men in white coats. Then the photograph of the girls again, one dark, one fair. One with her now familiar smile just wavering, just beginning to wobble.

The hallway is cold. Icy cold, as if the front door has been left open, which it hasn't. As if a violent wind is blowing through the house. On my back, at my shoulder blades, two small hands are pressing at me. Pushing. I know not to look around. A child's voice is softly calling to me. Fear catches at my throat. *Tina. Tina.*

So then I'm back to our doorstep, that's where it starts, Mandy just standing there, the crown of her head, the yellow paint. Then the chair, the moment when he shifts along, the weight lifting and redistributing on the sofa beside her, springs rudely squeaking, and she is uneasy but doesn't understand why and blurts out, worried that it might seem bad-mannered: maybe I should go home and Tina can come to my house and call for me for a change . . . and he says, let me give you a lift, that'll be just fine, we can put your bike in the van. I'm going fishing after, I can take you to Burnt Fen on my way to the river, and she, well, it would be rude to refuse a lift from Tina's father, even if she doesn't like him much, Mr Humber, even if she does always find him a bit creepy. She has been taught to squash this feeling down, to squash all rude and unfriendly feelings about other people's fathers and mothers, about anyone in fact. Once, she said that the minister at Tina's church was a freak and her mum stared at her fiercely and told her she was being unChristian and, worse than that, catty.

So she is late to register Mr Humber's breathing and the sweat along his dark curly hairline and the nasty smell in his van and the way he pants when he heaves her bike into the back and looks all around him, and the way his hands shake when he folds his cigarette paper. Mandy sits stiffly looking out of the van window and she doesn't protest when he drives first to the allotments, thinking he has something he needs to pick

270

up from there and it's really only when he asks her into his shed and says he needs her to come in and hold something for him, it's probably only then that she begins to feel he's acting in a way that makes her uncomfortable, and even then *uncomfortable* is the only word that will form, not frightened or wary, or anything more definite.

And I'm there with them, along that drove, that unfamiliar piece of land, the allotment, then the shed, somewhere I think I've been before. I know the river is here somewhere: I can smell it, the way I always smell it: earth and mud and something clean, something outdoors and then the hot warm wooden smell of a building, the sudden dark as we go in out of the sun. And at first, there they are, I see them both, the small girl, the man in his green fishing jacket, and at first it's true, the picture looks tender, what would someone else think, how should they look on this, if they were to peep in through one of those smeary glass windows, like a bird, tapping, tip-tapping on the window. But even a bird might feel it, as it comes closer, smell it. I want to go home now, she says, when he releases his hand. Go home now. Please.

And he says to her: put your hands around my neck. He likes this, this is what he wants her to do. The little enclosed fingers, her face close to his. The two perfect dark nostrils, the open pores, in the crease of her chin. And I'm watching and watching and I'm not really here, I never was *here*, only slipping between the tunnel and the surface and this time I really wish for darkness, wish the crack of light to close and blacken completely,

271

so there's not a thing I can see, so that I can stop having these hairline cracks, these glimpses, but it just won't happen. When her hands are linked round his neck, he puts his fingers around hers. I feel the warm pulse there. Now I'm closing my eyes, refusing to look. Even in dreams sometimes I can do this, wake myself in the middle of a nightmare, will myself to wake up, but I can't do it this time, I can neither slide away nor wake up, it just keeps on coming, *he* keeps on coming, he's coming towards me. He's closed the shed door, he locked it, it's not our shed but another shed, somewhere else, I don't know if this is a place I've ever been with him, but he's taking me there right now. This is the tunnel. This is the burning smell. This is where he wants me to go with him, to travel his loneliest journey, and he's a coward in this, too, even this, he's weak and self-pitying and somehow desperate; he wants me to see it, he put his hands just softly on my throat too, only this time it's a dream, but now he makes me watch him, shaking and shaking until her head flops back and forth, back and forth and it's loose, wildly loose like a rag doll but not a doll, I know it's not a doll, and so does he. There's a bubble of saliva at the corner of her mouth. Her eyelids are closed and paper-fine. Nothing flutters beneath them.

I'm sorry, Mandy, I scream to her. I'm really sorry. You have the Sindy hairbrush, keep it, honest, I don't mind! I'm sorry it was you, not me. I'm sorry you came to our house and I was out, at the beach, looking at the dead seahorse. Wake up, Mandy. Wake up, *please*. Please, Mandy. Let me go now.

★ ★ ★

Wendy gives me brandy, which I hardly touch, and then strong tea with three sugars.

It's always worse when the child is the exact same age as your own, isn't it, Wendy says. Poppy's ten, isn't she? Just like my poor Chloe. That's why she can't switch off about it, even though they're from a different school. It's too close to home.

Quietly, a half-whisper. She strokes my hand. Mum is smoking, ostentatiously flapping the smoke away from Rose. She never used to smoke. She's eyeing me warily.

I thought you'd stopped all that, Mum sniffs. Funny turns. I thought you'd grown out of them.

Chloe comes back in the room, bringing me a blanket, a blue furry one with stars and silver moons, from her room, draping it over my legs. Rose has her pyjamas on, her hair damp and curling from her bath, hair smelling of tea-tree oil. Nit lotion. They stare at me: the strange American aunt. No wonder we didn't know much about her.

Are you sure about flying back tomorrow? Andrew asks, for the tenth time. You sure it's going to be OK? Surely Dean won't mind if you change it . . .

When I shake my head, start murmuring about my seahorses, the crucial point I'm at, he says firmly: I'll drive you. At least, let me drive you to Heathrow.

Mum glances at him, quick, lightning quick, but I catch it, intercept. It isn't a glance she meant for me, and it's hard to read, but knowing her as well as I do, I think I just about get it. It's something like: so you're on her side, now? Of course, I know Andrew hasn't told

Mum we've been to the police, he won't have told her the conversations we've had, but it's subtler than that. She's slightly affronted, anyway. She can sense some *care* on Andrew's part, some special solicitude. She senses a story that excludes her.

Or rather, a story that has been growing beside her like a tree, these last thirty years.

It's dark now and the brandy is seeping into me, warming up my corners. Mum's eyes are so soft, the edges so creased that the whites, the irises, the pupils seem almost to melt into the peachy grey of her face. She's fifty-seven years old, in a purple velour dressing gown, leaning back into the cushions, watching the evening news. It's a childish fantasy, to keep hoping. To think there's still a chance she's going to turn into someone else.

I never told her that I went to see Dad before I left. Instead, I tried back then, for the first and last time, to talk to *her*. About Dad and girls. Not about Mandy but about Dawn Staples and an ill-defined, inchoate sense of something, something not right. Not Jenny, because I didn't know about Jenny. Nothing definite. No, I wasn't trying to tell her he'd molested me. That would be too specific, too fully formed for the sort of thing I was trying to talk about.

You've no idea, she said. Little girls, young as you like, some of them are terrible flirts! They can wrap men around their little fingers. You're not telling me they don't know what they're doing —

Easy to see now why I never confided in her about those boys in the lane, or told her about Russell, at the

274

time. She'd be sure to huff and snort and blame me. Girls with so much power, wreaking their own destruction. This is what she believes. Without her anger at these girls, she's bereft. She's the woman he left, she's nothing: she's air.

I can see Dad in his shed and he has his dressing gown cord; he's drunk, and he's been crying. This is not a slide I can hold up to the light, it's murkier than that. His hair isn't peppered grey or his hairline receding, the jaws puffing out, the hawk-nose now fattening, the way dough rises, left in the airing cupboard. No, he looks how he used to look, when he still lived with us. He's much younger, with all the features sharper, his dark thick sideburns but no beard, and his eyes bright, the way the light is, about five o'clock in the autumn, just before a storm, sluicing the fields and the trees into colours true and intense: brighter, darker.

She didn't fend me off, Dad says, whispering beside me. It's his fear I feel, not mine, *his* despair, palpable as his breath on my face, as a heartbeat right beside me. Bile rises in the back of my mouth, my temperature floods hot and cold, my eyes water as I struggle not to throw up.

If she'd been a good girl, you know, like a girl that young ought to be, she'd really fight, she'd fight like a hell-cat, he says.

He's not real, he's not like a real person beside me, I'm not saying that. He's vivid, but I know he's not real. There is a smell of him, just under my nose, the same old rough wool smell, and mud and cat-piss and tobacco and tomatoes in a greenhouse, the sour pungent sugar-beet smell.

Even a sow protests, Dad says. Squeals, honks, tries to run.

I didn't fight, when Danny did it to me, he says. I mean, I cried a bit, with the pain the first time, but then I got to like it. I was a dirty little lad, at heart. It's just a bit of affection really, it doesn't hurt. I knew she was the same. Some of them were, you could tell.

His voice rustles, coming from a direction I can't place, like a sound with nothing human in it, a husk.

Father found us one time, Danny and me, he says. Hiding round the back of the pig-sties. That's what Father said I was. No better than a pig. He made me sleep the night there and he threw my clothes in the mud after me and he made Danny leave. I never minded the smell, I worked with it every day, it was like the smell of cut grass is to other people. Father was wrong to call me a pig, though. You should never underestimate a pig. Pigs are clean and they're warm too. I was a dirty little bugger, much worse than any pig.

Now his voice is fading, like the volume slowly turned down on the radio.

She really ought to have fought harder, he says. Not play dead like that, make it worse, so sleepy and so quiet. If she was a good girl. She ought to have fended me off. Big as I am, I'd a never managed it, if she had, he says.

That's when I keel over. Auditory hallucinations, Dean calls them. He has his words, names, useful ones. I have mine.

276

Russell and I try again, many times. He can be patient, he says, but I've got to understand. Prick-teasing is cruel. The pain gets worse and worse, and last for hours afterwards, my whole stomach and thighs stiff, so that I can hardly walk. Vaginismus. One of Mum's magazines, *Company*, has an article about it: "Extremely painful, involuntary spasm of the pelvic floor muscles, virtually closing the entrance to the vagina, interfering with sexual intercourse. Usually occurs in women who assume that penetration will be painful. A traumatic experience such as rape or sexual abuse as a child may be a contributory factor; also, underlying guilt or fear, due to a restrictive upbringing or an inadequate sex education."

I think my sex education, the bit that Mr Davies taught us, was pretty thorough. Still, I'm interested in that word: involuntary. Not my fault then. Of course I don't tell Russell that I've read about this curious spasm, this clamping. It doesn't feature in any of the magazines he reads, where the chief problem with girls seems to be our lesbian antics or our nymphomania, so I feel instinctively that he won't believe me. I'm sure he thinks I'm just faking the pain because I'm scared, or frigid or something. And anyway, I feel sure that he's cooling off, and don't want to give him a reason to finish with me.

I puzzle over it in my usual way, thinking about the words. *Virtually closing the entrance.* To me. That's right, really. That is exactly how it feels — as if my body is a closed fist. I like it when Russell strokes me and kisses me and tells me how gorgeous I am, but it's the entering bit that freaks me out. Who wants someone else to be *inside* them?

I mean, I haven't seen *The Exorcist*, it's an X so I'm not allowed, but I get the idea, we all do, of what it is to be possessed, to let someone really invade you, like an alien, take up residence inside you. I tell myself this isn't what it means, to be *penetrated*; I'm being too literal, as usual, being ridiculous. Maybe it's just the words that are causing me the trouble and that's silly because sex is not words. It's the Most Natural Thing in the World. Everybody's doing it — remember, even Mr Davies, the Science teacher, having sex more times than he's had a bath!

I haven't talked to Jenny or Cherry about my secret meetings with Russell. I really don't know why this is. In some ways, we tell each other everything, every trivial thing. But in others, well, they seem different to me. They seem like they should be: giggling over Donny Osmond and worrying about who's in the school netball team. I'm something twisted and strange, I'm far too interested in all these other things, and always have been. Even very small, I remember a comic with a little picture in it, a naked picture, and just looking at it could make my body fizz, could make feelings in me. It was before I could read. I must have been three or four.

One day at Jenny's Russell passes me in the kitchen and says nothing. We're on our own, he could easily come over and lift my hair from the back of my neck and kiss it, but he doesn't do it. What's wrong? I mutter, as loud as I dare. He's pouring himself a Cola

278

from a giant bottle; I'm fishing about in the Tupperware for the orange-flavoured Jacob's Clubs. We neither of us look at one another.

Your old boy, that's what.

My dad?

I haven't seen Dad for months. We know where he is living — over in Littleport — and we sometimes see his van go past the school bus in the mornings, on his way to the factory, but not apart from that. Russell, I know, drinks at the Sugar Social Club. It's the first time it occurs to me that all this time, while we've been not seeing Dad, Russell has.

He's told me to lay off, Russell mumbles. Someone saw us together. He threatened to deck me, Russell says, in a flat voice. He doesn't turn around, keeps his eyes on his glass of Cola. He's acting like it's nothing to him, that he doesn't mind at all. I know from *Jackie* that boys always do this, that they're actually hurting inside.

That's us finished, Russell says. I can't lose my job . . .

He blows me a kiss on his way next-door, back into the swampy living room.

I lean against the fridge, feeling the cool white seeping through my jumper, the most almighty pause seems to be happening: the fridge has stopped humming. Then it starts again with a shudder. The weirdest thing is not Russell, not his reaction, not his finishing with me. It's picturing Dad. Dad with his face up close, his blue eyes glaring, shouting, upsetting glasses, those thumping sounds of chairs tumbling over;

that sort of crackling, electricity feeling in pubs when men get angry, when something flares up. Dad still caring about me. Dad warning someone away from me.

It's my fourteenth birthday in two days' time. I've been wondering whether Dad will send me a card. Now I'm thinking: I don't even mind if he doesn't. I know it's not much. I know it's probably bloody hypocrisy, as Russell muttered, as he put the Cola back in the fridge. But I think maybe it's jealousy too, maybe I succeeded in *something* after all. Stuff Russell. I got a rise out of Dad. I made him remember me.

Once, aged about four, Poppy's lying on the floor with her Sylvanian Families, gifts from a grandmother she barely knows. She's arranging the Grey Bear Grandparents in the Village Sweetshop and she suddenly looks up and says: Mommy, do you remember me?

Of course I remember you! You're right in front of me, honey . . .

It's a funny sentence. I think of it now. She meant, I thought at the time, have you forgotten me? Or, perhaps, Mommy, why are you ignoring me? Now I understand it. I think it was: do I exist if you stop paying attention to me?

Wendy cooks us pasta with a garlicky sauce and I eat it on my knee in the front room with the television still on, Andrew bringing me a beer then going to eat in the kitchen with Mum and the girls. Mum seems to live at their house. Not literally, but a reluctance to go back to her own place is obvious, and it's hard to tell, at this point, whether this is resented by Andrew and Wendy or not. I hear a car outside, a taxi, I think, hearing the radio through the open windows, but it scrapes over the gravel drive at some speed and then the front door is flung open dramatically, and I hear Billy's voice in the hallway. Raised voices. Andrew's tone placating.

Then Billy's standing over me, steaming. I almost expect him to be pawing the floor with one foot, smoke pouring from his nose.

You're such a bitch . . . he's saying, while Andrew is behind him, like a scene from a pub brawl, saying: calm down, calm down . . .

What? I ask, sitting up, putting the beer bottle carefully on the table, wiping my mouth with my hand. My heart hammering though, my cheeks aflame.

Now you're concocting this! He's dead for God's sake, he can't defend himself. Is that why you came back, just to slur his name even further?

Out of the corner of my eye I notice Mum standing in the doorway, arms folded, just watching us. As if we're three bickering kids and any minute now she's going to burst in and split us up, but she's biding her time.

Billy, leave her, Andrew says. She's just saying what she thinks is true and if you don't like it —

Thinks is true! Thinks is true! Based on what? Based on her own fucking weirdo imaginings . . .

Billy, will you stop this foul language in front of my daughters? Tina isn't very well, calm down will you and come in the kitchen and — have a cup of tea —

This is Wendy. She's magnificent. She herds him back into the kitchen, a hand on his shoulder. The girls are staring at me. Rose begins to cry. I know my face is beetroot. The whole thing took seconds: slowed-down, painful seconds, like a parent watching a child have a tantrum in the supermarket, wondering whether to shout and bellow, join in, or walk out. Like most parents I chose the red-faced attempt at dignity. False, pretending to be calm, rational. I'd have liked to jump on his back, dig my nails into his neck.

On the drive back from the police station Andrew and I had talked about who else I might tell, if the police were not willing to pursue it. Should I talk to Sandy, Mandy's mother? But what good would it do, if it can't be proved, and the police aren't interested? Surely it will only make her feel worse, drag it all up again, only to frustrate her? We persuade ourselves that this is true but now, with Billy, the real reasons become terrifyingly clear. We don't want to dismantle things, take away their intricate scaffolding.

I cuddle Rose onto my knee and tell her not to worry, Uncle Billy just lost his temper, he's fine now. It's hard to look at her. I don't know if I'm ashamed or frightened: Billy flying at me, Billy's fierce, shimmering dislike of me; blame, whatever it is, always glitters just under the surface, but it's a long time since I saw it for real like that, saw the sparks. In the kitchen I can still hear his voice, a voice so deep and gruff; almost a cartoon voice. Because I can't hear the words, I hear the tone, the qualities of the voice in a way I hadn't until now. It's as if his voice is missing, as if he needs to cough, to get his real voice back. I've never noticed this before. I listen to this for a few minutes, again not understanding the words, and remember Gaynor mentioning Billy's illness, and that, yes, indeed, he did have an operation a few years back on his throat, and I'd forgotten, in fact I'd not tuned in to how serious it might have been. *She always had it in for him* reaches me, suddenly, in this same gravelly emptied voice. Then Wendy's reasoned tones, something soothing followed by Mum's voice, hot, indignant, her usual snorts of disbelief. It's the first she's heard of it, but even so she sounds . . . what? Prepared.

He used to play a trick on me, Billy. Whenever we sat in Dad's van, waiting for him to do some errand or other, in Ely, pick up one of his mates, buy a paper, or whatever it was, Billy would wind down the window and shout out rude things to anyone who passed. Then he'd duck down really fast so I was the one sitting there, staring out at a shocked Mrs Aitchinson, the words Big Fat Bum! ringing down Market Street.

I'd stare straight ahead, hot-faced, furious. Now I suddenly want to laugh. I wish I could say: Billy, that was brilliant. That was a pretty good trick.

Chloe too comes to join me, quietly sloping in, spying, trying to gauge my reaction; biting the skin around her nails. She stares at her sister, snuggling on my knee.

What's Uncle Billy so mad about? she asks.

Oh. Something I said.

Something about your dad?

Yes.

Was your dad a paedophile? That's what Mum says.

283

I glance at Rose. She is sitting up, eyes dry, listening. Such a plain sentence. Flat. Bleak.

I suppose that's what you'd call him, today, I say. We didn't really use that word.

Chloe makes a noise, a sort of *weeee* sound, a whistle. She tugs her mini-top down, trying to close the gap between top and jeans. I see that the flesh is goose-pimpled. It's just as I always suspected, like I lectured Poppy. Your kidneys get a chill, wearing that look.

Maybe you'd better go in the kitchen. Make it up with Uncle Billy. You're going back tomorrow, aren't you?

I'm startled. Probably simply that a ten-year-old girl dares speak to an adult like that, advise me what to do. But then I realise, it's more than that. It's what she's suggesting that startles me. The idea that I don't have to sit in here, cowering in front of the telly, both hands hooked around my beer: floating. Sulking, fearful, embarrassed, whatever, but basically just floating. I could get up, I think. She's right. I could walk into the kitchen, start talking. I could tell Billy what I know, what I think. He's bound to disagree, Mum is bound to go postal. They'll stick to their versions, I'll probably never persuade them of mine. I know I can never prove it. But it's my childhood too. I was there.

At Heathrow, Andrew takes the car back to the hire place for me while I check in and then joins me again for a coffee at a Starbucks stall.

I'm stirring sugar into my latte and my eyes fall to the table beside me, a folded up *Telegraph*. Front page headlines: Man and Woman Arrested for the Murder of

284

Girls. The same case again: they already have their suspects. Andrew picks up the paper, reads in silence for a minute or two, flaps it down with a sigh.

God, how awful. Chloe's going to be beside herself, now. She's had a terrible time getting to sleep at night, it's really got to her. I suppose it's being so close. You never expect these things to happen on your own doorstep.

I say nothing.

God, what makes people do something like that? Andrew says, trying again, thumping his finger on the photograph. His hands, I notice, are shaking.

Like, you're asking me? You're really, seriously asking *me*? I say.

I read the article, some of the details. The murderer had a baby daughter, by another woman. He is known for his relationships with younger women, who were usually fragile in build and boyish. Neighbours heard violent fights between him and his girlfriend; but then others describe him as "friendly" and "helpful". His boss says he cried easily, was often sorry for himself. As for the woman, his girlfriend, here the journalist is un-equivocal. She's surely complicit too. She must have known.

Andrew rubs at his forehead with his shaking hand, his characteristic gesture. The creases in his forehead roll under his fingers: he's rubbing new ones in, not smoothing them out.

I mean, he says, agitated. It's obviously a sexual thing. Why doesn't he just leave it at that? Why does he have to kill them?

I don't know! I say, my voice doing this weird panicky loop at the end of the sentence, as if someone plucked the words from my mouth and tugged them up and away from me.

"*But when the goal blinds you, suffocates you, parches your throat, when healthy shame and sickly cowardice scrutinise your every step . . .*"

Oh God, I mutter. I really don't know — what do you want me to say? Like, you really expect me to know the answers. You're the one who works with the troubled boys, isn't that your job, turning the bad boys around —

His eyes swim with water, the whites glittering under the fierce airport light, and so I stop, mid-sentence, feeling cruel, and try to speak more softly.

I don't know, Andrew. I guess he, I hope, maybe he — fought with himself . . .

Andrew leans towards me, puts his face close to whisper: we did our best, Tina. We went to the police. There was nothing. No evidence, nothing to say that we were right . . .

He's staring at me. It's a begging look. Can't you just take it back home with you, can't you take it all back, keep it again, for us? His eyes are so tired, and I notice that his pupils today seem tiny, with the irises looking hazy somehow, unhealthy. Weak, I think. He's tried, he's considered it, he's allowed the idea to form, he's re-examined some things, held them up to the light. But he can't carry on like this. He can't go back to his life, with the girls, with Wendy, and readjust everything so that it can accommodate the idea that, after all, his father murdered Mandy Baker. It's too much. It was too much to ask someone to do, in one weekend.

A loud female voice reminds us from a loudspeaker, in the interests of security, to keep our luggage with us at all times.

Andrew glances one last time at the front page of the *Telegraph*, then folds the paper, folds the face away from him. I see Dad, Dad with his big, crayon-blue eyes, with their dark hollows. I'm closing my eyes now. Yes, it would be nice to do what Andrew is suggesting, to seal it up again. I can't see Dad, the whole of him, even though I looked at him all those days, all those hours, all those times over all those years and now when I narrow, half-close my eyes, what do I see: only floating parts of him. Him dancing in front of *Top of the Pops*, getting in the way of the programme, doing it stupidly, to deliberately make us laugh. His dark sideburns, curling up the side of his face in front of his ears. I know what they felt like: the tickle of them, the roughness, the Brillo-pad bristle, the maleness. That ring he wore, a glint of gold at the edge of his hand, dark nests of hair at his knuckles, the knobbly, raised up veins, his hands fixing a toy of Billy's, fiddling with the wheels of a truck . . . but before I can stop myself, before I can abort it, it's here, the unasked for thing. He's not holding a truck or a toy at all, but a length of fishing twine, and he's holding it taut between both hands, and it's lethal, it cuts like cheese wire.

Be quiet, it's nothing bad, it's just a game. It happens sometimes, just be quiet.

Something shifts once again from Andrew to me and with it comes a deluge of utter weariness. I need to lie down for the longest time. I want to go home and tell

Dean and then I want to go diving with him and fall into the deepest purest sea we know.

Andrew flicks a glance at the TV screen above our seats to check the flights, to check that he has time. A moment's indecision crosses his face and then he plunges, with a question I can't help feeling he has wanted to ask for a long time.

Tina — I've wondered. Do you think Dad killed himself because you left? I mean, I know we all thought — we were told — it was about that girl leaving him. But it did coincide, didn't it? It wasn't long after you went to America, and I know from Billy that Dad knew about that. Billy says you went to see him. You told Dad you were leaving.

I stand up, shake my head without replying. *Boarding at Gate B for American Airlines Flight 22.* As if I could answer Andrew's question anyway.

I don't know, I say firmly. I've no idea.

Perhaps I'm allowed to give up now, being the custodian for Dad's secret thoughts, secret motivations? That is, it strikes me there's nothing particularly exceptional about the way Dad poured himself into me, the way so many parents pour their dreams, their anguish, their desires, their anger and disappointments into their children, as if we were just little vessels waiting to be filled up with *their* feelings, as if we were put on this earth precisely as repositories for *them*. But enough already, as Poppy would say. I've filled to overflow.

We leave the newspaper on the table. I hug my brother. We break apart, smile at one another. I wheel towards the security gate with my one pull-along case, and I blow Andrew a kiss, and he waves at me, and tells me to give his love to Dean and Poppy and to have a safe flight, and to stay in touch.

You could come over, I say. Come and visit us! With your new wife!

He breaks into a grin at the word "wife". We glance quickly at one another; hungrily, a last look, a storing up look. I have a flash of him, in our old living room, a boy of about eight, standing in front of me, holding out his Explorer Stamp Collection. I can see the cover clearly, with its picture of a rocket and an astronaut, holding what looks like a motorcycle helmet. Where's Abboo Dabbi? Andrew wants to know, and he's showing me his best stamp ever: the one with the red and white flag, that goes right on the very first page. He thinks I'm the brainy one, he thinks I've got the answers.

Thanks for coming to my wedding! he calls.

I'm glad — it was great . . . Have a happy marriage, Andrew! Be lucky! Thanks for everything!

I can't see him any more. I'm still waving, looking back through the crowd, my back to the boarding gate. Of course it's not really a gate but a screen, and so I can still see my brother and a throng of passengers, as I move towards Security, towards the table flanked by guards nursing their brand new guns like babies. As I'm putting my bag down and sifting through it for my cell phone and change, I have the strongest sense that he is still behind me, still staring after me, and I turn around to wave one last time. But I'm wrong, and the space between us has ruptured, chock-full of people.

★ ★ ★

On the plane, briefly, as the landing gear lifts, it all swills up again. London falls away and blankness, cloud inflates beneath me. Drawing a veil, I think, yes that's it, that's what I must do: draw a veil, on the most exhausting, terrifying weekend of my life. I yank the grey blind shut. Just don't look out of the window, I tell myself. But I know that now I've seen him there's no un-seeing him. I might be going back to my cherished life with Dean and Poppy, but it's really just the beginning, now that I've allowed the thoughts to form, how could it be otherwise? There he will be, if I look, his face just over the wing, floating up, an untethered ballon. Crooning softly. Green grows the laurel, soft falls the dew. Sorry was I, love, when parting from you . . .

Here I am in my lab, home with my seahorses. I missed a great adventure while I was away: last night Henry gave birth to nearly twenty babies. This morning he's ready to mate again. That's nearly always the way: seahorses tend to give birth at night and we remove the babies as they're so tiny and just float there, with no help from either parent. They have a better chance of surviving if they're not around Daddy. That's the thing about this romantic image people have of seahorse fathers carrying the young. They're just as likely as fathers in other species to devour them once they're out. The difference is, with seahorses it's likely to be accidental. The babies can be wafted into their mouths by a current.

And here's Anais, bobbing up to him for her morning greeting and carrying a new load of eggs. Then the pair begins this nine-hour ballet.

Students come and go. I'm refuelled with cups of coffee and a new pen when mine runs out. The video tape in the machine is changed. Really, since we record all of it, there's no need for me to be here, my chair pulled up to the tank, my knees crushed against the cupboards beneath. It's just that it's mesmerising. The pivoting and twirling, the rising, the transfusion of colours. The lifting, nodding of their heads, the spiralling upwards (they tend to mate travelling upwards, we don't know why). You know, for some of the time, they make a shape exactly like a heart, with their heads the curved top, their tails entwined at the bottom. When we first met I gave Dean a photo I'd taken, underwater, of mating *Hippocampus kuda*. Be My Valentine. He had no idea how rare it is, that shape; how fluky I am to have seen it, captured it. Once in a lifetime. If you're very very lucky.

Seahorses flexing and flowing like ribbons in the water: how could I have found that first dead hard crust of a seahorse fascinating compared to this? It's 10p.m. before I get up and tear my eyes away from them, stretching. I realise I'm here on my own. The lab windows are squares of black sky, silvery trees.

There's a knock at the door and it's Dean, he's worried about me so he's brought Poppy and some beers and when I tell them why I'm still here, they pull up chairs and join me, our three heads directed at the one tank like a television set. Henry is flapping his empty pouch, filling it with water and really puffing it out, as if to say: look at me, look at me, I'm ready, come on *please*, I'm gagging for it! I murmur something along these lines to Dean. He puts his arm around me, kisses my neck, opens the beers.

While I was away Yelena started some research with the clicking sounds, I say, softly. It's a project off the coast of Turks and Caicos, taking a microphone down into the water and taping them, trying to discover whether they're actually communicating . . .

How will she know? Dean says, whispering too.

Ssssh sshsh. Look . . .

It's hot in the lab. I've switched off the fans as the noise was grating. As the three of us lean forward, holding our breath, I'm aware of the clammy feel of my skin touching the bench, the smell of my sweat.

So now, lit from above, Anais has become a diffuse green, the colour of a shallow lake. She's virtually transparent: she could almost be a trick of the light. But here she is, lifting her snout, and sidling up to Henry, carrying her gift. As I breathe out, she does what we've been waiting for all this time, presses her oviduct right up against him.

Poppy gives a little gasp. Dean's hand, in mine, is sweating. Anais is inflamed, she's batting up close, her tail hooked, her body extended, pressing towards him. She wants *him*, Henry, and her arousal, whatever is going on in her tiny body (I don't call it desire, I mustn't call it desire, seahorses don't feel desire) is powerful, it's absolutely equal in nature to the force of his. Henry's proved himself, in the last nine hours, and

292

morning after morning. He's been loyal, he's been responsive, he's been there, his timing is perfect. She didn't have to drop her eggs, disastrously, on the bottom of the tank, give up on him. He can't persuade her or overpower her if she's not willing, but she is, she's made her choice. He's the one.

Two weeks after my flight and Poppy and I are walking home from Hampshire Mall, along the cycle path that runs through the trees and leads directly to the campus. It's a very safe route, I've walked or cycled it many times since moving here. Nothing remote or cut-off about it: there's even an ice-cream stall halfway along where I bought Poppy and me a Banana Seat (blueberry banana shake). She's now trotting behind me, bouncing a basket-ball. A comforting thud lets me know she's following, dawdling though she is. And then the thud stops. I turn around and there's no sign of her. Under my nose is that smell, the one that always comes first. I look into the trees: expecting to see one burning. Is that Poppy's high black pony-tail, pulled through the hole of a blue cap, disappearing? Was that a scream, or just a shout from the tennis courts up on the campus?

Poppy, I say. Once, in a not-too-worried voice. I stare into the cool green wall of pines that surround the path. I notice for the first time that really, the cycle path feels just like being inside a green tunnel, carved into the middle of a forest. Green overhead and on either side. I sniff, and the burning smell is stronger still. A yellow line is painted down the middle of the path: a chipmunk skitters across it, in front of me, like a fluttering leaf, heading for its hole.

And then there's a movement in the canopy of trees, and here's a girl and she's not Poppy at all, but a fair girl around the same age, with a slightly wonky, faint smile, and she's eating a lolly, and wearing a hat, and her eyes are obscured so that I can't really see them, but she's moving determinedly towards me.

My heart skitters too, fast and hard.

I thought you would leave now, I think. This isn't right. Surely, you're — what — you're a symptom? Now I'm back, and I've told my family and did my best and it's over in some way and — and I'm on different medication. Surely now you should leave?

She smiles broadly. She's friendly. There is red ice dripping down her dress; her socks are drooping and wrinkled. She's moving smoothly, her weight shifting from side to side: she's on roller skates, and she's holding her hand out, the one not holding the lolly: there's something in it. She keeps right on skating. And as she looms closer to me I think, maybe she's not Mandy at all, I'm not sure now. It's like being in a room with green velvet curtains drawn and a cine film running from your family archive, and there she is, someone you know so well and then don't know at all. Or like looking down a well and being shocked at the sight of your own tiny reflection: the blonde, rat-tail hair, the big grey eyes, the bitten, folded-over lip.

As she approaches the sounds around me sharpen. My brain is telling me I'm wrong, she's not what I think at all, she's real, an American girl, maybe holding out her arm for balance; but my body refuses to believe it. As the girl passes, I'm ice-cold. Then I'm suddenly sprung with sweat. She makes a gesture towards my empty hand, as if she wants to give something to me.

Mandy? I murmur, but I don't know if I really say it aloud. She's hurtling past with confident speed, her prominent knees pumping. I open my palm to see what was dropped there, then close it again, bewildered. And in the place along the cycle path where I'm staring after her, my legs wilting to cooked spaghetti beneath me, finally, thank God, Poppy appears, emerging from the trees, grinning and waving. My ball disappeared! she calls. I was just looking for my ball.

Acknowledgments

There are many people I should like to thank for help with this novel. I have received support from the Royal Literary Fund for several years and wish to offer the Trustees and the Fellowship officer, Steve Cook, the warmest possible thanks. I am also grateful to the Arts Council of England for a grant towards research.

My thanks are due to the Zoological Society of London (ZSL) for allowing me access to the seahorses. Dr Heather Koldewey, Senior Curator, Aquarium, ZSL, has been a most generous advisor. I'm particularly grateful to her for an early read of the manuscript and for her willingness to let me study the seahorses. I felt very privileged indeed to be allowed to observe Heather at work. Her expertise and openness in sharing information, experience and many unique insights into a subject in which she is extraordinarily eminent has been one of the unexpected bonuses of working on this novel. Jodie le Cheminant, too, has been a perceptive, creative guide to the aquarium and all its wonders. Acknowledgments are due to Jodie for the original research into elastomer tagging, subject of her own Master's research, and for many subtle understandings of seahorse behaviour and not least for allowing me to bring Felix and visit the secret chambers of the old aquarium.

I have made use of research into seahorses which is available on the Project Seahorse website. I'm particularly intrigued by the work of Dr Amanda Vincent, Dr Heather Mason-Jones and the marine photographer Denise Tackett and hope they won't mind the inadvertent references I've made to their discoveries. Interested readers can visit the site on www.projectseahorse.com and donations are always welcome.

I'd like to draw the reader's attention to three books which are especially fascinating and pertinent: Sandra Brown's *Where There is Evil* (Macmillan), *She Must Have Known* by Brian Masters (Doubleday) and *Memories Are Made of This* by Rusiko Bourtchouladze (Weidenfeld and Nicolson).

For vital conversations, advice and comments which have all made this novel better than it might have been, I'd like to thank Kathryn Heyman, Geraldine Maxwell, Sally Cline, Suzanne Howlett, Caryl Phillips, Louise Doughty, Susie Orbach, Joel Jaffey, Carole Welch, Amber Burlinson and Caroline Dawnay.

The biggest thanks of all must go to Meredith Bowles, who will know what the novel owes to him.

ISIS publish a wide range of books in large print, from fiction to biography. Any suggestions for books you would like to see in large print or audio are always welcome. Please send to the Editorial Department at:

ISIS Publishing Limited
7 Centremead
Osney Mead
Oxford OX2 0ES

A full list of titles is available free of charge from:

Ulverscroft Large Print Books Limited

(UK)
The Green
Bradgate Road, Anstey
Leicester LE7 7FU
Tel: (0116) 236 4325

(Australia)
P.O. Box 314
St Leonards
NSW 1590
Tel: (02) 9436 2622

(USA)
P.O. Box 1230
West Seneca
N.Y. 14224-1230
Tel: (716) 674 4270

(Canada)
P.O. Box 80038
Burlington
Ontario L7L 6B1
Tel: (905) 637 8734

(New Zealand)
P.O. Box 456
Feilding
Tel: (06) 323 6828

Details of ISIS complete and unabridged audio books are also available from these offices. Alternatively, contact your local library for details of their collection of ISIS large print and unabridged audio books.